MAYBE BABY

"Not much masculine stuff in here." Jack's voice carried in from the living room where he was caulking a window that had leaked during a storm the night before.

In the kitchen, Delaney froze.

"What?" she called back, hearing guilt in her voice. She hated lying—which was a real inconvenience considering how she'd set herself up to live an enormous one.

"I said there's not much masculine stuff in this house," Jack said. His voice and body became large as he strode into the kitchen. "Your husband's not going to feel very at home when he comes."

She handed him a glass of water. "His stuff hasn't arrived yet."

"Sure, but he's going to visit, isn't he?"

He brought the glass to his lips. Delaney watched his throat as he swallowed and allowed her gaze to travel down his neck. She could tell his biceps were wide and his _____

She took _____ id of
Jack. Show _____ er life
other than a

She had

ELAINE FOX

Maybe Baby

AVON BOOKS

An Imprint of HarperCollins*Publishers*

This is a work of fiction. Names, characters, places, and incidents are products of the author's imagination or are used fictitiously and are not to be construed as real. Any resemblance to actual events, locales, organizations, or persons, living or dead, is entirely coincidental.

AVON BOOKS
An Imprint of HarperCollins*Publishers*
10 East 53rd Street
New York, New York 10022-5299

Copyright © 2001 by Elaine McShulskis
ISBN: 0-380-81783-7
www.avonromance.com

First Avon Books paperback printing: August 2001

Avon Trademark Reg. U.S. Pat. Off. and in Other Countries, Marca Registrada, Hecho en U.S.A.
HarperCollins ® is a trademark of HarperCollins Publishers Inc.

Printed in the U.S.A.

10 9 8 7 6 5 4

Chapter 1

The only sure thing about luck, Delaney Poole's mother always said, is that it'll change.

Delaney was starting to believe that was true.

After a year of bad luck—wherein she'd endured an unhappy relationship; lived with parents who barely spoke to each other, let alone her; and worked for peanuts as a resident in a busy inner-city hospital emergency room—it looked as if it might all turn around.

First, she'd dumped the guy. Then she'd gotten her own apartment. And now she was up for an assignment in the most beautiful place she'd ever been: Harp Cove, Maine.

As she stood across the street from a bar called the Hornet's Nest, Delaney couldn't help but smile into the darkness. She *loved* this town. Loved it with the excitement of a kid getting exactly what she wants for Christmas.

This backward little two-stoplight town, bathed in sea salt and populated with eccentrics, was exactly what she had in mind when she checked "Rural" on her National Health Service Corps questionnaire. No high-profile, big-city emergency room for her. No sprawling suburban hospital with professional hierarchies and stepladders to success. Sure, they offered an intense form of professional stimulation, but they couldn't give her what she really wanted: community.

She wanted to work somewhere she felt needed. Not by the staff or administration, but by the people, the neighborhood, the town.

And here it was. Harp Cove. Population 5,000. In the winter, that was. In summertime, that number probably tripled, but it was still a friendly, manageable town. A town in need of a doctor who, in a little over a year, would be fresh out of residency with state-of-the-art medical knowledge.

Music from the bar thumped across the April night, stumbling through the air like a clumsy drunk, begging her to revel in the teeming energy of the only watering hole in town.

Delaney tilted her head back, hugged her arms around her middle, and looked up at the stars. The sky was carpeted so thickly with them they looked like shattered glass, splintered and bright. So different from the dim sparks visible through the murk of a D.C. night. She breathed in slowly. Salt, pine, soil. Intoxicating earthy scents.

Harp Cove.

She imagined herself telling people back home, when she returned for the occasional visit. "It's just a tiny town on the coast of Maine," she'd say, smiling wistfully, "but I love it."

And they would picture her in some wild, dramatic setting, resourcefully saving lives with pinecones and twine. Pioneering.

Delaney laughed. As if she cared what the people in D.C. thought of her life. Most of them were just people she worked with anyway. Between med school, her internship and residency, she'd lost touch with most of her old friends. And she'd really only dated one guy since college—the disastrous Lonnie she'd gotten rid of six months ago.

So now she was free—free to start life fresh, in a brand new place. And *this* was the place she wanted. This odd, mystic, northern town, so unlike the predictable suburbs and myopically driven city she'd known all her life.

She smiled and realized she was happy. Irrationally, deliriously so. She couldn't remember another time in her life when she felt so hopeful. It was the most centered feeling she'd ever had. And it was because she knew exactly what she wanted to do, and where she wanted to do it. Odd, she thought, how the place instantly made her feel as if she'd been lost her whole life, until she happened to come here.

She just *had* to get this assignment.

Delaney had been in Harp Cove for four days, exploring the town in which she hoped to be assigned to work by the National Health Service Corps, the organization that had paid most of her med-school tuition. NHSC required one year of service for every year of tuition they paid, so, since Delaney had saved and paid for the first year herself, she could be in Harp Cove for three years. More, if she chose.

Granted, she had one more year of residency to go—in the frantic hustle and revolving-door busyness of a D.C. hospital—but after she finished up next June she might be here, living her dream of being a country doctor. And all it took was four years of med school, one year of internship, and three years of residency.

She smiled to herself. The end was in sight. Soon, she told herself, soon she would be a real, certified doctor. Not a student, not an intern, not a resident, but a *doctor*.

Chances were good she would get the assignment. Apparently most people chose locations in warm climates, or towns not too far from a major city. This town—nearly four hours up the coast from Portland—was too cold and too remote to interest anyone but her. She hoped.

If she got it, she would start in July of next year. Perfect timing for this northern clime. She imagined herself moving in, unpacking her boxes, and getting to know her neighbors. They would be happy to have a doctor so close, she thought. And she would be happy to be the one these kind, quirky folk came to when they needed help.

Delaney's whole body quivered with anticipation. She wished she was already settled here and this was her first weekend as a resident. She wished that, instead of leaving tomorrow to go home for another year, she was going to start work at the clinic here in town. She wished the waiting were over and it was all starting *now*, because up to now it seemed she'd done nothing but prepare for life. But here . . . here she would live it.

She spun suddenly in a circle, her arms outstretched, her shoes scrunching on the sidewalk— like something from the opening sequence of a sitcom—and came to a stop facing the tavern. She laughed to herself and glanced self-consciously around the square. But no one had seen her, and it wouldn't really matter if they had.

Music from the bar grew louder as the door of the Hornet's Nest belched a small crowd of people. They laughed and hung on each other as they meandered down Milk Street, no doubt to walk along the piers in the unseasonably warm weather and stare out into the vast blackness that was the Atlantic Ocean.

Part of the tourist trade, most likely. She'd been told by more than one person this weekend that tourism had started early this year, thanks to an unusually warm spring. Most of the people at that bar right now were probably "from away," and it was only going to get worse. Summer, people had warned her, was far different from the frozen, snowy winters in Harp Cove. But that didn't scare Delaney. She didn't need throngs of people. She certainly didn't need the loud music and smoky press of a barroom crowd. In fact the only reason she was here right now, contemplating entry into the melee at the Hornet's Nest, was because of the guy in the red sweatshirt.

She'd seen him all over town this weekend—not always in the red sweatshirt, of course—and what a treat that was. He was exactly her idea of good-looking. She'd noticed him the first morning after she'd arrived, when she'd woken up early, as usual, and walked from her B&B to the marina in the crisp air. He was the only thing stirring other than herself, his red sweatshirt catching her eye across the empty boats anchored in their moorings. She watched him moving around his sailboat, tying stuff up, unfurling things and furling them back up, moving boxes from the dock into the cabin.

As she'd strolled along the walk within view of where he was docked, he'd looked up at her from the cockpit of the boat, dazzled her with a smile, and said, "Good morning" in a tone that seemed so intimate in the early stillness that she'd actually blushed.

Later she'd seen him at the post office, then the Clam Shack, the pharmacy, the hardware store, and, finally, this morning, the coffee shop. At first they'd exchanged hellos and short pleasantries—each interaction unaccountably making her palms sweat—until this morning in the coffee shop, when he stopped by her table and asked if he could join her.

He had dark blond hair and greenish brown

eyes. A rugged, slightly weathered face—from sun-drenched days on the boat, she presumed—complemented by white teeth and serious cheekbones. And he had hands that looked more than capable of producing any knot the Boy Scouts could dream up. They'd produced a few in her stomach, that was for sure.

Jack. That was his name. Sailboat Jack, as she referred to him in her mind. They had hit it off immediately, their senses of humor bouncing and feeding off each other so easily that their conversation had taken off like a shot and never gotten back to the basics. She didn't even know his last name. She only knew he owned the sailboat and it was named the *Silver Surfer* after some comic-book hero he'd read as a kid. And that tomorrow he was sailing back to Cape Cod.

"I decided to stay for the weekend because I know the band playing at the Hornet's Nest, down the street," he'd told her, "but tomorrow it's back to Massachusetts to spend a week putting a roof on my sister's house. She'll have my head if I'm not finished by the end of spring break."

Ah, a guy who knew his way around a toolbox. Good.

"Where in Massachusetts are you heading back to?" she asked, simultaneously relieved and disappointed that he did not live here in town.

"Wellfleet." At her obviously blank look he added, "It's a little town on the Cape." He stirred some sugar into his coffee.

"Wellfleet," she repeated. It sounded familiar.

His eyes flicked up to hers, his mouth quirked into a small smile, and she felt a quiver run through her. Everything about him was attractive, she thought. Even that tiny little glance.

"You probably wouldn't know it, unless you've been to Cape Cod." He glanced at her again, questioningly—the look somehow hitting her in the solar plexus—and she shook her head. "It's not much more than a couple of streets and a harbor, but it's nice." He shrugged. "Real artsy. Not much going on if you live there year round, though."

"I imagine this place is the same way," she said, looking out the window of the diner to avert the unaccountable blush she felt coming on. If she moved up here, maybe they could see each other again. How far was Cape Cod, anyway?

He laughed. "Sure. It's not as bad as Wellfleet, but it's pretty dead. Summer's a different story, though. I usually spend half the summer here because the crowds on the Cape are so much worse. That and my sister's kids are hellions. I'm usually ready to get away from them after a few weeks."

She laughed. "That's charitable. I'm sure your sister appreciates that."

"Believe me, she feels the same way."

"Well, it must be nice to have the whole summer off," she said, wondering if she'd found the fatal flaw in this seemingly perfect man. Sailboat Jack— unemployed drifter.

"Biggest reason I became a teacher." He flashed a smile as mischievous as any fifth grader's.

"Oh my God." She laughed. "Don't tell me you're paid to influence young minds."

He leaned his seat back on two legs and looked at her through amusement-narrowed eyes. "Don't worry. They only give me the hardheaded ones."

"Like your sister's kids?"

He laughed. "God, no. Not as bad as that. There seems to be a gene in our family that produces demon children. No, I like other people's kids fine, but the ones related to me are insane."

"Oh you'd feel differently if they were your own." She smiled, thinking it would be a shame if no one got the chance to inherit those beautifully lashed eyes.

"That's what everyone says, but I'm not sure I want to find out. I've avoided it so far, anyway." At this he stopped, tilted his head, and looked at her. "You have kids?"

"Oh no. I've been too . . . busy, I guess."

"I bet you'll get around to it," he said then. "You seem like the type to produce nice, quiet children." He smiled slightly, his eyes warm on hers.

For some reason the look had addled her brain because after that he'd invited her to the Hornet's Nest, and she'd declined. For what? she'd thought later. Another night alone in her room at the B&B? Twelve hours to think about leaving?

He'd tried to talk her into it. The band was terrible, he'd said. She really shouldn't miss the opportunity to get a headache without having to consume even one sip of alcohol.

But she'd continued to demur, mostly out of

habit, saying she had to get up early to leave the next morning. Which was true, but still. Why not go?

Unfortunately, her practical side told her exactly why not. He was too good-looking, he lived too far away, and the *last* thing she needed right now was the distraction of a man. Besides, even if she moved here, it wouldn't be for a year, and he would still live several hours away. And once she started working, she'd have no time for any kind of relationship, least of all one that would require a lot of driving. So what would be the point?

There was no point, but here she was. Standing outside the bar whose roof should be shaking from the force of the bass guitar inside, ready to take this last night and paint the town red.

She crossed the street and took hold of the door handle. Music blasted as she pulled it open and pushed into the bar. She was immediately enveloped by a blanket of smoke, heat, and humanity. All around her people with fresh sunburns and thick sporty sweatshirts laughed and bellowed at each other over the music. Delaney kept one eye peeled for Jack as she snaked her way through the crowd.

The bartender spotted her immediately as she bellied up to the bar. He sidestepped a coworker and called across the noise, chin jutting upward with the word, "Yeah?"

His forearms were enormous and covered with tattoos. A bird with upstretched wings slipped under her gaze as he took a cursory wipe at the bar in front of her with a dingy cloth.

"Beer," she called back, and gestured toward the tap with the Geary's lobster label on it.

He nodded and slid a pint glass under the tap.

Delaney leaned back against the round varnished edge and looked through the crowd. It was unlikely Jack would be wearing the red sweatshirt she'd first seen him in, but she found herself looking for it just the same. A surprising number of people were wearing red and each time she spotted it her stomach gave a little leap.

Simple physical chemistry, she told herself. Nothing but raging pheromones and overreacting endorphins. Still, she hadn't felt so infatuated with anyone since she was fifteen. But then this whole weekend had been spent enjoying life in a way she hadn't since childhood, so it should hardly be surprising.

She handed the bartender a five when he slid a dripping beer across the bar to her, and let the change sit in the puddle it had left. She'd be wanting another, she thought. She'd give Jack two beers' time to show up before she left.

"Hi, I'm Phil." A tall, pudgy fellow with a bright pink face squeezed next to her at the bar and held out his hand. His light hair was thinning, and his high forehead looked painfully sunburned. She automatically thought of cautioning him about the incidence of malignant melanoma in people with his coloring, but nobody liked a spoilsport.

"Delaney." She shook his hand.

"Come here often?" He smiled, revealing a row of smallish teeth.

Delaney smiled. Definitely not from around here, she thought. The accent was too New York, not enough Down East.

Then she caught sight of him. *Jack*. He shouldered through the mob with a grin here, a wave there, a short conversation over one shoulder, and a familiar clasp of hands with the bartender. His hands were tan against the sleeves of his white shirt, his left one—as it had been on previous occasions—ring free. His hair was windblown but fell into an unstudied style, and his sweatshirt bagged attractively to his jeans-clad hips.

As Delaney's eyes scanned lower, the thought came to her, unbidden and completely surprising: What would be wrong with a one-night stand?

Blushing, she looked at her beer. Empty. She ordered another.

"I'm sorry?" she asked. Phil had said something to her. She dragged her eyes from Jack's face and tried to look attentive.

"I asked if you were here with someone." He scratched his forehead, leaving a momentary trail of white in the scorched area.

"Ah yes, actually. I just saw the person who invited me." She inclined her head toward Jack and picked up her new beer, leaving the change for the bartender. She paused. "You know you can use calamine lotion for that burn. Or aloe vera."

"Oh." Phil raised a hand to his forehead and laughed self-consciously. "Yeah, thanks."

She smiled. "Would you excuse me?"

Delaney made it through the crowd to stand just behind Jack before she noticed the petite redhead beside him. They were talking while Jack leaned both elbows on the bar, watching the bartender draw a beer from the tap.

She stood uncertainly, wondering if he'd hoped she wouldn't actually come when he'd invited her, which was ridiculous. She let her eyes drop down his wide back to his legs and back up when the redhead turned and nailed her with bright blue eyes.

The wretched woman nudged Jack with her elbow, and said through an amused smile, "Hey, Jack, someone's checkin' you out."

Delaney shook her head and exhaled, then forced a smile as Jack turned around.

The look she got in return was well worth the embarrassment. His face lit up at the sight of her, and he gave her that killer smile.

"You made it!"

Delaney was pretty sure she was glowing. "I may be sorry in the morning, but I made it."

He pushed back to make a space for her in the crowd, and the redheaded girl behind him jabbed him in the back.

"Oh, sorry Carol." He adjusted his stance to face both of them. "Delaney, Carol. Carol, Delaney."

Delaney held out her hand. "Nice to meet you."

Carol's mouth formed a one-sided smile as she

shook Delaney's hand in a strong, bony grip. "You too."

"Carol was just complaining about how often she's had to listen to this," Jack explained.

"The bass player's my husband," Carol said.

"Oh." Delaney nodded politely, relieved. Then added, "They sound good," which was a lie so blatant both Carol and Jack started laughing.

"I told you she was nice." Jack shifted his eyes from Carol to Delaney.

"Or deaf." Carol smiled at her. "I'll leave you to your date, Shep." She threw a quick wink at Delaney, then turned back to Jack. "And don't forget, I have some stuff to give you before you go tomorrow."

"Might be early," he warned.

"I don't care. Wake me up." She pushed off into the crowd.

Jack let her go with barely a glance. "So what changed your mind?"

Delaney shrugged, unable to repress a smile now that she had him to herself. What was it about him that turned her into a grinning idiot? "I'm not sure. I packed my bag and sat on the bed and thought, what the hell."

Those hazel eyes, so unthreatening yet so unnerving, smiled back. He raised a brow. "What the hell, Jack? Or what the hell, beer?"

Delaney swallowed some of her beer. "That's a very leading question."

He raised his brows and crossed his arms over his chest. "I know."

"I think I'm going to have to give you the safe answer and say beer."

He shook his head and picked up his glass. "Story of my life."

"Oh I'll bet."

They both laughed.

They stood next to each other for a long minute while Delaney searched for something to say. But all she could think about were his hands. What would he do if she took one in hers? she wondered. If she just held it, felt the breadth of its palm, the arrangement of its bones . . .

He leaned close. "Hey, this is about as slow as this band gets. Do you want to dance?" He gestured toward the packed dance floor.

Delaney glanced at the dancers locked in close embraces under a couple of dim strobing lights, and looked back into his eyes. "Yes. I would."

He took her hand, enfolding it in his, and she squeezed it, feeling a sudden, overpowering hunger to be touched. They weaved through the crowd.

"I find myself wishing I'd decided to spend the week here," he said, drawing her toward him with one hand and putting his other on her hip. "But then you're leaving tomorrow anyway, aren't you? It wouldn't have done me any good."

He was tall, at least six feet because Delaney at five-foot-five had to look quite a ways up to meet his gaze.

"Yes. I've got an 8:00 A.M. flight." She wondered if she should mention that she might someday be back, but decided against it. Too many ifs and assumptions in that. Besides, he was probably just being polite.

"So we're destined to be two ships passing in a weekend, huh?" He cocked his head.

"Well, one ship and a rental car."

He laughed. "Right. Unfortunately the rental car's moving a lot faster than my ship. So, what is it you do for a living? No, wait, let me guess."

She gazed up at him, brows raised.

"You're a vet. Veterinarian, that is, not a war veteran. You've got that scientific look in your eyes."

The guess was so close she was momentarily taken aback.

"Wow, I'm impressed," she said.

He bent his head toward her to hear as she spoke, and she could smell the shampoo he used, or maybe it was the fabric softener from his sweatshirt. Clean.

"So I was right? No kidding—hah!"

She'd been about to correct him, but he looked so happy to be right she didn't have the heart.

"You know," he continued, "I went against the obvious. Since you're from D.C., I might have gone with lawyer, but you seem too human for that," he said over the music.

She blinked up at him. "How did you know I was from D.C.?"

He smiled. "There are very few secrets in a town this small."

"Goodness." It was all she could think of to say. Why hadn't she found out anything about *him*?

He chuckled. "Don't look so nervous, now, I'm

only kidding. You told Lois, at the diner, and she told me right after we had coffee this morning. Actually, I think her exact words were, 'Don't even think about it—she's from D.C.' "

Delaney breathed a small sigh of relief. For a second she thought he might have called up the rental-car agency or somehow riffled through her purse. It would be just her luck to pick some great-looking stalker to flirt with.

They moved to the music, a vague, easy sort of rhythm. Her hand was on his shoulder, her palm small against its width.

She wanted to look up at him, to study his face, try to detect a flaw, but she couldn't just stare up at him from so close. It wasn't that he was perfect. No, he was not a pretty-boy. It didn't even look as if he'd shaved today. But he had the kind of face that intrigued. Masculine, expressive. The flick of an eyebrow, the flash of a glance, the smallest smile, all communicated with an eloquence she found mesmerizing.

"Are you here on vacation?" His breath brushed her ear as he leaned in.

She had the ridiculous urge to turn quickly and catch his lips with hers.

She spoke loudly toward his ear. "Yes. It's beautiful here. I've had a great weekend."

"And you sure got some great weather," he added.

She nodded, again toying with the idea of telling him she might be back. But the unusual and illicit idea of a one-night stand was still strolling around the back of her mind and revealing too much about herself somehow seemed to compromise that.

"You're very pretty, you know."

Delaney's eyes flicked back to his.

He shrugged, as if he couldn't help but pay her the compliment. "I have a weakness for blue eyes and dark hair. An Irish fixation, you might say."

"Hm, that doesn't sound healthy."

One side of his mouth kicked up. "Is that your medical opinion, or a warning?"

She lifted a brow but could not stop herself from smiling. "You decide. You're very pretty too, by the way."

He laughed. "If that's true, then I guess there *is* a secret or two left in this town."

She smiled. Great-looking and self-deprecating. The guy couldn't be shaping up any better.

She leaned toward his ear again, ostensibly to speak over the music but also because she liked the way his hand ran lightly up her back when she did so. "I don't know about you, but I could use a little fresh air. Do you want to go for a walk?"

He cocked his head and regarded her speculatively. "I don't know. Would I be safe with you?"

She shrugged. "Guess you're going to have to take your chances."

He shook his head, his eyes warming in a way that sent her heart racing. "I'm nothing if not a gambler. Let's go."

Delaney gave him the keys to her rental car. She probably wasn't supposed to, but she didn't care.

She wasn't in a mood for rules tonight. They rode through the night with all the windows down and their hair blowing wildly about their heads. Jack's would probably look fabulous at the end of this beating, she thought, but hers would look like something out of Greek mythology.

But she didn't care about that either. She felt too good. Delaney took deep breaths of the sharp, clean air. A twinge of coolness in the breeze had her cradling her arms across her chest, but the scent of pine and sea salt was so intoxicating she leaned her head on the seat back, looked out the window, and relished the feel of the wind in her hair. A half-moon sat high in the sky as the car flew down the road to the sea.

She looked over at Jack, saw his hand draped easily on the wheel, and she laughed out loud, stretching one hand out the window. The wind grabbed her fingers, and the sleeve of her white shirt billowed. Jack laughed too. For some reason she was sure he felt exactly as she did.

They reached the shore—a wide and deserted stretch of sand that Jack knew about—and stepped out of the car. The closing car doors echoed like gunshots in the stillness. The ocean rolled blackly ahead of them, invisible but for occasional white-caps on the waves and the low *hush* of sound.

The beach, white in the moonlight and dotted with boulders, stretched out before a forest of dark towering pines. To Delaney it felt like an elaborate secret. Remote and primeval. She pulled off her shoes and ran toward the water, sand still warm from the day's sun, flipping up behind her bare feet and crackling against her jeans. She slowed when she reached the dampness near the surf and was caught from behind by strong arms. She hadn't expected him to follow, but the feel of his arms around her was so delicious she laughed as he pulled her from her feet and spun her.

"Do you know how beautiful you are?" Jack turned her around to face him. He bent his knees to look levelly into her eyes. "No, I don't think you do. I sure am glad I waited till tomorrow to leave."

His smile was open, and she surprised herself by putting her arms around his neck. "Me too."

Jack's hands ran down her sides, broad palms following her curves, warming the skin beneath her cotton shirt. Her body drank in the sensation, craving more, pushing close. She wanted to curl into his hands like a cat being stroked, wanted his touch everywhere, awakening her senses.

His lips touched hers, and she melted against him, opening her mouth as his tongue slipped past her lips. His arms tightened around her. She let herself go, awash in the feel of his hair in her hands, his chest on hers, his long, muscled thighs against her legs.

He cupped her waist, exploring the shape of her, making her feel small, sensual, and important. She wanted to disappear into his body, become nothing but a spark of heat and passion dancing along the waves.

Jack made a sound low in his throat and pulled away. "Damn." His voice was quiet, his hands tight along the small of her back. "My heart is beating dangerously fast."

"In that case, I prescribe a cold shower."

Even in the dark she could see his eyes smile as his hands traveled up her back. "You might be right." In one fluid motion he swung her up into his arms and started walking.

"What are you doing?" she demanded, but she could not help the laugh that skipped out across the beach.

She could just make out the dimples his smile made. "Veterinarian," he said, moving toward the water, "heal thyself."

Before she knew it, he was wading into the surf, cold waves crashing about his legs. She clung to his neck, screaming with laughter and giving in to the abandon that had taken over her soul.

Despite herself, Delaney heard herself squealing like a teenage girl who wanted nothing more than for the teasing to continue. "Don't! Oh God, don't do it. I'm serious. Please."

Jack waded farther in, until Delaney felt the icy water hit her in the behind. She shrieked with surprise, pulse racing, hands gripping his shoulders. Then an unseen wave whitecapped in front of them and she knew it was all over—at least the dry part. The wall of water pushed them backward until the wave broke over their heads, but Jack's arms were tight. He dunked them under the crest, the cold shocking, and they floated upward on the other side of the breaker.

Delaney sputtered, laughing, out of the water.

"I'm sorry." Jack flipped his hair out of his eyes, water spraying her face. His laughter sounded close in the vast night, and she clung gratefully to the warmth of his body against hers. "I didn't mean for that—"

Another wave caught them and this time they broke apart, rolling and bouncing in the surf. Delaney's palms scraped the sandy bottom and water tugged the shirt from her pants. They surfaced independently in the shallows and crawled out to the shore.

Delaney's hair and shirt were plastered to her body. Her jeans were stiff as wet cement and coated with sand. She got just out of reach of the waves and fell onto her back, shivering. Sand crunched beneath her as she gasped for air, laughing and coughing at the same time.

Then Jack was beside her, warm and potent, his lips on hers, salty, wet, and demanding. Passion exploded within her. She brought her hands up to his forehead, pushed back the hair that dripped water onto her face, then slid her fingers down his back, pulling him onto her. He stopped, sat up, and pulled his shirt over his head. Delaney's hands instantly reached for the cool skin of his chest and stomach.

He smoothed the hair from her face and bent to kiss her lips softly.

"Want me to help you out of those wet things?" he asked, his voice low.

Delaney wanted nothing more, but she hesitated. Habits of caution die hard, she thought, then said slowly. "You know . . ." A smile spread itself across her face. "I think I do."

She sat up and plucked at the buttons of her shirt. Jack stopped her, raised her arms and peeled the wet shirt up and over her head. She felt it go with a mixture of exhilaration and surprise. He unhooked her bra and tossed it aside with the shirt. The night air caressed her breasts, and the chill made her nipples stand hard.

"Jesus, Mary, and Joseph," he murmured. His hands skimmed her body, raising shivers of pleasure along her skin. "I don't know what I did to deserve it, but tonight I am the luckiest man alive."

Delaney touched his cheek. "It's not luck." She wasn't sure why she said it, or even exactly what she meant. All she knew was that she felt something stronger than the moment seemed to warrant.

He turned his head and kissed her palm, his eyes on hers. "No." His voice was quiet, and they looked at each other for a slow beat.

He moved his hands to cover her breasts lightly, then brought his head around to kiss beneath her ear. Her neck curved back as his lips moved down to her collarbone, then on to her breast. He took the peak in his mouth and she inhaled with the sensation, his tongue swirling around the aureole before pulling against the nipple. She arched back, and his hips pressed into hers, his erection obvious.

Part of Delaney's mind attempted to get her attention, tried to reason whether or not this was smart over the thrum of nerves and the humming of adrenaline. But her limbs were molten, and only her hands sought answers. Her body was in the grip of an instinct more powerful than reason, one she had no inclination to ignore.

She shifted to her side and her fingers fumbled for, then found the button of his jeans. The zipper opened easily, and she pushed her hand into his heat. He inhaled when she touched him, and she smiled at his obvious pleasure.

"I want you," she heard herself say, and knew for a fact at that moment that she was dangerously drunk. Drunk with abandon and excitement. Drunk with pleasure.

They parted and shed their jeans as quickly as they were able, laughing together at the effort it took to get the wet denim over their damp bodies.

As they came back together he stopped and gazed at her. "Delaney." His voice was deep.

"Jack." Her voice was just a whisper, and the word felt strange on her lips.

He pushed his hair back from his face and took her hand, looking down at it a moment. His thumb moved across her fingers as if counting the number of bones.

"I want you to know that . . . I find you incredibly attractive."

Silence hung in the aftermath, and while he looked like he might say more, the absurdity of the statement struck her, and she began to giggle. Here she was, naked in front of him, just as he was in front of her, and he decided to tell her he's attracted to her?

He smiled, too, but continued looking at her hand. "I guess I just want to say that I don't do this all the time."

Delaney paused, the smile still playing about her lips. Though she hadn't been nervous about him before, she felt even better about him now. He was a truly nice guy. Just as she'd suspected.

"I don't either," she said, glad to be able to make the admission. "But I sure want to tonight."

He kissed her, then, until they were both lying on the sand, the waves licking at their feet.

His hot skin warmed hers and the feel of his chest, his palms on her body, his tongue tracing her lips, exhilarated her. Their hands roamed, caught each other, squeezed, and moved on. Jack's fingers trailed down her stomach and into the hair at the apex of her thighs. Delaney opened her legs and felt his fingers slide slick inside. Her muscles stretched and contracted at the same moment, and in the dark she saw him smile. She breathed out with a satisfaction she hadn't felt in years.

He kissed her neck again and traced his tongue to her ear. She shivered.

"Wait." His voice was molten lava, his breath hot on her cool skin. He started to pull away.

"No." She held him. She didn't want anything to stop. Her body felt possessed, craving his hands, his lips, his touch inside of her.

He kissed her lightly. "Just for a second," he whispered. "Let's be careful." He reached for his pants.

She let go and watched him, missing the warmth of his body on hers. She folded her arms across her stomach.

He wrestled a wallet from the back pocket of his wet jeans and pulled from that a plastic packet. A condom.

Relief almost made her laugh. He didn't want to stop, she thought. *Thank God.* But what a fool she might have been, carried away as she was. She, the doctor, hadn't thought of a condom.

A wave broke low on the bank and tickled her feet. Jack opened the package with deft fingers and pulled the condom out. He hesitated. Her eyes scanned his body, from his chest to his hardened manhood, before she realized he'd paused. She looked into his face.

"Are you sure, Delaney?" His quiet voice carried over the sound of the surf.

She paused. This was a man who carried a condom in his wallet. A man who had a day and a half ago no fewer than three women on his boat. A man who, despite his words, probably did this all the time. She knew she should think harder about this.

She nodded. "I'm sure."

He smiled, then slid his hand behind her neck, under her wet hair, and kissed her soundly on the lips.

"I could really fall for you."

Her lips curved against his, and she fought an urge to laugh. What was it about this guy that made that kind of corny line so seductive? She pulled him down over her. When he entered her, smooth and sweet, she felt as if her body were welcoming him home. They fused and moved as one. Their breath coursed together, and their hands spoke volumes to each other, more eloquently than words ever could.

Maybe it had simply been too long a time, but Delaney didn't remember sex ever being like this. How in the world had she gone so long without *this*, she wondered, as her body and mind rolled in waves of desire. Her hips rose, and he thrust deeper and harder inside of her. His arms and chest flexed under her roving fingers, and his hips drove against hers in a driven, instinctive rhythm neither one could stop.

"I wish you could stay inside me forever," she whispered.

"I will," he said, then threw back his head with a deep exhalation. "Oh Jesus." The words floated on a breath as he pulsed deep within her. "Don't move. I'll stay. I promise I'll stay."

And he did, until Delaney thought she'd spun off the face of the earth to glitter with the stars so clear in the sky above.

Chapter 2

Six weeks later Delaney sat in the bathroom of her D.C. apartment and stared at the white-plastic stick in her hand.

A minus sign and a plus sign. First one, then the other, big as life on the narrow piece of plastic. Such childish, simple things. She pictured them written big and blocky on a schoolroom chalk-board. 1 + 1 = 3

"Dee?" Michael, her best friend since high school, called through the door, his voice tentative with concern. "Your mother's on the phone. Should I tell her you'll call her back?"

Her arm began to ache, and she dropped it to her lap, shifting her gaze out the bathroom window to the Dumpster in the alley.

"God, yes," she said, amazed that her own voice emerged so steadily.

"Right."

She heard his steps return to the phone in the kitchen, then his muted words placating her mother.

I've been on every other night this month, she thought, *the toughest call schedule I've had this year. That's why I'm tired. That's why I feel kind of sick in the morning. That's why my period is so late. I'm stressed.*

She dropped her head, her eyes closed.

"What did she want?" Delaney called back through the door when she heard Michael return to the living room. Surely if she thought about something else for a while the pregnancy test in her hand would disappear.

She was a *doctor*, for God's sake. Doctors didn't accidentally get pregnant.

"I'm not sure. Maybe it was her mother's intuition, but she said she was just calling to chat. How weird is that?"

Delaney frowned. Her mother rarely called "to chat." Maybe her father had left the house for cigarettes or something. Otherwise, Mrs. Poole would never dare have a conversation he was not aware of.

Michael's steps approached the bathroom door again. "Honey," he said against the crack, his voice muffled and close, dramatically intoned, "dare I ask?"

She took a deep breath. "I think it's wrong," she said finally, and heard him sigh heavily. "I should probably throw it away and start over tomorrow, or the next day."

"Dee." His voice, always gentle, was implacable.

"You've put this off long enough. Don't toy with me now. Did you get a result?"

He was right. It was already unavoidable. The vague nausea, the missed period, the sudden sensitivity to smells and foods, it all made perfect sense. Her body was behaving properly for the situation she had gotten it into.

"Yes." She closed her eyes and pressed a hand to her fluttering stomach. *Fear*. She stood up and opened the door. Michael's soft blue eyes and concerned expression nearly undid her. She swallowed hard and held out the stick for him to view. "I'm scared, Michael. I can't remember the last time I felt this scared."

Michael's face reflected the same shock and disbelief she felt. "Oh Dee," he said. "Oh God."

He opened his arms and she stepped into them. It felt weird. Michael was not a tall guy and his frame was slight. They'd never been physically affectionate with each other, but they'd shared so much in their fifteen years of friendship that she couldn't turn away from the gesture. Still, it felt odd to be held by Michael. Everything in this circumstance felt odd.

"This is wrong," she said into his shoulder. "Have you ever had that feeling? That you're falling into a situation that is just utterly wrong?"

He laughed ruefully, and they stepped apart. "All the time. But I know you don't. I can't believe this is happening to you."

She backed up and sat down on the toilet lid. "It could be wrong."

Michael shrugged, and she knew neither one of them believed it.

"When I was a kid," she began slowly, "I always had the feeling that things were out of my control. That's why I spent my entire adult life managing things so meticulously. You know how I worked in high school. How I saved every dime to get to college, and then medical school. And now, when I'm finally close to getting out of residency, when I'm finally going to get to live a life of my own choosing and control, now I'm supposed to deal with this? How could this have happened?"

She glanced up and saw a dubious look on Michael's face and had to laugh. "All right, I know how it happened. But I had sex one time in the last seven months. *Once*."

"I know," Michael said gently.

Delaney swallowed back tears. God, when was the last time she'd cried, for pity's sake?

"Oh hell," she said then, forcing a wry smile to her lips. "All right, it's not as if this happened without my participation. Nothing immaculate about this conception." She tried to laugh.

"That's right, at least you got the benefit of some great sex first. You did say it was great, didn't you?"

Her rueful smile became real for just a second before she squelched it. "Yeah, so I had some great sex with a good-looking guy who had a little charm. A one-night stand with a guy whose last name I can't even remember . . . though I think someone called him 'Shep' at some point. And now

I'm going to have his child. Can you beat that? God, when I screw up, I do it right."

It was inconceivable. So inconceivable, in fact, that even as she sat there, stunned, she could not work up the requisite panic the situation seemed to call for. *Thank God for Michael*, she thought. Just seeing his concerned face kept her from feeling as if her life was over. At least she wouldn't be alone through it. Michael would help her.

"So you were responsible for what happened. It almost doesn't matter now," Michael said. "The facts are what they are. So what are you going to do about them?"

She looked up at him and shrugged. "I'm going to have a baby."

He raised one brow, a hand on his hip. "Are you?"

She knew what he was implying, that she had another choice. But she knew in her heart she didn't.

She nodded slowly. "Yes. I am." After a second she added, "It's funny. I always assumed I'd think about having children later. It was one of those 'maybe someday' things, you know?" She shrugged, then smiled wryly. "I guest someday is today."

He stood silently a minute, their eyes on each other. "You know what?" he said finally. "I'm not even worried about you. If anyone can handle this, you can. Now come on." He leaned into the bathroom, took her hand, and pulled her up.

Delaney tossed the pregnancy test into the trash can as he pulled her out into the living room.

"What are we doing?" she asked.

"We're going to figure this out." He sat her down on the sofa and seated himself in the armchair across from her. "Now. Remember how we worked through the problem of your getting out of your house to go to college? Remember how we found you that public-health money for med school? Remember how we got you this apartment for next to nothing?"

She nodded after each of these things.

"Well, we're going to figure this out, too. Now I'm going to ask you some tough questions, and I want you to give me your gut answer. All right?"

She nodded again, mentally thanking God that someone else was here to take charge of her chaotic thoughts.

"How far along are you?"

She counted backward to that balmy April night. "About six weeks." Her mind worked. "That would make the fetus about the size of a grain of rice right now . . ."

She paused, thinking how close that felt to being correctable, changeable, as if she could just take a tiny step back in time and alter reality.

"Pretty small," Michael said, watching her.

She nodded. But there was only one way to alter this reality, and she couldn't do it.

"So that puts the due date around . . . January 20," she said quietly.

There had probably already been some softening of the cervix and uterus, she thought. "I should start prenatal vitamins immediately. And there are some tests that should be done as soon as possible.

Hematocrit, rubella titer, Pap smear, urinalysis, albumin, white blood cell, blood and bacteria, and tuberculin skin tests."

She ticked them off as if she were taking an exam.

"Okay," Michael said. "Think of this clinically, if that helps you. Anything else?"

She felt a blush rise to her cheeks. "VDRL and gonorrhea tests should be done, too." *Because who knew anything about Jack Maybe-Shepherd?*

Michael frowned. "Honey, I thought you said you used a condom."

"I *did*," she said with all the feeling of injustice the situation provoked in her. "And it should have protected me from some of that, but let's face it. It's already failed—spectacularly—on at least one front, so the tests should be done." She pressed three fingers to her forehead and took a deep breath.

"All right, all right." Michael sat forward in the chair, his hands out patting the air calm in front of him. "Now, here's the toughie. Will the father be involved?"

A shudder ran through her. "No," she said immediately. "No, no, no. I don't need some man in here thinking he has a right to tell me what to do. Besides, I have no idea how or where to find him. I can't even remember the name of that town he said he was from. Something like Wellsley? Wellsmead? Who knows?"

"Dee, honey, that's sounding like an emotional response to me. Think about it now."

"No," she said, shaking her head, unwilling to stop and examine the anxious flutterings in her head and stomach. "I can do this on my own. After all, I'm going to be thirty years old in a couple of months. I've got a solid career and a stable income. There's no reason I can't have this child and bring it up myself."

"Except that he's the father," Michael said gently.

She rubbed a hand across her forehead again.

"He's got a stake in the outcome," Michael continued.

She exhaled firmly.

"He might be needed by your child down the road. He might want to help raise it, be part of its life."

"He might think he could tell me what to do," she objected. Adrenaline pumped through her veins so vehemently that she almost stood up. The only thing that kept her seated was knowing that Michael would think she was getting hysterical, and she hated anyone thinking she was anything but rational and logical. "He would think he could tell me what I'm doing wrong, or how I should be. He could have the mistaken idea that I owe it to him to alter my plans to accommodate *his* rights."

She stood up then, aghast, and walked in a circle, stopping next to the sofa upon which she'd sat.

"But what rights does he have?" she demanded. "He has no rights. We had a one-night stand. No strings. Neither of us said anything about seeing each other again."

Michael was wearing that dubious look again. He ran one hand through his hair, the tight blond curls springing instantly back into shape.

"And why should we have?" she persisted. "He lives somewhere in Massachusetts. I live in Washington, D.C. Who would pursue a romance over that long a distance? We had sex, that was all. One overexcited night that came and went like the weather. I know it sounds absurd, Michael, but I feel very strongly that he has little to do with this child."

For a second she remembered lying on the sand, feeling his hands smooth the wet hair back from her face. Strong, capable hands behaving so gently. She remembered his eyes, thick-lashed and kind, seductive in their attentiveness, and a faint fluttering kicked up again in her stomach. Not fear this time. No, she remembered all too well the passion he'd awakened in her.

"There," Michael said, standing up and jarring her from the memory. "What was that look for?"

"What look?"

"The look that was just on your face. This guy was more to you than a fun night on the beach, now, wasn't he? Come on, be honest. And remember, I *know* you, Delaney."

She turned abruptly and walked to the kitchen. "Do you want some tea? I'm suddenly in the mood for some tea."

"Delaney," he said in a warning tone, following her into the kitchen.

"Okay, maybe," she said as she pulled a pot from beneath the stove, "maybe I do owe him something—notice or fair warning that he's going to become a father. But how in the world will I find him?"

"Isn't there someone in that town who might know him?"

Delaney paused, her hand on the faucet. "There was this one woman I met in the bar that night. Carol somebody-or-other. Oh but God, Michael, imagine the conversation we'd have to have. And if I end up going back to Harp Cove for my assignment, it would be foolish to let anyone know the circumstances of the child's conception."

She filled the pot with water, put it on the gas stove, and waited for the flames to catch as the gas hissed against the pilot light. Then she turned around, leaned against the counter by the sink, and crossed her arms over her chest.

"Plus I don't know her last name either, so it'd be just as hard finding her as Jack. And even if I were able to track down a Jack Shepherd—and who knows how he even spells that—he could be a 'John' or it could be 'Sheppelini' or something—just imagine the conversation we'd have. 'Hello, Jack? Delaney Poole here. From last April—Harp Cove? One-night stand? Yeah, well, I'm pregnant, and you're the father.' How in the world could he respond to that, do you think? He'd probably say something like 'Who is this again?'"

Michael chuckled.

"Or this," she continued, nearly frantic to wipe the skeptical look off Michael's face. " 'Jack. Delaney Poole. One-night stand—Harp Cove? Guess what. I'm pregnant, and you're the reason. Yes, you did use a condom. But yes, I'm sure. No, I'm not a slut. No, I don't want anything—just letting you know. Okay, you have a nice life too.' "

"I have a hard time believing you'd sleep with a guy who had that in him. Do you really think he's that bad a guy?"

She sighed, panic making her tired. "I don't know. No, I guess I don't think he's a bad guy. Honestly, I have no way of knowing what kind of guy he is. I barely know him. But while I'm not going to say that he is a bad guy, I have to consider the fact that he *might* be. Don't you see that? He could be grossly irresponsible. Untrustworthy. A heavy drinker. A gambler. He could even be a child abuser. Good grief, he could be psychotic, a serial killer for all I know, or *worse*."

Michael frowned. "What would be worse?"

"I don't know. I can't think." She shook her head and pushed her hair back from her face. "I just believe I'm better off alone, raising this child in the safe, controlled environment I know I can provide. Don't you see, Michael? It's definitely best. I'm going to love this baby. I'll make sure it gets healthy, positive male influences. You, for example! But I will not subject it to a father who for all I know could be insane."

With a relieved exhale she turned to the boiling pot of water. "What did I boil water for?"

Michael leaned against the counter and crossed his arms over his chest. "Tea."

"Oh, right." She pulled a couple of mugs from the cabinet. "Plus—God, I'd forgotten about this— he practically *told* me he didn't want to have kids."

"You guys talked about kids?" Michael's expression was incredulous. "Wow, you do move fast."

She waved a hand and poured water into two mugs. "It wasn't anything serious. He was basically telling me he didn't like his sister's kids. But then he said—and this I do remember—he said, he'd avoided it so far, becoming a father. And something to the effect that he didn't want to find out if he'd like kids that were his own, the way everyone always says you will."

She turned to look at Michael. "Doesn't that sound to you like someone who doesn't want to have kids?"

Michael shrugged dismissively. "It sounds like something a lot of single guys say."

"I don't know," she said, shaking her head. "He sounded serious to me. The bottom line is, though, sure, the father may have some rights—and I could fire off a litany of them right here because I'm a liberated woman who believes in being fair—you know that. But those rights pale beside the welfare of a child, don't they?"

Michael said nothing. She turned away, not wanting to guess what the look on his face meant.

"Well, they pale beside the welfare of *my* child," she said, then paused. She stood for a moment facing the stove, hot teapot in hand. "Good God," she murmured as realization dawned, slipping like a tiny shaft of light into her brain. "I'm going to be *a mother*."

Chapter 3

Harp Cove, Maine
July, one year later

Jack Shepard sat at a back booth in the dim cavern of the Hornet's Nest. His fingers pushed a cloudy glass filled with Coke in a circle as he thought about the best tack to take in breaking up with Lisa Jacobson.

She would be there momentarily, with all her bounce, perk, and generally exhausting youthfulness, at which point he would have to have what he mentally referred to as The Talk.

Normally, he dreaded The Talk. The it's-not-you-it's-me conversation required to let women he didn't want to date anymore down easy. He had a hard time with absolutes, and an even harder time hurting people's feelings, which is why he always went so far out of his way to date people he wouldn't have to break up with. Like tourists. When summer people went back to their homes there were no hard feelings. Not answering a letter or returning a phone call was far different from telling someone *I'm just not interested anymore*.

But though Lisa, a cute, buxom blonde, had been fun for the last couple weeks, Jack was pretty sure he couldn't survive another night of nineteen-year-old bar talk without taking a swizzle stick to his frontal lobe.

He looked up as someone slid onto the cracked vinyl seat across from him.

"Kind of early to be sitting in a bar." His brother pushed an envelope across the table to him.

Jack moved his glass to the side. "It's just Coke, ask your bartender. What's this?" He picked up the envelope and saw his father's handwriting across the front. *Kevin Shepard, The Hornet's Nest, Harp Cove, Maine.*

"Dad's latest news. Read it." Kevin inclined his head toward the letter, his expression grim.

Jack exhaled and closed his eyes. "You'd think he'd at least remember the zip code." He turned the envelope over in his hands without pulling the letter out. It was not good news, he knew. Aside from the fact that it was never good news, he had spoken to his father a couple months ago and had a feeling he knew what the letter contained. For some reason his father always called Jack and wrote to Kevin.

The postmark was Boca Raton, Florida, where his father had been living the high life for the last year. Up until then it had been hard to keep track of the old man, but for some reason Florida had stopped his twelve-year whirlwind tour of wealthy retirement communities.

Jack rubbed his forehead. "Why don't you just tell me what it says."

"All right. Are you ready?"

Jack leaned back. "I'm sitting down."

"He's marrying her."

Jack squinted across the table at his brother. "Marrying *who*?"

"That *girl*. Whatshername . . . the latest bimbo." Kevin's face grew red as he shook his head, agitated, and looked toward the door. A few dusty rays of sunlight squeezed in around its imperfect edges.

Jack felt a dull surprise momentarily stop him. This was something his father hadn't mentioned, though it now made sense why he'd stayed so long in Boca.

"But that's not the worst of it." Kevin took the envelope back and shoved it into his breast pocket.

Jack waited a second. "Okay, I'll bite. What's the worst of it?"

"He wants to sell the place." Kevin glared at him, chin raised, as if Jack might dispute the fact.

Ah, Jack thought, this was what he'd been expecting. Still, hearing the words out loud again made something inside of him lurch. The place— the only one the brothers had in common—was the house where they'd grown up, where Jack lived now. The fieldstone house on the coast where his family had flourished and floundered for the last hundred and fifty years. Give or take.

For a second Jack thought of his mother, thousands of miles away in California, free from the shrinking band of struggling Shepards camped on the windy shore of Maine. He should do the same thing, he thought. He should leave Harp Cove. Start fresh somewhere else. What difference did it make if your family had slept on the same piece of land for over a century? Really, he wanted to know, what *difference* did it make?

He took a deep breath and picked up his Coke. "I know. That's why I've been fixing the place up."

Kevin gaped at him. "What are you talking about? You *knew*?" The words were practically a whisper, as if he were too stunned to speak at a normal level.

Jack nodded and looked away, toward the door through which Lisa would pop at any moment. *I should move away*, he thought again.

He rubbed the back of his neck and looked at Kevin. "Look, it's just a house. You didn't want it. Dad doesn't want it. And I can live anywhere."

The words were colder than he felt. The truth was that when his father had told him about selling the house Jack had spiraled into an angry sort of depression. But his anger, unlike Kevin's, was not directed at their father, and his depression was something inscrutable even to himself. Both emotions, however, sprang from disappointment in himself. Why didn't he have a house of his own by now? Where was his future taking him?

But he was not about to get into listing his own

shortcomings with Kevin, who would be all too willing to help catalog them.

"Just a *house*?" Kevin slammed his palm down on the table and looked at the ceiling, his jaw working. "I don't know what the hell's the matter with this family. Am I the only one who doesn't want to throw away generations of work? If Great-grandfather Elias were here, this would not even be discussed. He's probably spinning in his grave right now."

"If Great-grandfather Elias were here, we'd be selling it to pay for his nursing home. But it's Dad's house now. He can do what he wants."

And he wants to sell, Jack thought. For a lot of money—much more than Jack would be able to scrape together. He knew. He'd checked.

"What Dad wants is to marry a bimbo," Kevin said.

Jack shrugged.

"He'll probably use the money to buy some prefab condo in Florida and a big fat diamond for his trophy wife. Makes me sick." Kevin scoffed and looked down at the table. "So that's why Dad told you to fix the place up."

Jack nodded. "Yeah. So he could sell. That's why I put in the new furnace and redid the front hall. I'm working on the carriage house now."

"Well, thanks a whole helluva lot for telling me."

Jack laughed once. "Call me crazy, but I was a little worried about your reaction."

"Jesus Christ," Kevin muttered. Then, with an

accusatory glare, he added, "I thought you rented the carriage house."

"I did. Or rather, Bill Knecht did. I decided to let Knecht Realty handle the arrangements. Being a landlord isn't exactly my style."

"No, I can see where there'd be a little too much responsibility in that role for you."

Jack didn't even blink at the familiar denunciation. "Yep. But I told him I'm going to have to work on the place while the renter is there, so I'm lucky he found a taker. And you know who it is? The new doctor. A Dr. Poole. He's moving in next week, after I finish the second bedroom. Apparently he's got a kid."

Kevin looked at him shrewdly. "How much are you getting?"

"Three-fifty."

"A *month*?" He pushed his hands back through his hair and looked scandalized. "That's ludicrous! You could get twice that, easily. Especially from a doctor."

"Not while I'm working on it. And when was the last time you were in there? It's pretty rough. The kitchen hasn't been updated in God knows how long, and the laundry room was home to a whole community of mice. Besides, in order for me to have access to it anytime I want while fixing it up, I had to rent it cheap."

Kevin sighed. "This is a crime. Jesus. So how long have you known about it?"

"That he's going to sell? About two months." Long enough to discover there was no way he could save the place, not without a huge influx of money from God knew where.

Kevin stared at him, shaking his head. "You know, this is *just* like you, Jack. You *and* Dad. Not only do you not care about losing the place, but you're not even valuing it while you're there. Is there anything on earth that *is* important to you? Three-fifty, my ass. Next thing you know you'll be marrying a bimbo yourself. Like father, like son." He slid jerkily out of the booth, knocking the table so hard Jack had to catch his glass with one hand before it could spill across the table.

"Kevin, give me a break." He scowled. "It's Dad's place, and it's Dad's decision. There's not much we can do about it if he wants to sell. You know how he is."

Kevin looked down on him. "Yes there is. You could buy it from him. He'd sell it to you."

Surprise, disguised as a laugh, escaped Jack's lungs. "What?"

"I said you could buy it. You're already living there. It's about time you put down some roots anyway."

"Roots? I don't need any roots. Besides, what makes you think I could even afford that place?"

"Oh come on. You've been working at that school for five years. You've got to be making decent money."

Jack laughed at his brother's naïveté. Didn't everyone know teachers were notoriously underpaid? Football coaches were even worse, but he had no intention of setting Kevin straight on the matter. Why give him yet another reason to consider his brother a failure?

"Why don't *you* buy it if it means so much to you?" Jack retorted.

"I can't. You probably don't remember since you obviously can't think about anything but yourself, but Carol and I are buying the salon so she can set up on her own. Besides, we've got her place. And this place." His arms flopped out from his sides as he momentarily surveyed the empty bar around them. "I even talked to the bank about it, but with three mortgages already they practically laughed me out of the office."

"Well, they've got a point. With all those places, what do you care about Dad's house?"

Kevin shook his head. "It's our history, asshole. Our heritage."

The bells on the front door clattered, and both looked over to see Lisa push through the door. She squinted into the dimness, clutching a large metal object to her chest, then smiled when she saw them and waved.

"Here comes your bimbo now," Kevin said.

"What in the world has she got with her?" Jack asked.

Kevin shook his head at Jack's latest mistake. "I can't be sure. It looks like a bust of some sort . . . Wonder Woman, maybe?"

Jack resisted the urge to bury his head in his hands. God help him, The Talk couldn't take place soon enough.

Kevin looked down at his brother and issued a

reluctant laugh. "Guess I'll leave you to your day-care duties. We'll talk about this later." He walked off.

"Hi, baby," Lisa chirped as she approached. She bent down to kiss him on the cheek as she dropped the metal bust on the table. It landed with a solid *thump*. "I got you something."

Jack stared mournfully at the chrome bust—and he did mean *bust*—of what did indeed appear to be Wonder Woman. The figure was sculpted down to just below a pair of impressively pointed torpedo tits, as they'd been affectionately known in junior high school. The chrome was pocked along the back of the flowing hair and on portions of the fore-head. One of the breasts was dented, too, creating a point at the nipple that looked lethal.

He glanced at Lisa. "Is that . . . Wonder Woman?"

Lisa's brow furrowed, and she tilted her head to look into the figure's face. "Who?" she asked, look-ing back at him, perplexed.

Jack sighed. No, The Talk couldn't take place soon enough.

Delaney put her hands on her hips and bent back-wards to stretch her spine. It was only her first day on the job, but it had seemed interminable. Emily had woken up at four that morning screaming her head off with a dirty diaper, and though Delaney had changed and fed her, she hadn't gone back to sleep.

"Can't leave yet," Nurse Knecht said with a tone of resigned irritation that was rapidly becoming familiar to Delaney. "We got a walk-in." She handed Delaney a chart and took the one Delaney had just finished from the examining-room counter. "A head laceration. Not too serious but probably needs stitches."

Delaney took the chart and bent over to touch her toes. Standing around on the tile-covered cement floor was doing nothing for her back, she decided. She should start doing yoga or something. Ever since Emily's birth she'd been meaning to get back to some kind of exercise program, but it wasn't easy. Especially with the move.

"You should take a hot bath when you get home," Nurse Knecht said. "I hear that hotel's got a whirlpool."

Nurse Knecht—who insisted on being called by the archaic "Nurse Knecht," pronounced "connect," instead of "Miss Knecht" or her first name, "Janet"—was the sister of Delaney's realtor, a wonderful man named Bill Knecht who cleverly used the name in his logo: Knecht Realty . . . Connecting People to Places. Bill was as friendly and warm as his sister was odd and had managed to find Delaney the most amazing little stone house to live in. Not only was it ridiculously affordable, it was right on the water. The only catch was it wouldn't be ready until next week.

"I'm not in the hotel. I'm staying at the Reynolds' B&B."

"Down there near the harbor? Why, they don't even have TV." Nurse Knecht looked irritated afresh.

Delaney smiled. "I know. That's what I like about it."

Which wasn't exactly true. She'd stayed at the B&B the last time she was in Harp Cove, which was the weekend Emily was conceived. Though it was probably a classic symptom of guilt for not providing Emily with a father, Delaney had the desire to expose her daughter to the things leading up to her existence. As if it would constitute some sort of communion with her history, Delaney thought, which was, of course, ridiculous. For one thing, Sailboat Jack was little more than a sperm donor, in her opinion. For another, he was nowhere to be found.

She knew this because after all her soul-searching of the year before she had eventually decided to try to find him. She'd looked up Shepards and Shepherds from Harp Cove to Provincetown, Massachusetts, and there'd been plenty. Three hundred and twenty-one of whom were Johns or J's. She'd even called a few—a John Shepherd in Truro, Massachusetts, on Cape Cod, who was sixty-eight years old and hard-of-hearing. And a J. Shepard in Harp Cove, whose number was disconnected. She'd even tried an L. J. Shepard in Harp Cove who turned out to be a woman and a Jack Shepherd-Johnson in Boston who was British.

Still, Delaney had mostly fond memories of her weekend with Sailboat Jack, and she was determined to keep them fond. Someday, maybe, she'd be called upon to tell Emily stories about her absent father and remembering him well would help that, she'd decided.

She'd already had to tell one story about him, but that was not to Emily, and it was fairly simple. To head off any questions about Emily's existence she'd told her employer, Dr. Jacobson, that she was divorced; and she was ready to tell anyone else who might ask the same thing. After all, this town was not about to accept the truth, and Delaney was not about to offer it.

It wasn't as if it was a huge lie, however. It just simplified things and was relatively easy to pass off. She was divorced, and Emily's father had very little contact with them. Sometimes it happened that way, and anyone who pressed her for more details would get a curt "I don't wish to talk about it" in response.

"Give me a minute before sending the head-lac in," Delaney said, straightening from her latest stretch. "And could you ask the receptionist to call Tiny-Tot Daycare and ask Cora to bring Emily here on her way home? She said she'd be happy to do that if I ever got busy. Of course I didn't expect to have to take her up on it the first day."

"All right."

Delaney tried to judge from the nurse's tone if she was annoyed at this request, but it was impossible to tell. The woman sounded perpetually annoyed anyway.

Oh well, Delaney thought. Too bad if she was annoyed. Delaney missed her daughter, and if Cora was willing to bring Emily to her, then Nurse Knecht was just going to have to deal with it.

Emily, Delaney thought with a smile. It was funny, after her shock and terror at finding herself pregnant it was amazing how much she enjoyed being a mother. Nothing had ever made her feel so useful—not even medicine—or so loved. Emily had become everything to her and she could not imagine her life without her.

"I'll give the head-lac a pressure bandage," the nurse said, and left, her back ramrod straight as she closed the door firmly behind her.

Mrs. Danvers, that's who she reminded Delaney of. Mrs. Danvers from that movie, *Rebecca*. Stern, sour-faced, malcontented. She suppressed a shiver and opened the chart in her hands.

Jack Shepard.

Delaney's heart skipped a beat. The name at the top of the chart leapt out at her and she dropped the folder as if it were poker-hot. For a long moment she couldn't breathe, then she gasped for air, realizing immediately that she was hyperventilating.

She moved to the edge of the examining table and sat, the paper cover crinkling beneath her. She put her head between her knees and breathed into her shirt.

Oh my God, she thought. *Oh my God oh my God oh my God*. Sweat broke out across her skin, and she found herself swallowing so many times her mouth went dry.

From the corner of her eye she saw the folder lying bent against the floor, the orange label unreadable from this distance. Surely she'd read it wrong. It must have said something else. Joan Shepard, for example. It was just that she'd been thinking about Jack, and so she'd seen his name.

She pushed herself off the table and gingerly picked up the folder, peeling back the cover as if a confetti snake might pop out.

Jack Shepard. Male. 34 years old. Allergic to penicillin.

Delaney placed the chart on the counter and laid her palm flat against it, holding it facedown against the Formica.

Oh my God, she thought again, and with that, the door behind her opened.

Delaney spun and saw a short, blond girl with some kind of metal head in her arms enter the room. The man next to her held a bloody bandage to his forehead, but Delaney could not look at him. Instead, she focused on Nurse Knecht, behind them, as she shut the door.

Delaney's eyes rose to the man's face at the same moment his descended to hers. For a moment, silence gripped the world.

For Delaney, the ground seemed to dip beneath her feet as she looked into the long-lashed hazel eyes she'd had so many dreams about, waking and sleeping. She didn't waver—no she still had that hand palm down on Jack Shepard's chart—but even though the dizziness had passed, she was unable to move.

He was not, as she'd grown to tell herself, an average guy who had simply caught her at a delirious moment. He was every bit as handsome as she'd remembered. And she found herself staring at him in stupefied silence while the little blonde rattled off an introduction of herself and the problem at hand.

"Hi! I'm Lisa Jacobson," she burbled. "You probably know the name because Dr. Jacobson, your boss, is my father."

For his part, Jack stood staring at Delaney, too, his mouth agape, bloody gauze at his head apparently forgotten.

"I brought this with me," Lisa continued, depositing the head on the examining table, "because my father always said the doctor needs to know what caused the cut, 'cause you can get diseases and stuff from them. So here it is, Doctor . . . what's your name?"

Delaney blinked slowly and shifted her gaze to the blonde, swallowing hard. "Yes, my name is—"

"Delaney."

The word from his lips shocked her anew and nearly made her shiver with . . . *what?* She wasn't sure. She remembered his voice so clearly from that night. Low and intimate . . . telling her how beautiful she was while his hands explored every inch of her naked flesh.

But at the same time ten thousand terrified thoughts careened through her mind. *Emily's father. A man with a claim. A resident of Harp Cove. A scandal waiting to explode. An unknown influence on her tiny daughter's life. An unknown threat to her defenseless daughter's future. The sperm donor suddenly come back to haunt her.*

"You *know* her?" The little blonde's face screwed up as she looked at Jack.

Delaney cleared her throat. "Dr. Poole," she said, holding an icy hand out to Lisa Jacobson.

Lisa turned back to her, scowling, and took her hand. "Yeah, nice to meet you. So here's the head—he can keep it when you're done. I don't care."

Delaney shifted her hand toward Jack like a robot while the girl talked. He moved the bloody bandage to his left hand, looked at his messy right hand, and took the gauze back into it. Then he reached out with his left hand, and took hers as if he were about to lead her from the room. And he gave her that dazzling smile.

"Delaney Poole," he repeated, his expression at once delighted and amazed. "You have no idea how many times I've wondered what your last name was. Or where you were and what you were doing."

Delaney nearly laughed—hysterically—at the statement. Oh if *you* only knew, she thought.

"When did you guys meet?" Lisa asked.

"So, are you visiting again from Cape Cod?" Delaney shifted her eyes to his chart, now somehow in her hands, and hoped her voice did not sound too hopeful.

"Visiting? No, I live here." He paused. "Oh. No, I was just visiting Cape Cod last year. Not visiting *from* there. I've lived here my whole life."

Delaney's eyes shot up to his. *Then why the hell don't you have a phone?* Not that she'd really *wanted* to reach him. And now it was too late . . . wasn't it? She didn't need to tell him now. She *couldn't* tell him now. Looking at him here, in the flesh, he suddenly seemed quite large. She had no idea what he was really like.

She cleared her throat again. "So, what seems to be the trouble?" she asked in her most clinical voice.

"Well, I seem to be bleeding." She could hear the smile in his voice.

"Yeah, and it's his own fault," Lisa added, her voice so caustic Delaney turned to her. "Well, his and this thing's." She laid a hand on the top of the head, disrupting its balance, and sent it crashing to the floor.

It hit with a loud, dull *clang*, and bounced toward Delaney's foot. She jumped, feeling like a raw nerve, and realized as the thing rolled to a stop against the cabinets that it was a bust of Wonder Woman. And her left cheek was a good bit flatter now than when she'd come in.

"Oh, sorry." Lisa bent to pick up the head, drawing Delaney's attention to her short skirt and young, athletic legs. "Listen, like I said, I'm not sure how it happened, but Jack hit himself in the head with this sculpture."

Jack gave Delaney a dry look. "I don't know what possessed me."

"I was trying to give it to him," Lisa continued, pushing the head back onto the examining table, "for his boat, but he didn't want it. Just like he doesn't want me. So I'm thinking he got what he deserved. In any case, it was this part here that caught him." Lisa touched the point of a dented breast with one pink-nailed finger.

"In some cultures it's probably a rite of passage," Jack said with a crooked smile, "to have a scar from the breast of Wonder Woman."

Delaney recognized that she should laugh at his comment, but she was frozen inside. Literally paralyzed with shock.

"You see, Jack was trying to tell me he's not the right man for me. Just like he's not the right man for any woman, not after a couple weeks anyway."

Delaney's eyes drifted back to Lisa's face. *This* was her daughter's father's girlfriend? *This* was the kind of woman Emily would be exposed to if somehow it came down to sharing custody?

"Lisa, I think you've helped about enough," Jack said, turning around and opening the door. "Thanks for bringing me over. I can get home on my own."

"Fine." Lisa shrugged and shot him a chilling look as she sauntered out the door. "Suit yourself. But don't bother calling when you get lonely 'cause I don't want *nothing* more to do with you."

"All right, thanks," Jack said amiably, closing the door behind her as if she'd just dropped off a plate of cookies. He turned back to Delaney.

The room was deathly quiet, the only sound the ticking of the plastic clock on the wall over the door.

"So," he said, "here we are."

Delaney's insides were quaking so hard she wasn't sure she'd be able to move without tipping over, so she leaned against the counter, his chart against her chest under crossed arms.

She cleared her throat once again. "I didn't expect to see you."

"No." He shook his head. "Me neither. You, that is."

Another moment of silence passed.

His brow wrinkled. "I thought you were a vet."

"Ah, no." Delaney glanced at the floor. "Since I didn't know you very well, I decided not to clear up that little, um, misunderstanding."

Jack's expression, that had been so open and happy to see her, was transforming inch by inch to one of confusion.

She nodded. "Listen—"

But he spoke at the same time. "It's just—"

They both stopped.

He grinned. "Go ahead."

"No, you." She wasn't sure exactly what she was going to say anyway.

He smiled and looked down. She noticed his cheeks flushing and for a moment felt a spasm of empathy for him.

"I just . . . I mean, I know we left on strange terms, last time we met. But I don't think we need to feel so . . . so awkward around each other." He looked up at her, his eyes crinkled into a danger-

ously appealing smile. "I mean, I'm really happy to
see you again."

"I'm married," Delaney blurted, then felt as
shocked as he looked.

The clock ticked even louder.

Jack's face went slack. "What?"

"My . . . I have a husband. Yes." She nodded, unable, it seemed, to stop.

"Oh." This time he cleared his throat. "Congratulations. Newlyweds?" He pulled the bandage
from his forehead and looked at it.

Delaney noted the cut and shook herself into action. "God, here, sit down. I'm sorry." She motioned for him to sit next to Wonder Woman.

This was good, she thought, nervously review-
ing her hasty lie. This was better. This way she
could just look at the cut, irrigate it, stitch it, and
not have to look him in the eye again.

She turned back to the counter and snapped on a
pair of gloves. Then she took the bottle of sterile so-
lution and a wad of gauze and turned back to him.
His eyes flicked away as she turned.

"So, are you newlyweds?" he asked again.

So much for hoping he'd forget the direction of
the conversation.

"Uh, no. Over a year, actually. Nearly two, in
fact."

"Two years?" he repeated.

Story details ran in and out of Delaney's mind as
she rapidly revised the story she thought she'd be
giving people. Okay, instead of divorced I'm still

married. Instead of my husband having no contact with Emily, he's a big part of her life. He's a *devoted* father, she thought frantically. And why wouldn't he be? Emily is his own daughter, his own flesh and blood, the product of their marriage, their decision to have children, their love.

So where the hell was he?

"Yeah, ah . . ."

He sucked in his breath as she moved a flap of skin.

"Listen, I'm sorry," she said again, manipulating the laceration so he would feel just enough pain to keep from being able to concentrate on her. "I was married when we met, but my husband and I had been going through a bad time. We were, uh, talking about separating." *Yes*, she thought, *perfect*. Someday when she wanted to be rid of this husband, she could then say she divorced him. "But we worked it out, and now we're fine."

"You were married?" His brows rose, and he tried to turn to look at her, but she pushed the gauze onto the cut and held his head in place. "That night," he persisted, "you were married?"

Delaney's cheeks flamed as she worked. An unfamiliar shame for cheating on this new husband engulfed her.

"Separated," she said defensively. "But now we're okay."

"So he's here now, too."

Damn. Delaney's mind scrambled. "Actually, not yet. He, ah, hasn't found a job here yet."

A knock sounded on the door. Delaney breathed an audible sigh of relief. "Come in."

She expected to see Nurse Knecht, but instead it was Cora carrying a happy, gurgling Emily. Delaney's stomach hit the floor.

"Here she is," Cora cooed. Emily beamed at Delaney. "Sorry, Dr. Poole. I wouldn't've interrupted except that I have to be home in ten minutes. Want I should give her to the nurse?"

"Yes, that would be fine," Delaney said, hoping Nurse Knecht didn't turn out to be some kind of cannibal. "I'll be with her in just a few minutes."

Cora left, and Delaney could not meet Jack's eyes. Did he know? she wondered. Had he sensed he was in the presence of his own daughter? Had the world actually stopped, as she'd felt it had, when the whole family was there in the same room? No, he must have thought it was just another patient.

"And that would be your baby," Jack said softly.

Delaney started. "What did you say?"

"Your baby. The one who needed the extra room fixed up at the house."

Delaney gaped at him as his eyes met hers. They were very close, and her hand rested on his forehead. For a second she imagined leaning into him, feeling his arms come around her to hold her up and steady the quaking his astonishing presence had induced in her.

"How did you know that?" Her voice was nearly a whisper.

He gave her a one-shouldered shrug and looked at her with eyes that looked sad.

Then his mouth crooked up into an obviously forced smile, and he said, "I'm your landlord."

Chapter 4

The moment Jack left, Delaney sank onto the rolling stool and covered her face with her hands. She had to get out of that lease. She couldn't possibly live so close to Jack Shepard. God, she'd even given *the landlord* permission to enter her house at will. *At will*. That meant anytime. When she wasn't there. When she was. Unexpectedly. Undesirably.

It also meant that in addition to fixing the roof, renovating the kitchen, and replacing the drywall, he could riffle through her things, find evidence that her husband was nonexistent, and discover the pertinent, damaging details about Emily.

Or rather, Emily's father.

Not that there was much of that lying around, but still. She couldn't give Jack Shepard that much opportunity to be around Emily. Because if he were around Emily, he would begin to think. To wonder. To *suspect*.

She had to get out of that lease. She balled her hands into fists and placed them on her knees. She could do it, she could get out of it. She hadn't even moved in yet. She *had* to do it.

But what excuse could she give? If it weren't completely believable, *that* could be the thing to cause him to speculate. It was a small town, after all. He would see her and Emily regardless. Would it be more dangerous, more suspicious to extricate herself from the lease than it would be to stay?

She exhaled and rubbed her temples with her fingers.

Where else could she go? It was the middle of summer, and Harp Cove, small as it was, was a resort town. The nicest houses were booked months in advance all the way through Columbus Day. That was why she'd contacted the Realtor back in March, and why she'd felt so lucky to find the "lovely stone carriage house by the sea" Mr. Knecht had so enthused about.

Lucky, she thought. *Hah*. Lucky to find herself right smack in the middle of the spider's web. Of all the places, she thought, rolling the heels of her hands along her temples. *Of all the gin joints in all the cities in all the world . . .*

She grimaced. Suddenly *Casablanca* didn't seem so romantic. Maybe Ilsa was horrified to find herself back in such close proximity to Rick. Maybe the whole affair with him had been a lie, and it was a grave inconvenience for her to have to deal with this skeleton from her closet on top of the war and the letters of transit and everything else she and her husband were going through. Suddenly it was clear the movie's writers were masters of ironic satire. *Casablanca* wasn't a romance—it was a parody.

A sharp knock sounded on the door. Delaney jerked upright. "Yes?"

Nurse Knecht opened the door. "I'm leaving now. Emily's asleep in her car seat in your office, and Maggie's here to clean up."

"That's fine. Thank you, Nurse Knecht," Delaney said, sitting stiff as a poker on the short chrome stool, like a disobedient child in the corner.

The nurse's hawk eyes surveyed her for a moment. "You leaving yet, or should I tell Maggie to leave your office for last?"

"I'll be leaving soon, thank you. I'll tell Maggie." *Just leave*, Delaney's mind shouted. *Leave so I can wallow in my shock and consternation.*

The nurse nodded once and left, somehow managing to close the door with disapproval. Or perhaps that was just Delaney's guilty conscience. Because despite what was undoubtedly an unhinged expression on Delaney's face, even Nurse Knecht would never suspect her of harboring the illegitimate child of a hometown boy.

Not that it mattered. Nurse Knecht was but one person in this town. If the truth about Emily were to come out, how many others would treat her with disapproval? Most of them, Delaney was sure. For this town was nothing if not conservative. And the unwed mother of a child conceived during a one-night stand would hardly be embraced as a valuable member of the community, let alone be considered a trusted and respected physician.

Which was the whole reason she'd concocted the *ex*-husband to begin with. Was it really so much more complicated to have an absent husband? No, she was just panicking because she hadn't expected to run into Emily's real father at all.

She should have planned for this, she told herself. After all, she'd met him here last year: why hadn't she considered that she might meet him again? Well, she had, sort of. She just hadn't considered that he'd be living here instead of visiting. That he'd be able to find out about her child by looking out his own damn window. That he'd turn out to be her landlord, for pity's sake. In her imagined scenario their meeting was brief, cool, and information-free.

Now that she'd told him she was married, however, the words could not be taken back. So she was stuck with a new lie—a much grander, more complicated, less malleable lie—and she had to make the best of it.

"Hey. You must be the new doc."

Delaney looked up to find a short woman with a dark mass of shoulder-length hair standing in the doorway. She leaned one hand on a mop, the other on the doorknob.

"I'm Maggie Coleman. I clean up here at nights. That your baby in the office?"

Delaney took a deep breath and rose, extending

her hand. "Yes. I'm Dr. Poole. That's my daughter, Emily. Was she still sleeping?"

Maggie took Delaney's hand in a strong grip, her brown eyes direct. "Oh yeah. She's out. Cute little thing. What is she, four, five months?"

Delaney's mind spun with the implications of the question. Having so recently acquired a husband as defense against Jack's sudden presence, she now needed to consider her daughter's age. Emily was six months old. Should she lie to throw him off? And by how much?

Delaney nodded. "About that."

"I've got a kid myself. Blake. But he's seventeen now."

"Really?" Surprise tainted the word. Maggie couldn't be much older than Delaney was herself. Maybe thirty-one or thirty-two, Delaney guessed.

Maggie chuckled. "Yeah. I had him young. High school, you know. Things got out of hand pretty quick for me, I guess. But I gotta say, I'm still glad when it takes people by surprise. Some days I feel as old as the hills."

Delaney gave her a professional smile, the one she'd trained herself to use no matter what state of mind she happened to be in. "Well, you don't look it. But right now I've—"

"Hey, was that Jack Shepard I saw leaving here?" Maggie jerked her head, curls bouncing, toward the front door through which she must have seen Jack leave.

"I'm afraid I'm not at liberty to disclose who my patients are."

Maggie laughed, a boisterous, uninhibited sound, and ambled into the room. "Boy, you *are* new in town, aren't you?" The paper cover crunched as she rested one hip against the examining table. "Your patients are everyone in town, just about, so it's not like you'll be letting any big cat out of the bag. I was just wondering because I heard his girlfriend gave him a black eye at the Hornet's Nest this afternoon. Guess it musta been more than that if he was here, huh?" She laughed again. "Serves him right, the lout."

Delaney schooled her face to a bland expression, though sweat broke out on her palms. "He's a lout?"

Maggie snickered. "Yeah, he's a lout all right." But her mouth curved and her eyes held what could be called an affectionate glint. "It's probably safe to say he's dumped nearly every woman in town, one time or another. 'Cept the ones too old for him. Doesn't seem to have any trouble going the *other* direction, though, if you know what I mean. That girl who hit him today isn't but nineteen. And him a ripe old thirty-four."

Delaney swallowed over a lump of mortification. The guy was a playboy, great. "Sounds like you know him pretty well."

"Sure. Everyone does. We follow the adventures of Jack Shepard like it's a friggin' soap opera. But I do know him a little better than most. We've known each other since high school, after all."

Delaney affected a casual tone. "And he's been, ah, a ladies' man since then?"

Maggie shrugged. "Oh sure. It's easy in high school. And now . . . well, you know, he's a good-looking guy. Big fish, small pond. He gets his pick. Plus he coaches Harp Cove High's football team, and if there's one thing you should know about this town, it's that it's football *crazy*. Coach Shepard's gotten them to the state finals every year he's been coaching, so in this town that makes him a celebrity, believe me."

"He's a *football coach*?" Delaney frowned. "I thought he was a teacher."

"Sure, that too. He teaches something, I don't know. Phys Ed, I think."

Delaney scoffed, the sound out of her mouth before she could stop it.

Maggie gave her a curious look. "Sure, it's not much to someone like you. But here it's a big deal. Lot a these kids wouldn't never get outta this town but for football scholarships."

"Maybe they'd get academic scholarships if they devoted that time to their studies," Delaney said, wondering what sort of father a football coach could possibly make. A *womanizing* football coach. Who taught gym. Not even English, or math, or history. He taught—trampoline and—and rope climbing.

Visions of her high-school gym class flickered through her mind. Awful afternoons in a sweat-scented gym, running around in blue-and-white shorts sets at the command of a large, angry woman.

Jesus, what had she been *thinking*? The very idea of Emily discovering she was the offspring of a two-bit playboy made her heart stutter with anxiety, not that Emily was about to understand any of it at the ripe old age of six months. Still, there was no way her child was going to grow up in a place—even for the three years it took Delaney to fulfill her NHSC obligation—where everyone knew she was the love child of the town rake. No, this secret had to be kept, at all costs.

Besides, how great of a role model would she, Delaney, appear to be if her daughter found out that her mother had gotten knocked up by an ignorant, small-town Lothario with no aspirations?

Maggie drifted toward the door. "I guess someone who goes into medicine's got to be pretty into books and stuff, huh?"

"I suppose." Delaney dragged her attention back to the woman in front of her.

Maggie smiled. "That's good. Me, I watch too much TV. Somehow it always seems easier, you know? But books are good. I'm trying to get my Blake to read more."

Delaney nodded. "It's important."

"I don't know, though, all he ever wants to do is play sports or watch 'em. Personally, I think they're as addicting as cigarettes. This country ought to be organizing a suit against the TV people. You know—"

"Listen, it was very nice to meet you, Maggie. But I've got to go. Shall I leave this door open?" Delaney stood and moved toward Maggie and the door, suddenly unable to sit still a moment more. She had to get Emily and go home. She had things to do. She had a husband to invent.

Maggie stepped back to let Delaney pass. "Yeah, I still gotta do this room. Good to meet you too, Dr. Poole."

Delaney walked quickly down the hall to her office. She didn't like leaving Emily alone, even at such a short distance, but gleaning what she could from Maggie Coleman had seemed important. Because now she knew.

Now she knew that Jack Shepard was an opportunist. A cheap—albeit good-looking—sexual opportunist. She was lucky she hadn't ended up with some disease. Whatever remote—and they had been *extremely* remote—thoughts she might have harbored about that night on the beach being somehow special, she now knew they were false. That night was special only because it had brought her Emily. And now was the time to protect her.

Delaney gathered up her purse and Emily's diaper bag and slung them over her shoulder. Then she picked up Emily's car seat and eased from the room.

Emily's petal pink cheeks were flushed in sleep, her dark lashes smoky against the pale baby skin. Standing outside her office, looking down on her daughter, Delaney felt such an overwhelming rush of love and protectiveness there was no question in her mind that what she was doing was right. She had to convince Jack Shepard and the world that Emily was her "husband's" baby. She had to keep Emily to herself no matter what.

Delaney jumped and glanced up as Maggie clattered from exam room one with a rolling bucket at the end of her mop.

"See you tomorrow!" Maggie waved a rubber-gloved hand.

Delaney gave a halfhearted wave. "Yes, see you tomorrow," she murmured as Maggie rattled down the hall.

Jack sat in his truck outside Sadie's Diner the following morning and fingered the spot near his shoulder where Delaney had jabbed the needle. Had it been his imagination or had she been a little too zealous in popping him with that tetanus shot? Yep, there was a bruise, he could feel it. She had been upset upon discovering he was her landlord, that much was certain. She couldn't have looked more shocked, or displeased.

Come to think of it that's pretty much how she'd looked the moment she'd laid eyes on him. Shocked and displeased. Which was a long way from how he'd felt upon seeing her. He shook his head, trying to remember how they'd left things after that night on the beach.

Not that he hadn't done that before. No, he'd gone through it a thousand times in his head. *Why didn't I ask for her phone number? How in the world did I not get her last name? Why didn't I find out exactly where she lived? Did she know anybody here—anybody I could ask about her? How did none of this come up in conversation?*

Yes, he'd kicked himself over and over for not being able to find her, because he sure hadn't been able to forget her. That night had been incredible. After days of seeing her flitting about town like a ghost sent to haunt him, he'd finally gotten up the nerve to ask her to join him at the Hornet's Nest. Granted, he'd suffered several mortifying hours of rejection after she'd told him she wouldn't come, but then *there she was.* Beautiful, elegant, nymph-like. She was mesmerizing with her clear, intelligent eyes and subtle smile. God, the mere thought of how she'd looked at him as she'd asked him to get some air had his muscles tightening in all the right places.

Or the wrong places. Because he'd wondered that, too. If they hadn't had sex, would she have gotten back in touch with him? Was it the suddenness of it that made her disappear? The stigma of giving herself on a first—what was it?—not even a date? Because for him it had felt like much more than sex. Even before they'd gone to the beach it had felt to him like a *connection.* Like something he'd never felt before with any other woman. He'd looked into her eyes and he'd seen comprehension. A deep, soul-stirring recognition.

At least that's how it had seemed. And he'd understood her, too, he'd thought until yesterday. Yesterday, when she'd told him she was married and had been even at the time they'd been together.

Disillusionment swept over him again. He supposed he could be angry that she hadn't told him, hadn't been honest, but that would be pointless. Besides, what he felt wasn't anger, it was sadness, and that profound, confusing disappointment.

None of it made sense to him, either, though he was willing to concede it could be because he didn't want it to. *Face it, Shep,* he thought, *you would have found something about her that bugged you if you'd had anything more than a few short—passionate—hours. Why would you think she was right for you when every woman you've ever known has been wrong? Thinking about her all this time's been nothing but wanting what you couldn't have.*

Still, he couldn't give up the idea he had of her. For the first time in his life, he thought he'd met The Impossible Woman—the woman he wouldn't eventually want to dump. Though he'd never spoken of it to anyone, his perpetual unhappiness with women was actually a great source of despair for him. It wasn't that he didn't *want* to find Ms. Right, he just hadn't been able to. And he'd started to believe she didn't exist.

Until last summer, that was.

He could still see Delaney standing by the bar in that oversize white shirt, her eyes large and vulnerable in her lightly tanned face as she agreed to dance with him. She'd been free that night. Emotionally, spiritually—and yes, sexually. He inhaled sharply at the memory. God, making love with her had been like nothing he'd ever experienced. And it had ruined him for other women ever since.

Yeah, right, he told himself. The *fantasy* had ruined him. And what he needed to do now was discover the reality. If only to save himself.

Delaney sat at the counter in Sadie's Diner and mechanically chewed a piece of toast. Barely aware of what she was putting in her mouth, she sat riveted to the conversation of four old men going on behind her.

"Beaned him with some big piece a metal's what I heard," one of the old voices creaked.

Actually it was a table of five old men, she could see in the mirrored wall behind the counter, since one had come in late and pulled a chair up to the corner. They were gleefully recounting the story of Jack's injury the previous day at the Hornet's Nest.

"That little Lisa's got a temper on her, always has," another, raspier voice chimed in. "She may be cute, but she's tough."

"No tougher'n Jack," a third said. This was the one with the red hunting cap, complete with earflaps like Elmer Fudd's, Delaney was fairly certain. She'd heard him speaking when she'd first come in and noticed him because he'd watched her with undisguised interest. "That there's the new doc," she'd heard him stage-whisper as she'd passed to sit at the counter.

"Oh, Jack ain't so tough," the raspy voice said. "He's just a sucker for a pretty face, but it never lasts. And disinterest always trumps interest."

"Disinterest—what? What the hell are you talking about, Sam?"

"I mean," raspy-voiced Sam continued, "that Jack only appears tough because he's a love-'em-and-leave-'em kinda guy. Ayup. Nothing they can do if he doesn't want 'em. But if he ever meets up with a woman he wants, *then* we'll see who's tough and who's not."

Delaney forced another forkful of eggs between bloodless lips as the bells on the door chimed.

"Now Myrtle, she's got a recipe for clam chowder'll make you think you've died and gone to heaven," Elmer Fudd said.

"I believe you're right," Sam chimed. "I had that last year at the VFD chowder fest."

Delaney swallowed, then nearly choked as she heard Jack's voice.

"Morning, Sam. Norman, Howard. How you boys doin' today? Marvin. Joe."

She glanced once in the mirror, then quickly away when she saw Jack notice her. His footsteps behind her shifted, then approached.

"And good morning to you, Dr. Poole," he said, sliding onto the vinyl-covered stool beside her.

Delaney swallowed hard and turned to face him. He wore a calm smile, but his eyes were wary, not nearly as open as they'd been yesterday when he'd first seen her. Then there'd been hope, even gladness, in his expression. At least she'd thought there'd been.

Until she'd dropped the husband bomb on him. Which reminded her, she had to remember to tell Dr. Jacobson and Kim McQuade, the clinic administrator, about her newly minted marital status.

"Good morning." Delaney glanced at the fresh bandage on his forehead. The old men would have a field day with that after he left, she was sure. "How are you feeling today? Any headache?"

"Now, Doc, I'm not going to make you work over breakfast. How are *you* doing on this fine day?"

Delaney flushed, aware that the table full of old men was silent now, no doubt listening intently to their conversation.

"I'm just fine, thank you."

"Hey, Melinda," he greeted the girl behind the counter. "Just coffee, please." He turned back to Delaney. "I've got some good news for you."

She swallowed the last of her tepid coffee and motioned for the check. *Good news*, she thought, *what could that be? He's moving? He's accepted a position in Kuala Lumpur lasting at least three years? He's sterile and Emily was a conception all my own?*

"What's that?" She plucked the napkin off her lap and laid it next to her empty plate with an unsteady hand. Had she really eaten all that? she wondered, unable to remember a single bite. She must have just been shoveling it in as she listened to the old men talk.

Jack rested an elbow on the counter and shot her a look from the corners of his eyes. "When's your husband coming up?"

Delaney's stomach hit the floor, irrationally surprised to hear her lie coming back at her so quickly. She looked at her plate, then pushed it away from her. "Uh, I'm not sure, why?"

"Well, the house'll be ready for you to move in tomorrow. I imagine he'd been planning to get here in time to help move your stuff in, right?"

"Oh? Tomorrow? That's early . . ." Should she say something now about getting out of the lease? What could she say about her husband's not arriving? He, he had a job, in D.C. They were living apart at the moment until he could find something here. Something impossible to find here . . . he was—a lawyer! Yes! A D.C. lawyer. What in God's name would he do up here?

"Couple of days early." He shrugged and dumped a seemingly endless stream of sugar into his coffee, his large hand steady and sure. "I thought you'd probably want to get settled as quickly as possible, though, what with your daughter and all. So I moved a bunch of stuff out of the spare room last night and cleaned it up."

Delaney's pulse thundered at the mention of Emily. "It's not making much difference to her right now. She spends most of her time at Tiny Tot Daycare."

"Really? Tiny Tot?"

He looked at her, and she felt her stomach quiver. Why? There was nothing in the look. Just directness. Just curiosity. Just that bronze-green color and those long deadly lashes that had made him look so languidly passionate that night on the beach . . .

"Yes."

"My sister used to work there. Years ago, of course, when she was in high school. She didn't like it much, though."

"Oh?" Monosyllabism seemed to be the best Delaney could do, conversationally.

"No, something about too many babies needing a lot more than they could give." He shrugged, then seemed suddenly aware of what he'd said, and added quickly, "Not that they're like that now, probably. I'm sure it's great now." He laughed, and she thought she saw a tinge of pink hit his cheekbones. "I don't want you to feel like you have to worry or anything."

Delaney bit her lip. She was a bad mother, that's what he thought. She knew the place was too crowded, but she'd had little choice. The other, more desirable day care was full, and she didn't know any other mothers in town who might be taking on a baby or two in their homes. And having Jack point out a chink in her Good-Mother armor seemed especially dangerous.

Delaney picked up her check, then slid her legs to the side in order to rise. "It was the best I could do. The other place has a waiting list, and I've got Emily on it."

"Emily? That's her name?" Jack's eyes seemed to pin her where she sat.

She nodded, then grabbed up her purse to paw through it for her wallet.

"That's nice, a pretty name," he said. She looked back up at him. His lashes dropped and he gazed into his coffee cup. "Emily ... What's your husband's name?"

Her stomach clenched. "My husband? Why?"

He frowned, no doubt at her tone. "Just curious. He wasn't on the lease, so I was wondering . . ."

Suspicion, Delaney thought. *Good God, he's checked the lease.* She quickly looked back into her purse. What was his name? She picked up her coffee. *Joe*, she thought. *No, that was the name of one of the old men. Jim. Yes, Jim. James.*

"James," she said then, firmly.

He nodded slowly. "James. He go by Jim?"

She lifted one shoulder and nodded mutely.

"Jim Poole," he said, almost to himself.

"Uh," her mind spun. Poole? Or something else? Should she be a modern woman and have kept her own name? Or would that perhaps alienate her from the people of this town? Should she worry about that? Why hadn't she thought of all this for the divorce scenario? Oh hell, she should make it something other than Poole, shouldn't she?

But the moment was lost, she'd already appeared to have acquiesced.

"So was Jim planning to be up here for the move? Because if moving in early's going to leave you on your own, I can help you."

No! her mind screamed, and she opened her mouth to say it. But she certainly couldn't put off a move based on the arrival of a man who didn't exist. She should accept his help; otherwise, he'd be looking for Joe—*no, Jim*—Poole to show up.

"That would be nice of you. But I'm sure I can hire someone." She exhaled. This was ridiculous. She was starting to get a headache.

"No need for that. I'll help. How much stuff have you got?"

"Not much, really. I could probably do it myself. The place *is* partially furnished, right? Mostly what I have are books and, and personal stuff. A couple chairs. And Emily's things, of course. Her crib, and stuff . . ."

His eyes were on her, bronze and intense, like piping-hot ingots. "You can't do that yourself. Besides, you'll have Emily to look after at the same time. I'll help, just let me know what time."

Hearing Emily's name on his lips gave her a jolt. *What was she doing?* She couldn't move in next door to this man.

She looked down at her watch. "Oh my goodness! I've got to go." Delaney stood. "Have a good day, Mr. Shepard."

He watched her, bemusement in his eyes. "You too. I'll see you tomorrow. I should be home most of the day. Just knock on the door when you get there."

She stopped. "No, really. There's no need."

But he just smiled and shook his head, his gaze calmly amused. "I'll see you tomorrow, Dr. Poole."

It wasn't until she'd arrived at her office that she realized she'd never paid her check.

"Jack, you're gettin' awful friendly with that one," a voice behind him piped up. "You fixin' to ask her out or what?"

Jack turned on the stool, coffee cup in hand, and gave Sam an amused look.

"Now Sam, you know me better than that. When have I ever gone after a married woman?"

"Aw, hell." Sam scowled. "She's married? Well, ain't that a crime."

Jack nodded ruefully. "It sure is. So I'm just helping her move, that's all. Seems the least I can do, seeing as how we're going to be neighbors. She's moving into the carriage house."

Sam let out a whoop, then a delighted laugh. "You mean to tell me you're going to be living right next door to a pretty girl like that and not do anything about it?"

Jack laughed. "I can't, Sam. I told you she's married."

But what I can do, he thought, *is see just how married she is.* After all, things had been rocky enough for her to turn to him once. If things got rocky again, maybe she'd decide she had to leave the guy. And there Jack would be. The nice guy right next door, who even helped her move.

"Well," Sam said, after much shaking of his head. "Don't give up. Maybe she's got a sister."

Chapter 5

Ten minutes after she'd arrived at the clinic, Delaney stood on the threshold of Kim McQuade's office, knocking softly on the open door. "Excuse me, Kim. You needed to see me?"

Kim was the administrator who handled most of the financial and accounting aspects of the clinic. From the moment Delaney met her she'd thought Kim was strikingly out of place in Harp Cove. First of all, she was dressed in a way that screamed New York chic. Second of all—or second, third, and fourth of all—she was young, beautiful, and smart, with the look of a woman whose career aspirations would outstrip Harp Cove's potential in days, if not minutes.

She also had a sharp sense of humor that skewered small-town life in a way that made Delaney, a city native struggling with feeling out of place, feel better about the time it would take her to break into the community. Kim was the first person in town—with the uncomfortable exception of Jack—with whom Delaney felt a connection.

Kim looked up from her paperwork and pushed her wire-rimmed glasses to the end of her nose. Despite the librarian-like pose and the jumbled mass of hair piled on top of her head with a clip, Kim still looked pretty and stylish to Delaney.

"Oh Delaney, hi. Yeah . . ." She paused and straightened in her chair, re-collecting her thoughts. "This is a little awkward but"—she gave a small laugh—"it's, ah, come to my attention that you—you're married . . . ? Is that right?" Kim's perfectly arched brows rose.

Delaney took a deep breath and let it out slowly. So this was how small the town was; she could make up a husband one day and have him come back at her the next. She glanced out the office door behind her. "Do you mind if I close this?" she asked, hand on the doorknob.

Kim shrugged agreeably and motioned her in. "Not at all. Come on in. I don't mean to pry, of course, but if it's true there are a couple of things in your paperwork that need to be corrected."

Delaney closed the door and sat in the chair across the desk from Kim. A blush burned her cheeks. "Really? I'm sorry. Did I fill something out wrong?"

Kim shuffled through some papers on her desk. "Well, you checked 'Single' on your W-4. Hope that wasn't wishful thinking."

Delaney forced a chuckle. "No. Well, sort of, maybe. I—it's—well, this is kind of embarrassing. You see, I thought I would be divorced by the time I moved here and it—*he*—wouldn't be an issue. We'd been having problems, you see, and it looked like we were heading that way, you know, toward divorce, but we've sort of decided to put that on hold."

Hopefully, Kim wouldn't wonder when this "hold" decision came to be because she'd only just filled out the paperwork a couple weeks ago.

"I see." Kim regarded her sympathetically. "I don't know if I should say I'm sorry you've had trouble or I'm happy you're working it out. I guess I should say both."

Delaney smiled, the comment putting her a little more at ease. "To be honest, I'm not sure either, but we'll see."

Kim nodded for a thoughtful moment. Then she turned, pushed her chair over to a file cabinet, put her pen between her teeth and began to rummage through some papers in a drawer. Delaney noticed she wore a short skirt with dark, sheer stockings. Her high, spiked heels, the kind Delaney never wore, showed off perfectly shaped legs.

"I do need you to redo your tax forms, though," Kim said through the pen.

"My tax forms?" Delaney clasped her sweating palms in her lap.

"Yeah, the W-4 and all that."

"But Joe and I are going to file our taxes separately, that's why I checked 'Single.' And I did put Emily as my dependent . . ."

Kim pulled out several sheets, took the pen from her mouth and rolled back behind the desk. "I think you did, yes. But you'll need to check the box that says 'Married, filing separately,' instead of the 'Single' box. You did that at your last job, didn't you?"

Delaney froze. Good God, now she had to lie to the IRS? How could she get out of this?

She could come clean to Kim, tell her the whole story. But who knew if Kim could be trusted? And what kind of flake would Delaney appear to be, coming out with such an outlandish story her second day on the job? Not to mention the fact that she would, in essence, then be asking the woman to lie for her.

God, what a mess.

Maybe she could clear it up later. After all, wasn't there a "marriage penalty"? So she'd in fact be paying too much tax, which wouldn't get her in any trouble, and she could straighten it out with the IRS later. Surely she wouldn't be the first person to have "accidentally" checked the wrong box. At least she wasn't claiming more dependents than she had. That was the kind of thing that got people in trouble. Wasn't it?

"Uh, yes. I mean, I guess I must have. I don't really remember. I'm not very good at this kind of thing."

Delaney leaned forward and rubbed her damp

palms together. In any case, she at least had to fill out the form the way Kim wanted it for the moment. She could decide what to do later.

She plucked a pen from a holder on Kim's desk as Kim handed her the papers. With a shaking hand, she checked the other box, filled out the rest of the form and signed at the bottom.

"So who told you I was married?" Delaney asked as casually as she could manage, handing the papers back over the desk. But she let go too early and Kim grabbed too late. They fluttered to the desk in disarray. "I'm so sorry. I don't know what's the matter with me, I've been clumsy all day."

"No problem." Kim bent to retrieve a paper from under the desk. "Jack Shepard," she said, reemerging from the floor.

Delaney's heart skipped a beat. "Oh?" Her brain was empty of anything intelligent to say, though she'd known it had to be him. "My landlord?"

"Yeah. He's a friend of mine and just happened to mention that you'd said you were married, which for some reason none of us thought you were. I guess because you rented the place yourself. I don't even think Jack put together the fact that you were a woman. I think he just heard 'doctor' and assumed you were a man. Typical." She chuckled cynically.

Delaney laughed with her, her brain awash with what the word *friend* could mean. Were they in a relationship? No, they couldn't be, not if Jack had just gotten beaned by Lisa yesterday. But if they weren't in a relationship, why weren't they? Kim was much prettier than Lisa, and obviously smarter. Older. Then again maybe Jack was the kind of guy who preferred bimbos . . . which didn't say much for the mother of his child.

Delaney shook herself. Why should she care if Jack was in a relationship with Kim or Lisa or *any* woman? He wasn't in a relationship with *her*, and that was the important thing.

"Yes, he did appear kind of surprised to see me," Delaney said cautiously. After all, Jack could have confided a lot more to this woman. How close were they? Would he have mentioned that one-night stand? Another blush rose to her cheeks.

"I imagine he did." Kim smiled, looking speculatively at Delaney. "So how long have you been married?"

Delaney waved a hand. "Oh I don't know. Forever, it seems like." She hoped to get around nailing down this detail but Kim still looked at her expectantly. "About five years, I guess."

"Five years, huh? And your daughter's how old?"

What had she told Maggie?

"Four months." Delaney's palms moistened, and she clasped her hands together. For some reason, by altering the day Emily was born her Bad Mother Meter soared into the red. "How long have you known Jack?"

Kim leaned back, as if situating herself for some girl talk. "We've been friends since I came here, about three years ago. At first he tried to hit on me"—she laughed—"until he found out I've got a boyfriend in New York. Still, I was flattered."

A lump of disgust rose in Delaney's throat. Was there anyone in town Jack Shepard *hadn't* hit on? "Flattered?"

"Sure, he's a great-looking guy. Don't you think?"

Delaney looked down at her hands, writhing in front of her like a couple of snakes. She pried them apart and moved them, palm down, to the tops of her knees. "I don't know. I guess looks aren't everything."

"Oh sure. But still, he's got 'em. And he's got this way of looking at you, when he's interested, that . . ." Her gaze seemed to glance off Delaney's shoulder. She chuckled again. "Well, anyway, it's a good thing I'm pretty sure Chris is the one for me, or I'd have had some serious reconsidering to do."

"Really?" Delaney said. "Don't you think he's a little too, I don't know, too much of a playboy? That's what I've heard, anyway. I hardly know him myself. But I've heard it from *a lot* of people, and I've only been here a week."

Kim took off her glasses and set them on the desk, rubbing the bridge of her nose where they'd rested. "God, people love to talk, don't they? Small towns, I'm telling you. I'll be happy once I finish up at U of M and can join Chris in New York. People are especially bad around here."

"You're in school?" Delaney asked. "Isn't the university a long way away?"

Kim shrugged. "A little over an hour, and I only go twice a week. But the good news is I'll be finished next June and then I'll be out of this gossip cauldron forever."

Delaney paused, then had to ask, "So you don't think it's true, what they say about Jack?"

"Who knows? Sometimes I swear Jack does stuff just to keep those old coots in the diner happy. Things get a little slow, Jack'll let them know about some failed date he's had, or he'll ask out some old biddy right in front of them just to get them going. God knows what they'd find to talk about if Jack weren't around."

"How altruistic," Delaney murmured.

Kim smiled and shrugged. "He has fun with it, I think. For some reason the gossip doesn't bother him. I guess he's been the butt of it for so long he's used to it."

"You'd think he'd learn to tone down his behavior some. You know, just to maintain his own privacy."

"Actually, I think he has. He hasn't really dated anyone in town—not that I know of, anyway—in the three years I've been here."

"No? What about Lisa Jacobson?"

Kim snorted. "Well, *that* was a mistake. And I don't know if you could call what they did 'dating.' She took him way too seriously, and he wasn't thinking at all. But that only lasted a couple weeks, and I guess he's paid for it now. I'm sure he'll go back to his old policy."

"His old policy?"

"Yeah. Used to be he'd only date summer girls, and I have to say it got him in a lot less trouble. But then, anyone could've seen the trouble with Lisa Jacobson a mile away. Anyone but him, that is."

"What do you mean, 'summer girls'?"

"Tourists. Girls who won't be here when the music stops, if you know what I mean."

Oh boy, did she know what Kim meant. *Summer girls.* It made her sick to think about it. She was one of Jack's "summer" girls. And he had no idea how loud that music got before it stopped.

Anger shot through Delaney's limbs, and she stood up abruptly. "I guess I'd better get to work."

Kim straightened in her chair. "Oh okay. Yeah, I guess I should too. Sorry I kept you so long. It's just so nice to talk to someone from away, for a change."

"Yeah, thanks. I enjoyed it too." Delaney hesitated, wanting to know so much more, so much that Kim could probably tell her, but she couldn't ask. Not then, anyway. Not when she barely knew the woman. She turned on stiff legs to leave.

"Oh, Delaney? One more thing."

Delaney turned, schooling her face to a neutral expression. She hoped.

"I don't know if Doc Jacobson's mentioned it to you yet—my feeling is he hasn't, since he's barely been around the last week—but you're committed to teach a couple health classes at Harp Cove High. They start in . . ." She shuffled through papers with one hand and pushed her glasses back on with her other. "About five or six weeks. Around the time school starts, I think. There are four different classes and you'll visit each one twice during the semester. That amounts to about one every other week, last period of the day."

"Health classes? At the high school?" *Where Jack Shepard works?* Her overworked adrenal gland surged to life again.

"Yeah. There's a syllabus around here somewhere, I'll get it to you. It's pretty simple stuff, really. Since it's high school, they already know about menstruation and erections and all that." She flipped through a tall stack of papers on a far corner of the desk.

"So . . . nutrition, that sort of thing?" Delaney's heart sped up. *Oh please don't let it be a sex ed class,* she pleaded silently. She was the last person on *earth* qualified to preach contraception.

"Sure, but the regular teachers will cover a lot of that. Mostly they want you to handle some of the more awkward teenage stuff. Like there's no such thing as blue balls and girls *can* get pregnant the first time. That sort of thing. I guess they think the kids will take it more seriously coming from an actual doctor."

Delaney's heart sank. Then she felt an almost overwhelming urge to laugh. Maybe she *was* the best person on earth to teach that lesson. Certainly she had enough firsthand experience. "So, contraception."

Kim looked up over her glasses and gave her an

exaggerated look of horror. "God, *no*. Not in this town. Here they preach abstinence. First, last, and always."

Delaney frowned. "That seems a little . . . unrealistic."

Kim pushed the hair from her face and gave a wry smile. "Girl, you're in Harp Cove, Maine, now. The Way Life Should Be," she added, referring to the state motto that was printed on everything from bumper stickers to the highway WELCOME TO MAINE signs.

"What about The Way Life *Is*?" Delaney asked.

"Has nothing to do with life in Harp Cove. I can't tell you, though, how nice it is for me finally to have someone here who understands the way they do things in other places. And why. Maybe between the two of us, we can give Harp Cove a little reality check every once in a while."

Delaney laughed. Boy, did *she* have a reality check for them. "Maybe. I don't know. I've always found people are pretty resistant to change."

"No kidding. But I guess if you already know that, you should do all right here. Listen, I'll have to get you that syllabus once I unearth it. But like I said, it's really basic stuff and there are materials at the school from last year all ready to use. Jack can help you with that."

"Jack?"

"Yes. The first class you'll be teaching is his football team, just before school starts."

Chapter 6

Delaney pulled into the drive, up to the open wrought-iron gate with its ornately curved "S," and stopped the car. In the middle of the wide lawn beyond the gate an American flag on a tall pole snapped in the brisk ocean breeze. Glancing in the rearview mirror Delaney couldn't help but smile at her daughter in the car seat behind her, despite the trepidation beating in her breast.

Emily's eyes were bright in her creamy pink face, taking in the world around her as she gurgled happy sounds into the cool morning air. Gnawing on two saliva-covered fingers with a sublime smile, Emily had no idea she would soon be in the company of her father.

"This is it, Em," Delaney said, gazing back out the front windshield.

Across the expansive lawn to the left stood a large stone house. To the right and just behind stood the little stone cottage that was to be hers. Beyond them both sparkled the sea.

"So close," she murmured, shifting her eyes from the house to the cottage.

The driveway ran along the edge of a wood, then curved in a semicircle in front of the larger stone house. A side drive cut straight back to her cottage and branched off to a service entrance behind the main house.

"So close." She took a deep breath.

He was probably down there, she thought. Waiting for her and her truck full of belongings to show up. She glanced at the clock on the dash. The truck from the storage place wasn't due for another twenty minutes, however, and she was not sure she wanted to arrive with that much time to spend in conversation with Jack Shepard.

Not that it would be as dangerous as yesterday's conversation. Last night she'd sat down and hammered out some details about her husband, "Jim," though she did wish she'd called him "Joe." For some reason the name "Joe" seemed more real to her than "Jim" did, more like someone she would have married. Which was silly, of course, because they were just names. But still, Joe sounded like a regular guy whereas Jim sounded a little yuppie. Why had she changed it? She couldn't remember.

In any case, reconciling herself to "Jim," she'd

quizzed herself about him as if she were preparing for a play.

What does your husband do, Dr. Poole? He's a young, up-and-coming lawyer in D.C. Unfortunately, he couldn't possibly find a job that would do his career any good in Harp Cove. So for the moment we're living apart.

After all, she'd thought, who would blame a *man* for not giving up his career to follow his wife? Certainly no one in this town.

Does he plan to come on weekends? No . . . (sad shake of the head) . . . not at first because he's in the middle of a really important case right now. We're going to have to go a couple months without seeing each other.

What a shame. Won't this be hard on your marriage? Depending on who asked, Delaney would either say she hoped not or she would confide that in fact they'd been having some trouble anyway, and they both thought that time and distance might do them some good.

This would be perfect, Delaney had decided, especially if those gossips at the diner ever got hold of the information. Because eventually she'd be divorcing old "Jim Poole" and setting up the marriage like this to begin with would ensure it all made sense.

And it *had* to make sense, especially to Jack.

In addition, she'd decided, she needed to talk about him a lot, her Jim. To make him more real not just to herself, but to Jack. Bringing him up in conversation should be natural, the way couples always spoke in terms of "we." She should talk about what "Jim thinks" and frequently add what "Jim says" to the topic at hand.

"My husband really wanted a larger house," she said out loud, testing the words on her lips, "but since he wasn't to be joining me anytime soon, I decided to go with this place." She nodded to herself. Yes, that kind of thing.

She took her foot off the brake and eased the car forward. She could do this. She could have an imaginary husband.

The day was incredible, with the sky a deep, cloudless blue and the sun splintering on the water. She couldn't have asked for a better one, really. If it weren't for the Jack Shepard problem, she thought wistfully, she'd be ecstatic about moving into this idyllic little house.

She tried to look at it with the enthusiasm she would have had, had she not known that disaster lived right next door. She might have thought about putting up window boxes and filling that old half barrel next to the drive with petunias. She might have contemplated getting a hammock for the backyard, and a set of furniture for the patio. She might have thought about the friends she'd make and the parties she'd have out here, overlooking the sea.

But all she could think about now was Jack Shepard.

So she would live here a few weeks, maybe a couple months if she had to, she told herself. Then she would come up with some reason she had to move. An allergy of Emily's, or a phobia of hers about living in such relative seclusion. She scoffed at the thought—the place wasn't nearly secluded *enough*. Or she could say she thought her husband might be coming so she'd need a larger place, then his arrival could fall through at the last minute.

She pulled up next to the house and spent a moment regarding it sadly—it might have been so perfect—when a movement in the rearview mirror told her Jack had emerged from his house.

She gathered her purse and the diaper bag and got out of the car. The salt-stung breeze whipped her hair around her face as she rounded the hood. She was careful to keep her eyes on Emily in the backseat so Jack wouldn't know she'd seen him.

The sun was warm on her back, but not nearly so warm as the sensation of Jack's gaze. God, she thought, hefting Emily up and out, he was probably looking at her butt and thinking pregnancy had done nothing for her figure. Then, feeling disloyal, she clutched Emily to her chest and gave her a big smacking kiss on the cheek.

So what if she had hips now, she thought. Emily was worth every pound and more, something someone like Jack Shepard would never understand.

One little fist grabbed a handful of Delaney's hair, and she was prying at the tiny fingers to extricate it when she felt Jack relieve her of the diaper bag.

She turned swiftly, as if surprised, and gave him a smile. "Oh, it's you."

"Expecting someone else?" His hair ruffled in the breeze, and she had a sudden picture in her mind of how he would look in high seas on the deck of his boat.

She gazed up at him, feeling small, and tried to stop remembering how he'd lifted her up on that beach with no effort at all and held her body close to his. She'd forgotten he was so tall.

Joe would've been tall, she thought. Jim, in her mind, was thin and somewhat short. Someone she'd feel bigger than.

No, she'd make "Jim" tall. And handsome . . . ridiculously handsome, she added as she took in Jack's sun-warmed skin and dropped her eyes to his muscular forearms.

"No, of course not." She closed the car door. "But for a second I automatically thought it was my husband. He usually carries that stuff for me. But since Jim couldn't make it, that was impossible. Of course. In fact I wasn't expecting you either. You really don't have to do this, you know."

Jack glanced into the empty backseat of the car. "Yes, I can see you really don't have much stuff."

She laughed and peeled another lock of hair from Emily's fingers. She should have pulled her hair back in a ponytail, as she usually did. But she hadn't—and why? Because of Jack, she admitted with disgust. Because she hadn't wanted him to notice that the baby might not have done her figure any favors.

She glanced at her watch. "Actually, the truck's

due any minute. The storage place said they'd bring it out for a pretty reasonable fee, so I went ahead and paid it. They should be able to unload it too, so if you have something else to do . . ."

"Trying to get rid of me?" He was still smiling, but his eyes narrowed, perhaps against the sun.

"No!" She laughed. Shrilly. "Why would you think that?"

As soon as the words were past her lips she wanted to shove them back down her throat and clap her hand over her mouth. *Idiot*, she cursed herself. *Stupid, stupid idiot.*

He leaned one hip against the side of the car. "Well, for one thing, our meeting again and living so close is bound to be awkward, at least at first. Don't you think so?"

It didn't seem awkward for *him*, she thought sourly. *He* appeared as calm as a funeral director.

"Yes, yes I do." She took a deep breath. "Listen, Jack, since you brought it up, I want to apologize for that, for what happened that night on the beach. I should have been . . . more forthcoming, I suppose. It was a foolish thing to do and—and I regret it now."

He paused a long moment, studying her, before he laughed lightly. "Yes, I suppose you would." He shifted the diaper bag on his shoulder and looked away. "I didn't, not until you told me about your husband. I guess I've never been an adulterer before."

The comment took her by surprise and her eyes

shot to his. A blush of shame for her own "adultery" crept over her. "Yes, I can see where you might be reluctant to add to what I hear is already an extensive résumé." She straightened her shoulders and lifted Emily higher on her hip.

The look of surprise on his face was momentarily gratifying, then almost instantly mortifying. She'd never said anything so mean in her life. Not to mention antagonizing. Even if she cared nothing for his feelings, drawing battle lines at this stage in the game was a bad idea.

She shook her head, pulling more of her hair from Emily's fingers. "Listen, I'm sorry—"

"No, I'm sorry. I didn't mean—"

"Look, let's just forget it, okay?"

He lifted his hands in surrender. "Forgotten already."

She looked him dead in the eye. "No, I mean all of it. That weekend I was here, that night on the beach, all of it. I know what's done is done, and I'm really not trying to sweep anything under the rug, but if we don't forget about it, every meeting we have will be strained like this one. And I don't think either one of us wants to live that way."

He pushed his hands into his pockets, the pale pink strap of the diaper bag incongruous against his olive drab tee shirt.

His face was somber, his eyes soft. "No," he said slowly, "I definitely don't want to live that way."

She thought he was about to say something else, when the storage truck pulled into the drive and their attentions were diverted. When she glanced back at him, Jack had already turned away.

The last thing Jack planned to do was sweep *any-thing* under the rug. Even if he'd been inclined to do it, he knew from months of experience that he was incapable of "forgetting all about" anything when it came to Delaney Poole.

Besides, he'd sat up the last two nights thinking about her and her sudden husband. Why wouldn't she have mentioned him at least once that weekend she was up last year? They'd had several conversations before that night on the beach and he was sure he would have remembered the mention of a husband. Her finger had been ring-free, too. Free of the indentation or tan line that a normally beringed finger frequently had as well. He knew. He had trained himself to notice such things.

Of course, that could be because they'd been separated a while, but to show up now, shocked to see him and suddenly aware of her vows . . . well, it pieced together in an odd way, he thought.

Plus, there was the baby.

Certainly there was no better reason to claim you were married, even if perhaps you weren't, than a child. Maybe she'd *never* been married, he'd thought, and she worried about being a single mother in a small town. He had to admit she might be regarded differently by the general population if it were known she hadn't married the baby's father; but it wasn't as if she wouldn't have been able to do her job. People would have gotten over it eventually, just as they did every other scandal that came along.

Then again, maybe her one-night stand with him wasn't so unusual. Maybe she slept around and didn't *know* who the father was.

Hell, if he hadn't used a condom that night, he might have thought *he* could be the father. But he had and he wasn't and the kid was too young anyway. Just four months, his buddy Kim at the clinic had told him. The math didn't compute.

An hour later, Jack bent low to pick up the bottom end of a bookshelf that one of the movers tilted to lift.

"Where's it going?" he asked, as they shuffled from the gaping back end of the truck.

The mover—a guy named Ross who lived next door to Kevin—shrugged, looking slantwise behind him. "Upstairs, I guess. The master bedroom."

Jack grimaced for no one's benefit but his own. The *master* bedroom. Where Delaney and her husband would sleep.

They paused at the door while Manny, the other mover, trotted out for another armload of boxes. Jack squinted into the dark hallway beyond, but Delaney was nowhere in sight. Tending to the kid, most likely.

Despite his doubts about her sudden marital status, he had to admit she was doing an admirable job of trying to sell the idea. If she brought up her blasted husband one more time, he was going to break something, he was sure of it. Preferably something cheap and replaceable, but he couldn't be responsible. Everything was "Jim says this" and "my husband thinks that" until he was sure he was going to lose his mind. Blah blah blah blah blah.

If he existed, why the hell wasn't Jim here schlepping this hundred-pound bookcase up the narrow stairs of a carriage house, Jack wanted to know. What sort of husband was he if he shipped his wife and infant daughter off hundreds of miles without lifting a finger to help? Delaney hadn't even seemed that sure she could *afford* to pay the movers to stay and help. What kind of a lawyer was this guy? The broke kind?

Then again, doctors weren't usually so impoverished either, so what did he know.

"Wait."

The sound of Delaney's voice caused Jack and Ross to stop their crablike manipulations just short of the steps. Jack lowered his end of the shelf to the floor.

"I'm sorry." She smiled, her sky-blue eyes friendly and apologetic for Ross. "I'd like that shelf in the living room, not upstairs. I guess I should have marked things better."

Ross grinned back at her like a lovestruck idiot. "No problem. Wherever you want it, we aim to please."

Jack aimed to do a little more than that. He aimed to get to the bottom of things with Mrs. Poole.

Delaney's eyes sidled over to Jack, and he caught

the faint hint of a blush on her cheeks. Interesting, he thought. What was she thinking?

They maneuvered the thing into the living room and, with a self-conscious half bow as he passed Delaney, Ross hopped right back outside in his continuing effort to please.

"So, what do you think of the place?" Jack asked, as Delaney started to leave. He leaned one arm along the mantel.

Delaney turned back, slim fingers tucking a lock of hair behind her ear.

His eyes scanned the room as if pointing out his favorite details, from the exposed-beam ceiling to the white walls and dark wood trim around the windows. "This was the first room I did. We had to dig the fireplace here out from under layers of plaster. It works now."

Her eyes dwelled on the grate behind his left leg. "I love it," she said. Sincerely, he thought. She raised her eyes to his, all politeness. "You've done a nice job."

"Yeah, it's a pretty little place. Not much room, though, if your husband ever decides to come up."

Jet lashes framing sky-blue eyes narrowed. "What do you mean, 'if'?"

He shrugged, meeting her eyes squarely. "I don't know. It just seems up in the air right now. Or am I wrong? Do you guys have a date when he'll be coming?"

The faint blush stole across her cheeks again, and he wondered once more about the possibility of little Emily having no father.

She sure looked pretty when she blushed, though, he thought, and had the illicit idea that her color was probably high that night they'd made love on the beach. Did she think of that night every time she looked at him too? Did she remember the details as vividly as he did? If he were the blushing kind he'd be beet red every time she entered a room, he thought. Hell, every time she entered his thoughts, which was far too often.

"No, actually, we don't. But he *will* be coming." She turned again to leave, then stopped and turned to face him. "You know, I don't appreciate your . . . insinuations." Her tone was brittle.

He raised his hand, one elbow still resting on the mantel. "Hey, I didn't mean to insinuate anything."

She pinned him with those pale eyes, one brow raised. "Didn't you? I thought we agreed not to talk about this."

"We didn't say anything about not talking about your husband. Just that night. And have I said anything about that night?"

She glanced behind her as Ross and Manny tromped upstairs with armloads of boxes.

"You're saying it now," she said quietly, looking back at him, her eyes intent.

He met her gaze and held it. "No I'm not. As a matter of fact, I don't want to talk about that night either."

She glared at him, and he laughed.

"Fine, forget I said anything," he said finally. "Should we make your husband off-limits too?"

He watched her swallow as her eyes left his. "Maybe so."

"Good, 'cause I'll be more than happy to forget about him. But I suggest *you* stop bringing him up. Jesus, all I've heard all day is 'Jim this' and 'Jim that.' If you don't want to talk about him, you sure have a weird way of showing it."

She took a step forward and poked a finger through the air at him. "You see, that's *just* the point. It shouldn't bother you if I talk about my husband or not. I shouldn't even have to *think* about bringing him up in front of you. Oh God, I shouldn't be living here. This is all so awkward."

Jack straightened and crossed his arms over his chest, where the mention of her living somewhere else had set up an unexpected fluttering of dread. "Actually, that's *not* the point. But if you'd like to make it the point, go right ahead."

"It *is* the point."

"No, it's not. The point is you pull this husband out of your hat when you need him and get prickly whenever anyone else does. Why is that, Delaney? I don't think it's just because of that night we spent on the beach."

The flush that had seemed so sensual before was now angry, and her eyes flashed. She glanced once out into the empty hallway and stepped closer to him. "Would you *please* keep your voice down? I don't pull him out of my hat."

Jack straightened as she neared, resisting an urge to touch her. "Sure you do."

"No I don't. I just talk about him because he's—well, he's a fact of my life. And the sooner you get used to that the better."

Jack raised a brow. "I don't think I'm the only one who needs to get used to it."

Color rose to her cheeks again. "I don't know what you're talking about. You argue just like a man—in circles."

He threw out his hands. "Forgive me. But you argue like a woman with something to hide."

She took a sharp breath, her expression tight. "That's ridiculous. I can't even imagine what you mean, and don't try to tell me. I don't need you speculating about my life any more than I need you living next door. You don't know a thing about me."

"That's not true," he said, taking two slow steps toward her, close enough to reach out and run a finger down her soft cheek, though he didn't. "I know one thing," he continued quietly, as Ross clattered down the steps and out the front door. "I know you were once the type to have sex on an empty beach with a guy you'd just met."

At that the glow in her cheeks drained away. Her chest rose and fell with rapid, shallow breaths. She opened her mouth to speak but it was a moment before the words emerged, and then they were husky and low. "I was not the only one who was once that type."

"Yes, but *I* was not married." As soon as he said it, Jack regretted it. What if she really *was* married?

What if everything she said was true? If that were the case, then it was a low, mean thing to say, and he wasn't ordinarily a low, mean person. But something about her story just didn't jibe, and something inside of him could not let it lie.

He shook his head and glanced at the floor, unsure whether to apologize or press on. At least this way they were talking, he was finding out things about her. And for some reason he didn't want to analyze, he really did want to find out things about her.

Delaney stepped back, resting one hand on the back of an armchair. Her eyes darted to the window, resting on the two movers who were wrestling a chest of drawers from the back of the truck.

Jack thought about asking straight out if the baby had a father, then imagined offering himself as a comfort, as assistance in handling the town and the gossips. He could help her, he thought. He could be gentle and kind, he could win her over—

"You weren't exactly honest with me back then either, Jack." She spat out his name like a bad taste.

Her tone snapped him out of the silly reverie. Whether she needed him or not, she sure as hell didn't want him.

"What do you mean? It's not like I had a wife stashed in the attic."

Her pupils seemed to dilate. She looked like a wild kitten who, cornered, had no choice but to bite its captor. "You told me you didn't do that sort of thing all the time. But somehow ever since I got here all I've been hearing about are the sexual exploits of Jack Shepard. According to my sources you're Harp Cove's very own soap opera."

Jack gave her a delighted look. "I'm flattered to know you're so interested. Though I have to say I would've given you more credit than to put stock in rumors."

She folded her arms in front of her. "I'm not that interested, I just hear things. And it's hard to believe they're just rumors when everyone says the same thing. And I do mean *everyone*."

"Well, for your information, I *don't* do that sort of thing all the time. And if you continue to listen to the gossips, you're going to find out a lot more things I've never done."

She looked decidedly disconcerted, and her eyes cast around the room as if for something to throw. "And—and—you said you were a teacher."

He frowned, off guard. "I *am* a teacher."

She raised her chin along with one eyebrow. "You're a *coach*. There's a difference."

He took the words in slowly. "That's right. And I teach physical education. Something wrong with that?"

She looked at him from beneath lowered brows. "Well, it's—it's not exactly molecular biology, now, is it?"

"Did I ever *say* I taught molecular biology?"

"You said you were a teacher." She lifted one shoulder and let it drop. "When you say that, one naturally assumes math or history or something. Anyway, it doesn't matter. Just like it doesn't matter that you've apparently dated every woman who ever passed through Harp Cove and never mentioned that."

He cocked his head. So the kitten did know how to bite. "I'm sorry if I violated the terms of our disclosure agreement. But I think a secret husband tops anything I may or may not have said."

"Maybe. Maybe not. The fact is we each misrepresented ourselves. I think we're even."

He ran a hand through his hair. He had no one to blame but himself if the kitten bit him hard enough to break the skin. He was the one who'd started it, taunting her about her husband.

What he didn't understand was why her sudden jab bothered him so much. He loved what he did, and he didn't need her good opinion. If she had a problem with it, she was not the kind of person he'd thought she was, and that was that. He should be *relieved* she was married.

"Just because my job's not up to your high standards doesn't mean I misrepresented myself," he said. "We can't all be doctors and lawyers, *Mrs.* Poole."

He studied her face as she dropped her gaze to the floor. Her near-black hair shimmered in the light coming through the window, her left hand fingered a tattered spot on the armchair beside her.

He looked at her, and he couldn't help thinking there had to be something else at work here that would make her go on the offensive like that. Surely she didn't really think less of him because he was a coach. Or could it be her prettiness had him thinking she was a better person than she really was?

She frowned, then sighed. "I know. Listen—I know. I, ah, I'm sorry, about your job—"

"You're sorry about my job?"

"I mean, what I said about your job." Her fingers worked at the spot on the chair. "I don't mean to sound like such a jerk. I—I respect your work."

"Uh-huh." Did he really want her to change her tune? No, it would be better if she were a jerk, he told himself.

She shook her head. "No, really. I do. And I think you're probably a wonderful teacher. It's just . . ." She took a quick breath and seemed to come to a decision. She looked up. "I just don't like being made to feel . . . as if I was the only one who had a one-night stand that night."

He exhaled slowly. So she wasn't a snob. Dammit.

"You see, I've been feeling bad about Jim," she continued, "and I've been feeling bad about myself, and—and I don't need to feel as if I committed some horrible crime against you, too." She looked up at him, her lovely pale eyes full of emotion. "Besides, you didn't expect any more from it than I did. It's not as if you asked for my phone number or anything."

It was true. He hadn't asked for her number, and he'd kicked himself for it time and again. And now he was kicking her because she obviously hadn't spent the last year thinking about him the way he'd thought about her.

"Come on, Jack," she said softly. "We both knew what we were doing that night."

He looked down and laughed once, without humor. "I thought I did at the time, anyway."

She stiffened. "If you mean you didn't know I was married, can you honestly say that would have stopped you?"

"That's not what I meant," he said.

But he couldn't tell her what he did mean: that at the time he'd thought making love with her would be a lot less significant than it had turned out to be. That when he'd taken her to that beach he *had* thought it'd be a one-night stand, which was exactly why he hadn't asked for her number afterward. His mind and heart a tumult, he'd fallen back on habit. He'd taken her back to her B&B, given her a passionate kiss to remember him by, and left like a thief in the night.

What he hadn't counted on was not being able to get her out of his head once she'd gone.

"I can't say whether knowing you were married would have stopped me or not." He shook his head and looked at her. "I really don't know. Maybe not."

She looked relieved, and her expression softened. "Then let's stop throwing blame around, shall we? I want to blame you to assuage my guilt, and you want to blame me because—I don't know . . . ?"

She looked expectantly at him, but he said nothing.

"Well, maybe because I'm blaming you." She waved a hand that, he noted, still wore no ring. "So what do you say . . . truce?"

He gazed at her, at her pale, smooth skin, her guarded eyes, the brave tilt of her chin.

One corner of his mouth kicked up in a wry smile. "You ever think about wearing a wedding ring? It might stop a few problems before they start."

She allowed a small smile. "Rings get in the way, when I work."

"Then maybe a sign, or something. You're just too damn pretty to be walking around looking available. It's dangerous."

His compliment was rewarded with a genuine, if embarrassed, smile. She looked down, obviously disconcerted, and clasped her hands in front of her.

She *was* too damn pretty, he thought. And it was a shame how well he remembered that prettiness, from her head to her toes.

"Thank you," she said, and moved toward the door in a businesslike way. "And if I get a firm date when Joe will be moving up, I'll be sure to let you know."

He frowned. "Joe?"

She stopped—hesitated for what he found to be a crucial second—while her face flamed red. "Jim. My husband. I said Jim."

Chapter 7

Delaney's heart thundered in her chest, pushing blood through her ears with a sound like a freight train. She'd gotten her husband's name wrong. How much stupider could she get? The implications were overwhelming. And the look on Jack's face told her those implications were not lost on him. Despite his earlier investigative prodding, the realization that he might actually be onto something seemed to shock him.

"No you didn't." His eyes were pinned on what she knew were her scarlet cheeks, her deer-in-the-headlights expression. He took a step toward her. "No, you said 'Joe.' I heard you. It was very clear. You said 'Joe.' "

Delaney punched out a laugh and turned for the door, mostly to hide her face, for she knew he wouldn't let her leave without an explanation. Her mind spun like a hula-hoop out of control, awkward and desperate, in danger of hitting the floor at any moment. She heard a voice that might have been her mother's emerge from her mouth. "Don't be silly, Jack. I've got a lot of work to do now. I'll see you later."

"Delaney."

She turned at the door, her hand on the knob. "What?"

She tried to look bored but couldn't do it. The mental hula-hoop careened wildly. The look in his eyes was giddy.

"You said 'Joe,' Delaney. What's going on?"

Her pulse hammered in her neck, she could feel it, knew it was probably visible from where he stood. Was he tallying all the evidence? Was he even now figuring out what would cause her to concoct such an outrageous lie? Fear and suspicion combined to keep that vein beneath the skin of her neck pulsing with the tempo of a band full of castanets.

But it didn't matter, she thought, grabbing her tumultuous thoughts with two firm mental hands. It didn't matter if he suspected her of lying because he couldn't prove it and he could never be sure. Not without her admission, or a paternity test which she would never, ever, as long as she and Emily lived, give him.

She inhaled. She could have a poker face. She could, right now, perfect the perfectly unreadable expression. "*Nothing's* going on. What's the matter with you?"

Her voice was high and unnatural, but he didn't know her well enough to know that. Did he?

She endured his scrutiny a moment longer than necessary, then sighed. "Okay, maybe I did say Joe." She rolled her eyes and muttered, "This is so embarrassing."

He leapt on it. "What is?"

"It's—it's a little game we play. See, his middle name is Joseph. James Joseph. So sometimes I call him Joe, sometimes Jim. I don't usually slip up in front of other people, though. I'm sorry if I confused you."

"Sometimes you call your husband Joe?" He looked so incredulous she almost had to laugh. Hysteria, no doubt.

She shrugged and looked away. "Sure. Jim, Joe . . . Jim-Joe, whatever. Depends on my mood. It's a silly thing, you know. One of those silly little things married couples do."

His eyes narrowed. "I don't know many married couples who call each other by the wrong name."

She gave him an annoyed look. "It's not the *wrong* name. It's his middle name. Besides, not many married couples let you see the intimate games they play. It's just one of those things."

For a second she imagined herself and her phantom husband in the cottage's tiny kitchen calling each other by the wrong name and laughing over it. What morons, she thought. But part of her felt a pang for that missing camaraderie.

Jack nearly disputed her—she could tell by the

incredulous look on his face—but stopped short. "Yeah, one of those things," he said instead.

What did he think? she wondered. Could he possibly be figuring out she'd made up her husband? It was so outlandish, even to herself, she couldn't imagine anyone suspecting it. And yet, it seemed so obvious to her that she didn't have a husband she also couldn't imagine anyone believing it.

"Listen, I really do have work to do." Delaney opened the door. She looked at him, taking in the suspicious expression on his handsome face, and felt suddenly fatigued. "I hope it's not always so awkward between us, Jack," she added impulsively.

His eyes met hers, and her heart stuttered. Whenever he looked at her she felt so *nervous*, as if the direction of his gaze were one of those red laser rifle sights. Was this what Kim had meant when she talked about the way he had of looking at you when he was interested?

But no, she thought. She remembered *that* look. It was the one that had caused her to invite him out of the Hornet's Nest that night, ostensibly for some air. Out of the bar and onto the beach.

His eyes scanned her face. "I hope so too, Delaney," he said finally.

Delaney dipped her head, glad that he seemed willing to call a truce, and turned in the doorway. But he called her back, her name on his lips sending a shiver up her spine.

She turned back with a questioning expression. Polite, she hoped, revealing nothing about the effect he had on her.

He paused. "I'm sorry if I make you uncomfortable. It's really the last thing I want."

Relief coursed through her, and she realized that until that instant she'd been thinking of him as the Enemy. Words crowded her head—words of gratitude, relief, communion, understanding—but responses close to her heart would take too long to explain. Would be impossible to explain, really, without giving away the whole mixed-up reality within her.

Finally, she just smiled and said thanks, closing the door behind her when she left as if he were the one who lived there instead of her.

One of those things, Jack thought as he sat on a barstool at the Hornet's Next, twisting the base of his beer bottle in the circle of its own condensation. *One of those things that make people suspect your husband's a fake. How many married couples have that problem?*

Jim-Joe . . . One of those games married people play . . . It was the most ridiculous thing he'd ever heard. Which was the problem. It was ridiculous enough to be true. And Delaney had certainly looked embarrassed enough explaining it to him.

Jack took a sip of the beer and went back to swirling the bottle in the puddle on the bar.

No, the husband was probably real, and Jack

was just a fool with an overactive imagination. A fool and a jerk for pressuring her to explain things she shouldn't have to explain. After all, what business was it of his what she called her husband?

"Hey, Jack," Kevin said, emerging from the door at the back of the bar and heading toward the counter.

Jack looked up, raised his chin in his brother's direction, a perfunctory acknowledgment. "Hey."

The bartender moved to the end of the bar closest to the door. Elbows on the counter, he bent low to talk to Nancy Fuller, a woman who seemed always to be in the Nest, always in that seat, and always in a half-inebriated state.

"I'm glad you're here." Kevin's eyes took in the bandage at Jack's temple and he smirked.

As much as Kevin complained about Jack's lack of responsibility, he sure seemed to revel in every example of it. In fact, despite his protestations, Jack was pretty sure Kevin hoped he would *never* change, Kevin's own mortgaged life looking so good in comparison.

"I got a call from Dad today," Kevin continued.

Behind them, billiard balls clattered as the only other two patrons of the place racked up for another game.

Jack raised his brows. This was unusual. Usually Kevin got a letter. Or, rather, a postcard. Once he got a list of important documents and their whereabouts written down on a cocktail napkin. *Deed to the house—upstairs safe. Jack and Kevin's birth certificates—*

Fleet Bank safe-deposit box #41. Key in upstairs safe. Divorce papers—upstairs safe. And on and on.

Why their father had suddenly decided they needed this information was beyond them both, but they'd added the napkin bearing the Rusty Scupper logo—a marlin leaping improbably over a schooner—to the items in the upstairs safe.

"He called you?" Jack asked, pushing aside his empty chili bowl and popping a pretzel from a nearby basket into his mouth.

"Well, actually I called him. I wanted to ask him about the property, if he had a buyer yet, and he said no." Kevin looked at him significantly.

Jack knew where this was going and wondered for a second what Kevin would do if Jack took up the reins of his absurd scheme to buy the place. "Yeah, so?"

Kevin picked up a rag and began wiping down the already-clean bar. "So I asked him what he'd think about selling it to you."

The hand holding Jack's beer paused midway to his lips. His eyes met his brother's. A half dozen scenarios featuring his father's reaction flickered through his mind in an instant. It wasn't hard to pick the right one. "He laughed, right?"

Kevin's eyes skittered away, and Jack knew he was right on target. He drew a healthy draught off the beer.

"I got him to say he'd reduce the price if you wanted it. Make it easier for you to buy than the general public, in other words."

"Did he say he'd reduce it by half? Three-quarters? Did he happen to mention what that land is *worth*? I hate to be the one to tell you, Kev, but that land's worth a helluva lot more than you or I or even he's got."

Kevin eyed him. "You could sell the boat."

Jack scoffed even as the words sent a jolt of adrenaline through his veins. *Sell the boat.* Sell his lifeline, his passion, his gateway to the world. The idea was ludicrous. The *Silver Surfer* was his own mental oasis of freedom, the only thing that kept him sane in this little town. Moored at the ready, waiting for the moments when Jack needed perspective—or escape—the sailboat was Jack's equilibrium. Getting rid of it would be like letting go of a life preserver in the middle of a roiling sea.

But Kevin wouldn't understand that. Kevin, who had married at nineteen, had a child at twenty, and now considered himself the Shepard mainstay of Harp Cove, would consider it a sign of weakness. Another example of Jack's lack of moral fiber.

"It wouldn't bring enough," Jack said finally, reaching for another pretzel. "Even if I was inclined to sell it, which I'm not."

"I think it would. I took the liberty of drawing up some numbers, what the boat's probably worth, what Dad might sell for, interest rates, monthly payments—I think it's doable. I don't have them with me, though. I didn't know you'd be by."

Jack glared at him. "You took the liberty."

Kevin looked annoyed. "It's not like I went through your things. I just guessed at it, made a few calculations. I've done it a hundred times for things Carol and I thought about doing. And if you've got a few thousand in savings, I think we could get your monthly payments down to somewhere in the two-thousand-dollar range."

Jack nearly spit out his beer in a classic sitcom manner. He swallowed hard, coming up for air laughing. "Gee, could you? And did you figure out how many other jobs I'd have to get to be able to eat, buy propane, and have electricity at the same time?"

The bells on the door chimed, and Jack saw with relief that Kim McQuade had entered and was winding her way past the pool tables toward them.

"Finally," Jack said, pulling out the stool next to him for her.

Kevin nodded at Kim. "Hi, Kim. How's it going?"

"Great, you?"

Kevin nodded again, then looked at Jack. "I'll get you those numbers, Jack. Think about it, okay?" He moved down the bar with his rag.

"You bet." Jack took a deep breath and turned to Kim.

Kim sat, throwing her purse onto the footrail below the bar. "What was that about?"

"The house."

"Ah." She nodded knowingly. "He's still after you to buy."

Jack took another swig of beer. "Like the devil after my soul."

Kim laughed. "Something tells me you'll run

faster from Kevin." The bartender ambled over, and she ordered a beer. "So what did you want to talk to me about?"

Jack smiled slowly. "Oh, I don't know. Don't you want to get drunk first?"

Kim raised a brow. "Ah, I see this is going to entail divulging confidences. Does this, by any chance, have something to do with Delaney Poole?"

"Of course not," Jack said, turning to face her with an irrepressible grin. "But now that you've brought her up . . . Did you talk to her about her husband?"

Kim took up the beer the bartender slid to her and took a deliberate sip before answering. "In fact I did."

"And . . . ?"

She shrugged. "And she told me all about it. Or him, rather."

"She told you about Jim."

"Jim? I thought it was Joe. In any case, yes. We straightened it all out."

Despite himself, Jack felt his pulse accelerate. "She told you her husband's name was Joe?"

"I don't know, maybe she said Jim. I'm not good with names. Anyway, the good news—for you, anyway—is that they're not doing real well, apparently. So maybe you've got a shot after all." She took a sip of her beer. "God, I can't believe I'm doing this. Spreading gossip just like the diners club."

Jack smiled and patted her shoulder. "Don't worry your little head about it, Kim. At least this time it's for a good cause."

"This time?"

He started to laugh, and after a minute she joined him. Kim was, though she frequently denied it, a gossip of the first order. The difference between her and the old men at the diner, however, was that the gossip Kim spread was generally true. And not malicious. Which was what Jack valued most about her. He could give her the straight story when he thought it needed to be known, as well as get the true story about others when the need arose. Jack had always prided himself on his manipulation of the system in Harp Cove.

But because Kim couldn't seem to contain any news she heard, Jack didn't tell her about the Joe/Jim slip-up Delaney'd had with him.

"So what makes you think there's trouble in paradise?" Jack asked.

"She said so. That's why she checked the 'Single' box on her W-4. She thought she'd be divorced by now."

"She checked the 'Single' box? So she's getting a divorce?" Hope—or perhaps it was heartburn from the chili—flared to life in his chest.

Kim pulled the basket of pretzels toward herself and shook her head. "Not so fast, Romeo. They changed their minds. Guess they're giving it another try, though God knows how, living five hundred miles apart."

Jack rested an elbow on the bar and rubbed his palm on the side of his face as he assimilated the information. "She say when he was coming up?"

"No, but I didn't ask."

"Hm."

"Yeah, hm. Gives you some time, right? What are you going to do?"

Jack's gaze slid over to her. "About what?"

Kim laughed and used the moment of tossing her head back to pop another pretzel. "About your crush."

"I don't have a crush." But he hesitated, was that all this was? "I'm just . . . interested in my tenant's needs."

"As a landlord."

He nodded. "As a landlord."

They looked at each other for an extended moment, then both started to laugh.

After a moment, Kim sobered. "But seriously, Jack, there's one thing I need to know if I'm going to keep doing you favors like this."

"What's that?" he asked, taking another swig of his beer.

"I need to know . . . ," here her lips curved into an ironic smile, "that your intentions are honorable."

Jack started to laugh. "What?"

"I mean it. I like Delaney and I'm not going to help you if I think you're just going to toy with her and break her heart."

"Believe me," Jack said, leaning his arms on the bar and staring down at them, "the last thing I want to do is 'toy' with Delaney Poole."

"You know what I mean," Kim said. "Are you in love with her? Do you think she's The One? What?"

Jack turned and looked at her a long moment. She really did care, he thought, and the realization caused him a moment of weakness.

"If there is such a thing as The One," he said, smiling slightly, "then there's a good chance she's it for me."

Delaney sat at her kitchen table, a pad of paper in front of her, pen flipping mindlessly between her fingers. The words, printed with great care to make up for their scarcity, looked like a first grader's spelling list.

JIM
Lawyer
Married five years
Emily—four months, b. March 10

Was that all she had told people? she wondered. Was that all she'd *need* to tell people?

From the corner of her eye Delaney saw Emily's hands jerk slightly, then settle down once again to her sides. She was sleeping in her swing, her head tilted to one side, her cheek scrunched against her tiny shoulder. As soon as Delaney finished her list she would move her, but she looked so peaceful there was no need just yet.

The necessity of the list, on the other hand, was unequivocal. She'd already messed up twice, hopefully without consequences. She'd confused her husband's name while talking to Jack—a near *fatal* mistake. And she'd told Kim she'd been married five years, then remembered later she'd told Jack only about two.

The last wasn't as grave a mistake as the first, because she was pretty vague with Jack, she believed. Still, she *had* to get her facts straight, and keep them straight every time something came up.

After a few minutes of fruitless thought, she decided that what she needed was some brainstorming. She plucked the phone off the wall and dialed Michael's number.

"I need to get to know my husband. I need to decide what he looks like, what he wears, who his family is, everything," she said without preamble. Their conversations often started as if they'd never hung up from the last one. "I'm desperate, Michael. Please say you'll help me."

Silence reverberated over the phone. Then, "Who is this?"

"Very funny." She shifted her feet onto the chair across from her. "I'm not catching you in the middle of something, am I?"

Michael laughed. "As if you wouldn't expect me to drop it."

Delaney frowned. "God, am I that demanding?"

"No. Just that needy."

She groaned, and he laughed again.

"You know just where to hit a girl, don't you?"

"Come on, you're the least needy woman I know. Monks are needier than you are. Stoics are. Camels."

"Camels?"

"You know, in the desert. They've got that hump . . . never mind. So, what do you need?"

"I keep tripping up. Telling different people different things. I'm going to get caught in this lie, I just know it."

"Tell me again the reason for the lie?"

"What do you mean? You know the reason."

"I know you don't want this guy to know about Emily, but I don't remember why. Is he that bad?"

Delaney covered her face with one hand. "I thought you understood. I thought you *agreed* with me." Her voice rose emotionally on the last syllables.

"No, no, I do," Michael said quickly. "That is I remember agreeing, I just don't remember why."

"Because he as much as said he didn't *want* children the first time we met, first of all. Second, because I barely know him. Third, because he's a here-today-gone-tomorrow kind of person and that would do Emily more harm than good."

"Actually you were the one who was there one day and gone the next."

"Michael!" She sat up straight, her feet hitting the floor.

"I'm just saying."

She clutched the phone hard and threw out a hand with her words, as if Michael were sitting across the table from her. "He's a playboy, to say the least. My God, the things I've heard about him since I got here. It'd curl your hair."

"Then I don't need to need to hear anymore of *that*," he said, laughing.

.

"Seriously," she said. "He's got quite a reputation."

"So you want a guy without a past for Emily's father, is that it?"

Delaney gritted her teeth against a now-familiar fear. "What are you saying, you think I've done the wrong thing? You think I should tell him about her? This stranger—this philanderer—this—this . . . *God*," she exhaled explosively on the word, "if you could have seen the bimbo he was with when he came into my office. Do you think it would be good for Emily to have to deal with a succession of pseudostepmothers like that? I can't bear the thought. What sort of self-esteem would she grow up with, surrounded by fake boobs—and—and stupidity and hair spray? Nurtured by a father who can't say no to a pretty face?"

"Okay." He said it slowly, patronizingly. "But as one of those pretty faces, I would think you might have a little more sympathy for him."

Delaney shook her head. "I need women friends. Why don't I have any women friends? *They'd* understand the problem I have with this."

She thought of Kim McQuade. She could be friends with her, she thought. She could build it up slowly, then tell her the truth and have someone sympathetic to talk to.

"Actually, I do understand the problem," Michael said. "But it's yours. Not Emily's."

"What do you mean? I'm *thinking* of Emily."

"Yeah, and you're thinking of you. Of competing with women you don't understand. Of having to deal with a man you don't understand, and might possibly have feelings for."

"*What?*" She accidentally sent her pen skittering across the table. "Are you *crazy*? I don't have feelings for him. How could I? I don't even know him. And believe me, I don't *want* to understand him."

She got up and pushed the chairs aside, looking under the table for the pen but blind to anything but Michael's audacity.

"So he's a single guy who dates a lot. Tell me again why that makes him a bad father?"

Delaney stopped, leaned back in the corner of the kitchen beside the table, and felt a lump grow in her throat. What was the *matter* with her? She *never* cried.

"Whose side are you on, anyway?"

"Honey, I'm on your side. Yours and Emily's. And I'm just trying to understand. If you can't answer all these questions, maybe you need to do a little more thinking about what you're doing."

She put a hand to her mouth, holding back emotions that threatened to spill forth. After a second she said, "Do you honestly think I think about anything else?"

Silence reigned for a moment while Delaney collected herself.

"All right," Michael said finally. "All right. What have you got there? I know you've got a list. What's on it?"

She smiled, though tears beaded in the corners of her eyes. "Hang on a second."

She bent and retrieved the pen, then maneuvered herself out of the corner to sit back down. She read him the list.

"You changed Emily's birthday?"

She sniffed. "Yeah, I know. It was hard. But if I gave him the real one, the first thing he'd do is count backwards, wouldn't he?"

"I don't know. You said he used a condom. My guess is it would never occur to him she might be his."

She sighed, rested her elbow on the table and her forehead in her hand. "Well, it's too late now. I've already said she's four months old to a couple of people."

I'm a bad mother, she thought. *I stole my own daughter's birthday.*

"Okay, that's all right," Michael said, obviously aware that she was feeling raw about this. His tone was placating. "So, okay. This'll be fun. We'll just invent Mr. Right for you. Boy, do I have a few ideas about that."

She forced a laugh and it felt good. "Just make sure you make him straight, okay?"

"Oh don't worry, honey, your Mr. Right and mine would be completely different, in more ways than the obvious. So okay, first you should write down what this guy looks like, generally, because Emily might end up looking like him at some point."

She lifted her head. "Good point."

Handsome, she printed.

Tall, 6'2"
Blond
Greenish brown eyes
Strong jaw
Broad shoulders
Great shape
College athlete

"Okay, now what does this guy like do to?"
Michael asked after she'd read him the list.

"What do you mean? He's a lawyer."

"No, I mean for fun. You remember fun, don't
you, Dee?"

"Ha-ha." She tapped the pen against the table.
"He loves the outdoors. Hiking, fishing, camping,
stuff like that. He's really capable, too, you know
what I mean? The kind of guy who knows how
everything works. And he's happy. Really easygo-
ing."

She wrote it all down.

"Jeez," Michael said, "who wouldn't marry this
guy?"

"I know," she said. "Sometimes I think about
that. About how nice it would be to have this guy—
or you know, some perfect guy—to come home to.
Maybe we'd have a dog in the yard. A swing set for
Emily . . ."

"And he should be able to cook," Michael
added. "Really fancy stuff."

She laughed and wrote down *Gourmet cook*.

"And he'd never ask me if I've finished the laundry, or why the hell hadn't I noticed that the car

smoked every time I started it up. He'd never stomp downstairs in the morning asking, god-dammit, why didn't I *tell* him his only good suit was at the cleaners? And he'd never, *never*, shove his eggs across the table, scattering the silverware and overturning the milk, if the yolks were too runny."

They both paused. Delaney realized she was holding her breath.

"Delaney?" Michael's voice sounded far away. "Every romantic fantasy you have doesn't have to end with your parents' marriage."

She exhaled. "Doesn't it? Okay, so not everyone would become as belligerent as my father. And I wouldn't be as meek as my mother."

She ignored Michael's snort of laughter.

"But isn't it inevitable that two people trying to spend the rest of their lives together are bound to start taking each other for granted?" she continued. "*I* think so. That's why I'll never get married. And now that I have Emily there's no need to, thank God."

The irony of those words hung in the air for a moment before Michael spoke again.

"I don't think every marriage ends up that way. My parents' didn't."

Delaney thought for a moment. How many times had she wished Michael's parents had been hers? You couldn't find more understanding peo-ple if you'd tried. When Michael had told them he was gay, for example, his mother had offered to fix him up with her hairdresser.

"Your parents had money," she said, writing *Big bucks* on the list. "Maybe a spouse without financial frustration stays happier longer."

"Well, it would help," he said. "But your parents are still together. You've got to give them that."

"Yeah, I'll give them that, even though it's only because they're so set in their ways. My father wouldn't know what to do if my mother left. And my mother's been cowed by him for so long she'd never believe she could leave."

They were both silent a minute.

"Well, that'll never happen to you," Michael said finally. "You're too selfish."

Delaney laughed.

"Besides, why would you ever leave a guy like the one we're creating? Now tell me some more about him."

Delaney sketched out a few more details and read him the list. "Majored in PoliSci. Brilliant. I must have a brilliant man. Uh . . . Owns a house in Arlington, near his parents, who baby-sat a lot. Only child (it's simpler that way, maybe one brother, if the need arises.) Drives a Volvo. Loves dogs."

"A Volvo?" Michael's voice dripped sarcasm. "You can take the girl out of Washington, but you can't take Washington out of the girl."

"What do you mean? They're not unique to Washington."

"Come on, they are the ultimate yuppie car. And D.C.'s the ultimate yuppie town."

"They're *safe*," she said. "They're the safest cars on the road."

"Uh-huh."

"And they scream 'security.' I could use a little security right now."

"You think someone's going to ask you what he drives?"

"They might. Besides, I need to be like an actress preparing for a play. I should know more about my character than anyone's ever likely to ask."

"You're certainly well into that area now. Have you decided if he wears boxers or briefs yet?"

"Neither," she said dryly.

He laughed. "You going to remember all this?"

She ran down the list with one finger. "This is probably enough for right now. If anyone asks me something that's not on here, I'll just write it down on the pad in my purse. I got it just for that purpose. Then I'll add whatever it is to the list when I get home."

"And you'll study this list every night at dinner."

"That's right."

He chuckled. "I know you so well. You always need to be studying something. At least this way you're exercising your creativity."

"You don't think I'm creative?" She scoffed. "Heck, I just created a whole man, right here. Mr. Right. I can picture him in my head this very moment."

It wasn't until she'd said that, dropped the pen on the table and leaned smugly back in her chair, that she realized with a start that the handsome, happy dream man she pictured was none other than Jack Shepard.

"Well, good for you," Michael said. "I hope he keeps you warm at night."

"At least I'll know he's not keeping someone *else* warm." She folded up the list to put it in her kitchen drawer.

She needed to make friends with a woman, she thought again. A woman would understand this. Tomorrow, she thought. Tomorrow I'll ask Kim McQuade to go to lunch.

"Hey," Michael said before they hung up. "Have you been watching *Destiny's Children*?"

"Come on, Michael, you know I don't have time for soap operas. I'm depending on you to keep me up-to-date." She smiled thinking of all the times they'd gossiped about the goings-on in the small TV town of Destiny, as if the people and their ridiculous problems were real.

"Well, get a VCR, honey, because Sybill and Drake finally got together," he said, his tone as salacious as if the fictional people were actual acquaintances.

"No!"

"Yes!"

"But what about Kristin? Is he going to leave his wife? God, after all they went through . . ."

"Nope. He's not. And get this, Sybill's pregnant."

"Oh brother. I can't believe they're going to do that. Isn't that how they got Drake and Kristin together?"

"Yeah, but I'm serious, you really have to watch it. You, of all people."

"Why *me* of all people?" she asked.

"Because Sybill's not telling either."

"What?" It took a second before Michael's point became clear.

"Sybill," Michael said. "She's not telling Drake about the baby, either."

She was a soap opera. That's what he was saying. Her life was as screwed up and absurd as a stupid soap opera.

Chapter 8

"Not much masculine stuff in here." Jack's voice carried in from the living room on a warm summer breeze. He was caulking a window that had leaked during a storm the night before, a storm that had left in its wake a near-perfect Saturday morning.

In the kitchen, Delaney froze. The glass of water she'd just poured was suddenly weightless in her hand as a now-familiar streak of adrenaline raced through her.

"What?" she called back, hearing guilt in her voice. She hated lying. Which was a real inconvenience considering how she'd set herself up to live an enormous one for at least the next three years.

She'd been in the middle of watching five hours—the week's worth—of taped episodes of *Destiny's Children* on her tiny black-and-white TV when Jack showed up to do some work on the house. So she was feeling a little more defensive than usual. Ever since Michael had pointed out the similarity—the *small* similarity—between Sybill's situation and her own she'd felt the need to study the show for any possibly noble intentions on Sybill's part.

"I said there's not much masculine stuff in this house," Jack said. His voice and body became large as he strode into the kitchen.

He was smiling at her, his eyes warm, and tools chinked together from the canvas belt at his waist. He seemed to take up three times more space in the kitchen than Delaney did, with his deep voice and tools and muscles.

"Your husband's not going to feel very at home when he comes."

Now that she saw his smile she could hear the teasing tone in his voice, and her heart slowed down a fraction.

She handed the water glass to him. "His stuff hasn't arrived yet."

"Sure, but he's going to visit, isn't he? That sewing cabinet in the living room isn't going to keep him busy very long when he does. Unless, is he into embroidery?"

He brought the glass to his lips. Delaney watched his throat as he swallowed and allowed her gaze to travel down his neck to the few visible chest hairs above his shirt. Despite his obvious strength there was nothing muscle-bound about his body, she noted. He had an elegance to him. And yet she could tell his biceps were wide and his chest well-defined.

Maybe it was the way he moved, lithe, coordinated, silent. More than once she'd been surprised by him when he was working around the house. He seemed to move on cat feet.

She thought of her list, now tucked into the back of the kitchen drawer, and considered adding *cat feet* to it.

"What are you smiling about?" he asked, setting the empty water glass on the counter.

"Just the thought of Jim," she hesitated only briefly, checking, "doing embroidery."

"My aunt once taught me how to knit," Jack said, an easy smile playing on his lips.

Delaney's brows rose. "Did she really?"

"Yep." He nodded.

"And did you enjoy it?" She couldn't help the smirk that molded her lips. It was all she could do to keep from laughing at the idea of Harp Cove's heartthrob so domestically engaged.

"As a matter of fact," he said, looking to the floor with a self-deprecating chuckle, "I did. Until Kevin got wind of it, that is, and there was the end of it."

Delaney tried to picture a small Jack Shepard with knitting needles and yarn, winding and twisting the threads with little-boy fingers, studiously counting stitches. What had he been thinking? What had he been picturing as he worked? A blanket? A cap? Something he could show his friends?

"What did you make?" Despite herself she thought he must have looked very cute. She could imagine his eyes narrowing as he concentrated, the lashes appearing even longer in his boyish face.

"It was a scarf, actually." He leaned one hip against the counter and crossed his arms over his chest. "A black one. Very manly."

"Manly," she repeated, smiling.

"Yeah. No fringe."

She laughed. "Have you still got it?"

"Nah." He shook his head. "My mother probably does. She's in California," he explained, then grinned. "A good distance. I think my secret's safe."

"I don't know . . ." She gave him a sly smile. "The cat's out of the bag now. What's it worth to you for me to keep my mouth shut?"

He looked at her then. Not that he hadn't been looking at her before; it just seemed to her that at this moment he really looked at her. His eyes went soft and at the same time his gaze became somehow penetrating. *This* was the look, she thought, that Kim had mentioned. This had to be it because it made her stomach flip over.

His lips were curved but the eyes were intense. "All right. What's your price?" he asked finally.

She laughed and tried to move nonchalantly to the cabinet where the glasses were. She took one down and thrust it under the tap, nearly cracking the rim against the faucet as she flipped the water on with her other hand.

"I think I'll have to think about that," she said, glancing out the window at the sunstruck ocean. Her heart raced.

"I guess I'm at your mercy then." Though he'd moved no closer, coming from behind her his voice seemed intimate.

She turned. "Yes," she said. "I guess you are."

Their gazes met and held for what was, to Delaney, a painfully long moment. Then Emily's cry reached her.

Delaney took a deep breath and mentally thanked God.

"The queen summons me," she said with a wry smile, moving past him. "Is the window finished?"

If it was, she could just say, "See you later" and that would be the end of it. Jack Shepard and his penetrating looks would be gone, and she could attempt to get her nervous system back under control.

"Yeah. Do you mind if I come up with you?"

She paused in the hallway and turned back. "Where? Upstairs?"

"Yeah." He shrugged one shoulder. "I'd like to see her. Emily, I mean. I like babies."

Delaney struggled to come up with a reason to say no, but all she could think about was a young Jack knitting a scarf. "I don't know," she said finally, then allowed a slow smile. "Maybe if you knitted her a blanket sometime . . ."

Jack laughed, and the light and warmth in his eyes when he did made Delaney's breath catch.

A second later, surprised at herself, Delaney laughed too. She couldn't help it. Despite the fact that she was consorting with the enemy, she was enjoying their conversation. She'd never been able to come up with this sort of banter with men before. Seemed she'd always been tongue-tied. But with Jack, it was easy.

She motioned for him to follow and started up the stairs. Emily's cries grew louder.

It was only because he was so practiced at flirting, she told herself. The best charmers were the ones who made everyone else feel witty. Jack was clearly one of the masters. And here she was falling for it. Again.

What she was doing bringing him up to see Emily was beyond her. *Bringing the wolf to the lamb*, she thought. *Only I'm the one who could be slaughtered.*

Delaney reached the crib and bent over the rail. Emily's face was beet red and streaked with tiny tears. Her chin quivered between wails.

"There now, sweet pea," Delaney cooed, picking her up from the crib. Emily's cries became trembling inward breaths and her little fists grabbed Delaney's shirt and strands of her hair.

She kissed Emily's fat, wet cheek and turned to Jack standing in the doorway. The expression on his face was inscrutable as he watched them.

"I haven't seen her much the last couple weeks," he said. "You guys leave early and get home pretty late, I guess."

"We did." Delaney smoothed Emily's damp hair back from her face. "But we got some bad news yesterday. Cora at Tiny Tot quit, and she was the one who would bring Emily to me at the office after work."

Jack nodded. "Yeah, I heard she was moving to Boston. Something about a new boyfriend."

"That's right." Delaney had momentarily forgotten she was in such a small town. Of course Jack would know all about it. She wondered how long it would be before she'd know everything that was going on around town. Or would she always be an outsider?

She frowned, worried again that Cora was the only one at Tiny Tot who gave Emily individual attention. "So that's going to cut into my day considerably. I'm afraid Dr. Jacobson's none too happy about it either."

Jack scoffed. "I wouldn't worry about Doc. It's not as if he'd ever fire you. You've got your priorities straight."

Delaney shrugged her brows. "I guess."

But did she? Part of her, a growing part, believed she should be home with Emily. If it weren't for having to repay NHSC for her tuition, she would try to go part-time, but as things stood that was impossible.

Now the thought of dropping her baby off at Tiny Tot without Cora there to greet them, looking delighted at the sight of her all-time, number-one, favorite baby—as she always called Emily—frightened Delaney. Emily was getting so responsive now. What would it do to her development to be left in a crib all day long? Only picked up for feeding and the occasional minute of play . . .

Despite her reasoning, despite the irrefutable logic of having to provide for Emily and ensure her career, in the wake of Cora's departure Delaney felt as if she were going to be dropping off her daughter at a prison.

"What's the matter?" Jack's quiet voice startled her out of her reverie.

Emily chewed sloppily on her own fist, the downy hairs on her head as she moved caressing Delaney's cheek.

"Nothing." Delaney shook her head. "We'll just miss Cora, is all. Won't we, sweetheart?" She pulled Emily from her shoulder and kissed her forehead, her heart swelling with love and trepidation.

Jack nodded, watching them.

Delaney moved to the changing table and laid Emily down. Emily's fists flailed, grabbed each other, then flailed some more. Delaney handed her a small pink rattle, which Emily held up in front of her face for inspection.

"You're worried about the day-care place, aren't you," Jack said, moving into the room.

For a second, the opportunity to share her worries with Jack seemed like an enormous relief. The idea that he might help her and relieve some of the burden of always wondering if she were doing the right thing was nearly irresistible.

But that was stupid. Crazy even. Jack wasn't a friend. He wasn't someone she could rely on and confide in. He was the one from whom she had to protect herself. Herself and Emily, that was.

She'd already decided he wasn't father material.

After getting to know him a little she believed he'd probably say that very thing himself. In fact he *had* said that very thing, when they'd first met. Besides, he was undependable. A philanderer. A playboy. An underachiever. The words were becoming a mantra.

Delaney peeled the dirty diaper from Emily's behind, hoping the sight of it might send bachelor Jack back to the doorway. The last thing she needed was Jack Shepard acting like part of the family.

An unexpected pang hit her in the pit of her stomach as she realized that's exactly what they were. A family. Only she was the only one of them who knew it. The responsibility was overwhelming.

"I'll figure it out," she said, speaking mostly to herself but knowing the words would suffice for Jack as well.

Emily looked straight at her and hit herself in the head with the rattle, as if to say, *It's simple, bonehead.* But though Emily's eyes seemed to hold all the answers, Delaney couldn't divine what they were.

"You know," Jack said, fingering the corner of the dinosaur blanket on which Emily lay. His hands looked enormous so close to Emily's little body. "My aunt sometimes takes care of children. She's only getting social security, so she likes the extra money. But she's great with kids. Especially babies. She took care of twins last year until the parents moved."

A lump of fear rose in Delaney's throat. "No," she managed to croak.

At the ensuing awkward silence she looked up. Jack's expression was surprised, and a little offended.

She busied herself with the washcloth. "Thanks anyway," she hastened to add. "I appreciate it, I really do. But I don't want to put anybody out. She's probably enjoying her retirement, and babies are so much work."

"She likes doing it," Jack said.

Panic rose in her chest. She realized she'd been wiping Emily's bottom long after it was clean. She whipped a new diaper from the pile at the end of the table. "Tiny Tot's not so bad, really. And it's close to the clinic, so I can go feed her at lunch. That's the most important thing."

She glanced up at him. His eyes were on her. She fumbled for the talcum powder.

"But you have to drive there, right? I mean, for it to be quick."

"Sure, but it only takes two minutes." She dumped way too much powder on the diaper and struggled not to cough as a cloud of it ballooned upward toward her face.

"My aunt's is closer."

She forced a laugh. "Closer than two minutes? Where is she, in the lobby?"

Jack laughed mildly. "Just about. She's in the building next door. Second floor."

Delaney swallowed and concentrated on securing the diaper around Emily's dancing legs. "Oh?" was all she could think to say.

The building next door housed, ironically, a

combination piercing and tattoo parlor indelicately called In the Flesh. When she'd first seen the clinic she'd thought she'd probably have to treat a large number of skin infections and botched piercings, but it turned out the place was clean and well run. And the building was nice. An old brick structure with tall casement windows and an ornate brickwork cornice along the top.

"Yeah," he said. "Couldn't be more convenient, could it?"

She swallowed. "I guess not."

"And that's the most important thing, didn't you say?"

Delaney's mind spun, well aware of the irony in his tone, but she didn't look at him. "I wonder that you didn't let your aunt live here. If she's that hard-up for money, I mean."

"She's not hard-up, just on a fixed income. And I offered her the house, but she prefers living in town."

She glanced up.

Jack shrugged. "She doesn't drive, you know. Anyway, I'll ask her if she's interested, if you want."

Delaney pressed the Velcro closures on the diaper and grabbed the rattle for a light tug-of-war with Emily. Having Jack's aunt take care of Emily would be disastrous, she told herself. Nothing good could possibly come of it. She was already too close to him as it was, living right next door, in a house he owned and could overlook from any one of a dozen windows.

Besides, if his relative took care of their daugh-

ter, that relative could one day notice a resemblance, couldn't she? *Wouldn't* she?

"Well?" Jack asked, leaning slightly forward to
look into Delaney's face. He caught her eye, and
she looked up from her daughter.

"No really, Jack. I can't let her do it," she said. "I
don't want to inconvenience anyone. Emily's fine
where she is."

But was she? For a moment the idea of putting
off Jack's suggestion was somehow selfish. Emily
could be the sole charge of a retired older woman
living right next door to where her mother worked,
instead of being cared for along with a slew of
other small children by a couple of harried women
making six dollars an hour in an ex–convenience
store building on the outskirts of town.

Jack laughed and shook his head. "It's no trouble, Delaney. I'll just ask and see what she says. Do
you mind if I hold her?"

The abrupt change in subject threw her. "What?"

"Emily. Can I hold her?"

"Oh." She looked down at her daughter. "Uh,
sure."

Maybe he'd forget, she thought as she handed
Emily to Jack. Maybe the aunt wouldn't want to do
it. As she'd said, babies were a lot of work, the aunt
was probably too old. Maybe the whole thing
would blow over.

She stared at Jack as he took Emily, his hands tan
against her pale skin.

He looked awkward with her, holding her out
from his body and looking into her face. "Hello

there," he said, in a soft tone that sent shivers up Delaney's spine.

Emily's hands reached for him and he settled her—ungracefully but effectively—against his side. Emily stared up at him as if engrossed by the rare sight of a grown man up close.

"Aren't you pretty?" he murmured. He smiled at her a moment, then opened his mouth and eyes wide—an exaggerated expression of happiness— then scrunched them both up and blew lightly into Emily's face. Emily smiled immediately, and he chuckled, then did it again.

The third time Emily's eyes and mouth opened wide at the same time his did, mimicking his expression, and Jack laughed, delighted. He blew lightly into her face. Her eyes narrowed against the breeze.

They continued two or three more times while Delaney watched, fascinated. They *did* look alike, she realized with a start. It wasn't something you'd see right off, but standing there, wearing the same expressions, it was obvious to Delaney that they shared quite a few genes. The realization terrified her.

"Stop," she said suddenly.

Jack turned to her, surprised. "What?"

She reached for Emily. "It—it's not good to blow in a baby's face."

"Oh." Obviously chagrined, he stepped closer to relinquish the child to Delaney. "I'm sorry, I didn't know."

Emily's face screwed up in visible displeasure. She'd obviously been enjoying the game.

"No, no, it's okay. Listen, I have a lot to do." She glanced around the room, hoping to see something undone she could start doing to make him leave, but the place was tidy.

Glancing into the open closet, regretting that she'd just straightened it that morning, is when she noticed the picture frame. Hung on the wall next to the closet door was an engraved silver picture frame with Emily's first photo in it. Her friend, Mary, had given it to her and had had it engraved with Emily's height, weight, time and date of birth.

It was this last that caused Delaney's heart to leap to her throat. She froze.

Why hadn't she noticed it before? More importantly, why hadn't she realized when she was hanging the blasted thing that the simple gift gave away her secret and jeopardized everything she'd done to confirm her story?

She clutched Emily to her chest.

Had Jack seen it? Had he noticed the date was *two months* earlier than she'd let on? Could she possibly yank it off the wall now without him noticing? Could she throw something at it? Break it? Drape Emily's blanket over it as if she did it all the time? Maybe she could step in front of it and act nonchalant until he left?

No. She had to get rid of him now. She spun back toward him.

But Jack had taken her first hint and had turned

toward the door. His high cheekbones were tinged with red. "Yeah, no problem. I gotta go too. I've got plenty to do myself."

They both headed for the bedroom door, on a course to barrel through together, but Jack stopped, motioning her ahead of him. Delaney passed him and proceeded down the hall, his footsteps heavy on the floorboards behind her.

Her blood thundered in her ears as she considered the brief time they'd spent in the room. He hadn't looked around, or even glanced away from her and Emily that she'd noticed, a fact that had made her very self-conscious. Surely he'd been too far away to read the delicate engraving from where he'd stood anyway. And wouldn't he have said something if he'd noticed it?

She could tell Emily watched him over her shoulder and she wondered if he was making faces at her. She readjusted the child to lie in her arms.

She began to descend the steps, but Jack stopped in the doorway to her room.

"Oh no," he said. "Is that *Destiny's Children*?" He motioned toward the TV and the muted voices emerging from it.

She must have forgotten to turn the tape off when he arrived. She blushed.

"Uh, yeah." She forced a laugh. "I record it during the week and watch on the weekends. It's my secret vice."

He laughed and looked back at the TV.

She cringed. Of all the embarrassing programs to leave on. A soap opera. She felt as if she'd just told him she wasn't a real doctor but she played one on TV.

"It just helps me unwind, you know," she said. "The ultimate mindless diversion."

"Sure."

He looked back at the TV, and Delaney swallowed hard. How bad would it look if she edged past him and switched the damn thing off?

"So tell me," he continued, "do you think Sybill's a selfish bitch or is my mother just a prude?"

Delaney gaped at him. "Your mother called Sybill a selfish bitch?"

"Yeah." He turned to look at her. Looked her dead in the eye, in fact. "She's the one who's lying about being pregnant, right? My mother can't stand her and for some reason feels the need to update me about her behavior every time we talk. I guess you could say my mother's something of a soap addict."

Delaney could think of nothing to say. She felt as if Jack had just admitted his mother hated *her*.

In the background, Sybill's voice said something brittle that Delaney couldn't quite make out.

"How often do you talk to your mother?" Delaney asked, hoping to change the subject.

"Often enough to know way too much about this show." He laughed. "About once a week." He continued to stare at the TV, mesmerized. "I guess that's Sybill, huh? Man, she's a piece of work."

"What do you mean?"

He turned back. "Well, if my mother's to be

believed—and in this case I'm sure she's right on top of things—Sybill seduced her best friend's husband, got pregnant, and now she's not going to tell him the kid is his. I guess I'd have to agree that's pretty selfish."

Delaney's face heated. "I guess. Except, you know, it would screw up Drake's life with Kristin, so maybe she's being strong. Doing it for a good reason. You know. Maybe."

Jack looked caught between amusement and confusion. "Well, that's an interesting take. I'll have to pass that one along to my mother. Although I'm sure she'll say Sybill's doing it to punish Drake for staying with Kristin. Seems to me she just said that today, in fact."

Delaney swallowed. "Your mother's pretty hard on Sybill."

He chuckled. "Well, she also thinks Drake's an s.o.b. and he's getting what he deserves. And that maybe this new guy she's got will be better father material."

"There's a new guy?"

"Yeah, Ruark. She's passing the kid off as his. I guess you haven't gotten to that part yet."

She shook her head. "I guess not."

He started to head toward the stairs. "Maybe you should give up on the VCR and just talk to my mother. She'd be thrilled to know my tenant's as intereseed in *Destiny's Children* as she is."

"But," Delaney couldn't help asking, "do you think Drake would really *want* to know?"

He stopped at the head of the stairs and she looked up at him from two steps down.

"I mean, it's not as if he wanted the child he thought Kristin was going to have."

He frowned quizzically. "I don't know. He married her, didn't he? He did the right thing."

She took one of Emily's hands, felt the small fingers clutch hers. "But, I mean, he's happy the way things are, don't you think? Why would he care about Sybill's child? It's not as if he's in love with her or anything."

"You know, I haven't ever actually *seen* the show, not all the way through. But I guess I'd have to say if it is his child there's no way he'll turn away from it. Besides, whether he wants to know or not, you know he's going to find out."

"You don't think he'd rather she just keep the whole thing to herself? You know, not mess up his life?"

"Well, he *would* be an s.o.b. then, wouldn't he? What kind of guy wouldn't want to know about his own kid?"

She dipped her head, feeling an elephant step on her chest. "I don't know. Some men wouldn't want to know, I don't think. As long as they don't know about it, it saves them having to take responsibility, don't you think? Saves all that child support and everything."

He looked at her a moment before answering, causing her stomach to clutch.

"It's not as if these people are real, Delaney." A

smile touched his eyes. "He's going to want the kid because that's the best way to drag out the story."

She shook herself. "Of course. I just thought—well, sure, you're right."

She turned away and continued down the stairs to the front door, Jack following. Once she reached it Delaney grabbed the knob and opened the door immediately.

"Let me know if that window leaks again," Jack said.

"All right." Delaney nodded. A fresh summer breeze coursed through the open doorway, flinging a strand of her hair across her face. She tucked it behind her ear. "Thanks for fixing it so quickly."

"No problem. Thanks for letting me . . ." He gestured toward Emily. "You know, play with her. Sorry, though. Sorry I blew on her."

Delaney shook her head, ashamed of the lie, her mind in a turmoil. She'd been disconcerted by the similarity she'd seen between them. How long would it be before others saw it? And what did he mean when he said that *of course* Drake would want the child?

"No, no, it's okay," she said. "Thanks for coming by."

"Yeah, all right." He hesitated, looking from Delaney to Emily. Then, releasing the air from his cheeks, he stepped over the threshold. "Okay, see you."

"Bye." She shut the door firmly behind him, then turned to lean back against it. Emily gurgled and grabbed a button on Delaney's shirtfront.

Delaney closed her eyes, concentrating on the warmth of the body in her arms.

What was she doing? Emily's father was *right there*. He wanted to hold her. He wanted to play with her. He knew how to make her smile. He wanted his aunt to take care of her. He thought an s.o.b. like Drake Westmoreland would *of course* want to know about his child . . .

She was losing control, that's what she was doing.

She thought of him asking if she was worried about Tiny Tot, how for a moment she had so desperately wanted to talk to him about it all. As if they were friends. As if they were parents.

Delaney pushed off the door and quickly moved to the window in the living room. Standing diagonally behind the curtain, she peered out the window at Jack's retreating figure. He was looking at the ocean and moving very slowly. Contemplatively, almost.

The thought formed in her mind that she should tell him. Everything. Stop this endless lying that she wasn't any good at anyway. She should tell him that her husband was a figment of her imagination and Emily was his daughter. That she had lied to him and everyone in town because she didn't want him to find out that he was Emily's father. Because she didn't know him. Because she didn't trust him.

Her stomach lifted as if she had just stepped off a cliff.

A car pulled into the drive. Delaney took a step right to watch its progress. A small white sports car pulled in behind Jack's truck. Jack moved on toward the back of his house, oblivious, until the driver of the white car leaned on the horn.

Jack's head snapped up, and out of the car popped Lisa Jacobson.

Delaney's stomach plummeted.

"Hey," she heard Lisa yell. Then Lisa's head ducked back into the car. She reappeared with something in her hand, a black piece of material. "Hey, Jack," she yelled again, the words emerged like bullets from a handgun.

She sauntered toward where Jack had stopped, his eyes narrowed against the sun.

Delaney watched Lisa's back, the way her hips moved from side to side in opposition to her shoulders, like a model on a runway. The black cloth fluttered in her hand before she slung it over her shoulder.

Clearly, it was a shirt.

Apparently, it was Jack's shirt. Left, God knows where—the backseat of a car? a dark alley? certainly not Dr. Jacobson's house, where her boss had complained more than once that Lisa still lived—for Lisa to return.

Lisa approached Jack, and when she was about five feet away she flung the shirt at him, her chin jutting out. The shirt caught him across the chest and draped there momentarily. Jack's hand lifted and snatched it down.

To Delaney the scene was perfectly readable: The shirt was his and Lisa was returning it to him. The short shorts and tight halter top Lisa wore were just as obviously calculated to tease as that attention-grabbing walk.

Delaney could no longer hear their words, but she didn't need to. Lisa inched closer while Jack watched her, his head cocked to one side. Then she saw his head turn and his eyes shift to her house.

She sprang back into the living room. Could he see through the window? Surely not. Outside was bright sunshine, and there wasn't a light on in the house.

Fool! Delaney told herself. *Idiot, moron, jerk. You almost told him. Because he's attractive, you had a moment of longing and almost put your own daughter into the hands of stepmothers like Lisa Jacobson, for God's sake. Time to grow up, Delaney Poole, and realize no matter how much he may smile at you, no matter how appealing you might find him, no matter how much you may want a friend, you have to think of Emily first and foremost.*

Delaney rubbed her forehead with her free hand and bent her stiff knees to sit in the chair in front of the window. The wing chair's high back protected her from whoever might look in the window.

Emily grabbed a fistful of shirt and drooled down Delaney's shoulder.

Idiot, she thought again. It had been foolish even to let him go up and see Emily. She'd succumbed to a moment of weakness and it was during moments of weakness that she made her worst decisions. Case in point: the night she'd decided a one-night stand was a good idea.

She couldn't trust him. She didn't know him. He

dated children, for God's sake, how could he be expected to care for one?

She took a deep breath. Okay, so he was a nice guy. He had . . . some charm, she conceded. But he was *not* the kind of man you pick to father your children. He'd as much as said he never *wanted* any children. And since she was in a position—sort of—to pick whether she wanted him for Emily's father or not, she needed to evaluate the situation very carefully. And so far, all the evidence suggested to her—no, *compelled* her—to keep the information to herself.

What she needed to do, she decided, was find other people to confide in, other friends to talk over her problems with. Not that Jack was a friend. No, Jack was just . . . just an unexpected distraction. A distraction with great charisma and a dangerously magnetic smile. But that was all.

Unfortunately, Kim had been on vacation all week, so she hadn't been able to cultivate a friendship with her, as she'd planned. But she would. As soon as Kim got back into town she would make friends.

Because she had to get rid of Jack. The temptation to talk to him was getting too strong. She needed to put him off. Show him that he didn't have a place in her life other than as her landlord.

She had to remember her husband.

Chapter 9

Sadie's Diner was nearly full the day Delaney and Kim went to lunch, with the waitresses hollering at the cook and Rodney, the owner, scowling at everyone.

Kim and Delaney stood at the door a second before noticing that a booth in the back near the rest rooms was empty.

"Come on," Kim said, grabbing two menus off the counter by the register and taking her by the arm. "We'll just slip into that one before Rodney tells us he's too full to take anyone else."

Kim marched across the room in her stiletto heels and short skirt, drawing not a few stares as she went. She definitely looked more New York than Harp Cove.

"He'd do that?" Delaney asked. "Turn away business?"

"Oh yeah. He's the laziest son of a bitch ever to own a successful restaurant. Not that you can exactly call this a restaurant."

Kim took the side of the booth looking out into the dining room while Delaney slipped onto the vinyl bench seat across from her. Salt stuck to her palm as she slid across the seat and she brushed it away.

"I don't think I've ever seen this place so crowded. I wonder what's up?"

"August," Kim said with a grimace. "Biggest vacation month of the year. And this last week before school starts is always the worst." She propped up a menu in front of her while her eyes scanned the room. "Oh God, the diners club is here. Well, at least it's too crowded for them to hear anything."

"The diners club?" Delaney craned her neck around to look at the teeming room.

"See the guys at the middle table? Bunch of old men?"

Delaney saw the men she'd heard talking about Jack the first week she was here, the morning she had breakfast at the counter and he'd joined her. "Oh, yes. Why do you call them the diners club?"

"Because they're an institution in this town. They're always here and they know just about everything about everyone. I bet they've got a file on you already, figuratively speaking."

Delaney turned back to Kim, alarmed. "What do you mean? Why would they be interested in me?"

Kim laughed. "Because they're interested in everyone. That's what they do. They're like journalists who can't stand anyone else scooping a story from them."

"But there's nothing to know about me."

Kim gave her a patiently amused look. "Are you kidding? The new doctor in town? You were news before you even arrived. But now, you're here, and you're a female with a kid—which took them by surprise, I'm pleased to say—and without a husband . . . well, it's kept them going for weeks."

"I'm not without a husband," Delaney said, aghast.

Kim shrugged and looked at her menu. "To them you are. If he's not here, he doesn't exist." Kim's eyes shifted to Delaney's face, and she laid a hand on Delaney's forearm. "Hey, don't look so worried. Everyone gets gossiped about sooner or later. They don't do any harm."

Delaney forced herself to smile and give a little laugh. "Oh I know." She waved a hand nonchalantly. "I'm not worried. I'm just not used to small towns like this. Coming from D.C., I guess I'm used to a lot more . . . anonymity."

"Tell me about it," Kim said, nodding. She slapped her menu shut and laid it on the table. "Rueben for me. I don't know why I even look at the menu anymore, I get the same thing every time."

"I'm going to have the chicken salad." Delaney placed her menu on top of Kim's. "So who are those guys, anyway? The diners club."

"Oh just a bunch of local guys, retired lobstermen, mostly. I think they're here because their wives don't want them hanging around the house all day long. But they're all nice guys—Sam especially, the guy with the white hair. He's a merciless teaser. Always looking for a good joke. But really nice."

Delaney looked back and noticed the man with the raspy voice she'd heard that morning. He had seemed sort of the ringleader of the group.

"And Norman," Kim continued. "He's a little odd—always has that cap on—but just as sweet as can be. He makes a living clamming now. Boy, talk about a tough life."

The waitress arrived, breathless and harried, with two cloudy glasses of ice water and a tattered pad. She took their order and as she wrote down Delaney's chicken salad, she paused just long enough to look toward the door, roll her eyes and say, "Ah jeez, here comes Mother Hubbard."

Delaney looked back over her shoulder, wishing she'd taken the seat Kim had, to see a robust woman in her sixties with steely hair and a steely look in her eye push assertively through the door.

Delaney turned back to Kim, brows raised, as the waitress marched off. "Mother Hubbard?"

Kim's red lips curved and her eyes glittered. She leaned forward. "Mother Hubbard is Rodney's mother. She's the one who started this place. When she comes in Rodney damn near shits a brick and the waitresses all have to step lively or be in for a lambasting."

Delaney laughed and sipped her water.

"I wonder what brought her in this time. Last

time it was because Rodney's wife had caught him cheating on her with one of the waitresses. Lola, if you can believe that. She lives in Machias now. Mother Hubbard gave him an earful that time."

Kim watched Mother Hubbard apparently long enough to determine she wasn't going to do anything interesting, then turned back to Delaney.

"So this is fun," she said, leaning both elbows on the table and smiling at Delaney. "I'm glad we did this. I've been wanting to get together with you."

Delaney smiled. "Me too. You know, I don't know many people in town yet, and you and I seem to have some things in common."

"Like being from a place with more than thirty-six people in it?"

They both laughed.

"Exactly."

The waitress arrived with their sandwiches in record time. Mother Hubbard's influence, no doubt.

"So tell me," Kim said, plucking a potato chip from her plate and eating it. "How are things going with—Jim is it? Is he coming up soon?"

Delaney looked down at her sandwich and pulled the ribboned toothpick from its center. She didn't want to get into anything about her "husband," didn't want to compound the lies she'd told to Kim because she wanted to get to the point of telling her the truth. But she couldn't just dive right into it, not without Kim thinking she was nuts, could she?

Delaney sighed. "They're not going great, to be honest. I'm pretty sure he won't be coming up anytime soon."

She had an almost overwhelming urge to come clean to Kim. Just tell her the truth and see what happened. Kim, of all people, was in a position to help Delaney, both with the legalities of the lie— not having to give false information to the IRS, for example—and the logistics of it. Having one good friend in town and in the office who knew the truth could help keep unwanted questions at bay.

Kim thoughtfully chewed another chip. "Hm. It's gotta be hard to mend a relationship when you're five hundred miles apart."

"Impossible," Delaney agreed. "And it's seven hundred."

"Wow."

She could lean over right now, Delaney thought, and say *Kim, I've got something to tell you that I really need to share with someone.* Kim seemed like the type who might take it in stride, the type who was not easily shocked. But then, Delaney probably didn't seem like the type to make up a husband. And what would she tell her the reason for the Faux-Jim was? Should she confess about Jack and Emily at the same time? No, that would be too much. And that secret wasn't just hers, it was Emily's too. She'd just say she was worried about being a single parent in this small town. Girl talk, after all, was the icebreaker for all good friendships.

"You guys have been married five years?" Kim asked.

Delaney nodded and took a big bite of her sandwich. Maybe if she kept her mouth full, she wouldn't be expected to say much. More time to think about her course of action.

"How long have you been having trouble?" Kim spooned coleslaw onto her Rueben, causing Delaney to wonder how she stayed so thin, eating such extravagantly fatty foods. "If you don't mind my asking, that is." She gave Delaney a mischievous smile, the kind of smile that, Delaney suspected, allowed her to ask all manner of probing questions without seeming nosy.

Delaney shook her head, swallowing. "I don't mind. There's just not much to tell."

Now would be the time, she thought. *Just say it now. Actually, Kim, I don't really have a husband* . . . But her caution was hard to let go of.

"The only part that was good was the beginning, really," she continued, thinking about Jack, about how easy it was that first night, and how awkward it was now. "But ever since the baby I've begun to realize that he's just not responsible enough for me. I think that's what it boils down to."

Kim looked at her with interest and nodded. "Uh-huh. I can see that. You need someone you can really count on, especially with a child."

Delaney's thoughts strayed further, seeing in her mind's eye the black tee shirt, thrown by Lisa Jacobson, draping across Jack's chest. Maybe she could talk about this without really talking about it. Get Kim's input without telling the whole truth just yet.

She looked up at Kim. "Plus there've been . . . other women."

Kim's eyes widened appreciably and she leaned forward. "*Really*."

Delaney's cheeks burned, and she looked back down at her sandwich. A blob of chicken salad fell out the back as she picked it up.

"Yeah. It's just the way he is, it seems," she continued. "And while I know that's really my problem, and not Emily's, I can't help thinking his infidelity makes him a bad father. Do you know what I mean?"

"Sure," Kim agreed, nodding heartily. "If he can't be honest and upright with you, how will he be honest and upright with Emily?"

"Exactly," she said, then thought, "though to be fair he hasn't exactly been dishonest."

"You mean he *tells* you about these other women?" Kim looked scandalized.

"Not exactly. But still, it's a matter of integrity, isn't it? I mean, if a man's a playboy, it shows a certain lack of character, doesn't it? Even if he's up front about it?"

"Certainly if he's a *married* man." Kim looked confused. "Plus, I've got to tell you, the very fact that he won't come up to see you has got to make you think he's not committed to making things better. I mean, if he can't even be bothered to help you move . . ." She shook her head and picked up her sandwich. "Well, I can see why you forgot all about him on your W-4."

Delaney froze, chicken salad stopping halfway

down her esophagus and threatening to crawl back up. She was suddenly sure beyond all reason that Kim suspected her lie. What had she said earlier, about the diners club? Something about if her husband's not here, he didn't really exist? And now, saying that she'd *forgotten* him on the W-4, why had she put it that way? Who *forgot* their husband on a tax form?

Delaney swallowed hard. "You know how it is. Someone gives you trouble, you try to put them out of your mind."

Kim laughed. "You sure did that! Wish I had as much luck with that when I'm mad at Chris. And I'm mad at Chris a *lot*." She paused thoughtfully. "But seriously," she said then, coming directly back to the point with a concerned expression, "it sounds to me as if you've kind of made up your mind. Or is there actually a chance he might show up?"

Delaney hesitated so long, caught up in wondering if Kim suspected something or if she was just being paranoid, that Kim added, "I mean, I'm worried about you. You seem so stressed. You're in a new town, a new job, a new baby. Your husband's nowhere to be found. I can see where it must be really hard on you."

"It's a little difficult," she said vaguely. She had to tell her, Delaney decided. She couldn't possibly build a friendship with the burden of this lie on her back, driving herself crazy with paranoia. She took a deep breath. "Kim, I've got something to tell you that I really need to share—"

The sound of a ringing cell phone piped up from

Kim's purse. Kim, who had just taken another bite of her sandwich, rolled her eyes, wiped her mouth on a napkin, then dug through her monstrous purse.

"Sorry, hold that thought, Delaney." She swallowed. "Hello?" she said into the phone, winking at Delaney. But the look on her face changed when the voice on the other end of the line spoke, and she shifted uncomfortably.

It was one of those phones that are amplified enough that anyone nearby could hear the other party, and hear him Delaney did.

"Are you done?" a male voice asked.

Jack's voice, Delaney was sure. She stopped breathing, not wanting to miss a word.

"Not yet . . ." Kim said musically, her tone obviously trying to tell him she was in the middle of something. Her eyes skittered to Delaney's, then she turned sideways in the seat, looking toward the men's room. She was apparently unaware that Delaney could hear the other end of the conversation.

"Well hurry up. Meet me on the boat when you're done."

Definitely Jack, Delaney thought, inhaling slowly.

"Keep your pants on," Kim said. "You don't want me to cut my lunch short, do you?"

"God no."

Delaney heard him laugh, and her stomach lurched. She pushed her plate away.

"Then leave me alone." Kim laughed. "I'll call you when I'm finished."

"No, come to the boat."

She smiled, flipped her eyes at Delaney apologetically. "Jeez, you're demanding. I can't. I've got to go back to work. *I* have a job, remember?"

"Just for a minute."

Kim sighed heavily.

"All right, where are you?" Jack asked.

"Sadie's. And I've got to go. This is rude."

"Okay, okay. Over and out."

"I'll talk to you *later*." She hung up. "Sorry," she said to Delaney, the color high in her face. "That was my mother. She's always bugging me on this thing."

She pushed the power button and the phone beeped off.

Delaney's skin felt cold. Had Jack been trying to set up an assignation? Were Kim and Jack involved? Why else would Kim lie about who it was? Thank *God* she hadn't said anything about Jim. She might have been confessing the truth to one of Jack's *girlfriends*.

She'd been saved, literally, by the bell.

"So, you were saying?" Kim asked, looking at her with great interest.

Delaney shook her head. "I . . . I can't remember now." She laughed lightly, feeling sick.

"We were talking about you and Jim. Were you mad when Jim didn't come up to help you move? Jack said it seemed you thought he might come, and then he didn't, so he helped you move in. That would have pissed me off no end."

"Yeah . . ." Delaney picked up her sandwich, then put it back on the plate and wiped the corners of her mouth with her napkin.

"Not that he minded," Kim said quickly. "Jack, that is. No, he'd do anything to help anyone. Salt of the earth kind of guy, is our Jack. He just mentioned, you know, that he was concerned because you seemed so all alone."

Delaney watched the juice from her pickle soak into one of the nearby chips. "So you and Jack are—are friends."

"Oh yeah. We're buds. I think the world of Jack. He's a great guy. Just a great guy." Kim downed another hearty bite of Reuben.

Delaney felt what chicken salad she'd eaten compress into a ball as her stomach turned into a fist.

"You guys do a lot together?" Delaney asked, picking up a chip.

"We do. He's always picking me up to do something . . . he's just considerate like that. Sometimes I think I'd go nuts in this town if not for Jack. Last week, for example, after that crazy day in the clinic? You know when all those old people and babies were in—and all of them, I'm telling you, every single one, wanted help filling out their insurance forms—well, Jack took me out on his boat, and I swear it saved my life. It was the most gorgeous night, and there was one of those tiny little moons out and the stars and everything . . ." She sighed heavily. "Well, it was fabulous. Just exactly what I needed. He's always coming to my rescue like that."

Delaney pictured them under the stars on Jack's boat. She could picture Jack most clearly, his hair ruffled in the breeze, tee shirt molding to his muscled back, hands steady on the wheel . . . or on Kim. Suddenly Delaney was back on that beach at night with Jack, but instead of seeing herself in his arms she saw Kim. Kim, who was always mad at her boyfriend Chris, who thinks *the world* of Jack, thinks he's just a *great guy*, who is rescued by him apparently on a regular basis.

Something unnervingly like jealousy nibbled within her chest, and she wondered if she were going insane. First she's paranoid that Kim suspects something, then she's worked up because she thinks Kim and Jack might be involved.

This last seemed to be the most immediately important, however. Because how could she be friends with Kim, how could she possibly tell Kim the truth or even part of it, if Kim was involved with Jack? Disappointment swept over her, but whether it was for the lost friendship with Kim or this further proof of Jack's lack of moral fiber in helping her cheat on her boyfriend, she wasn't sure.

"So," Delaney pressed, an odd mix of bad feelings getting the better of her, "seems you and Jack are pretty . . . well, you're pretty *close* friends, huh?"

"*Close* friends?" Kim asked. She looked surprised by the question, as if she hadn't expected Delaney to notice she had a thing for Jack. "Sure, we're close, I guess. We've been friends for a couple years now. But we're not *too* close, you understand. I mean there's nothing, you know, *going on*, though you might hear some people say there is. Why do you ask?"

Delaney shrugged, thinking the lady doth protest too much. "Curious, mostly. Of course you know he's my landlord."

Kim nodded, her brow furrowed.

"So I see people coming and going at the house a lot. And I've heard so much about him since I've been here. About his . . . exploits, I guess I should say. I'm not sure what to make of him."

"Oh, well, I wouldn't listen to the gossip about him, if I were you. You know how gossip is, it never tells the whole story."

"But it often tells part of the story."

How could Kim be involved with him, knowing what a womanizer he was? But then, maybe she didn't know, not really. Not in the firsthand, one-night-stand way Delaney knew.

Kim leaned back in the booth and picked up her pickle, her eyes narrowed thoughtfully. "Sure, some of the basic facts are true, but the situations and how he felt about them are not what the gossip would have you believe."

"Really? How do you know? I mean, how did he feel about them?"

Kim sipped her Coke. "Well, let's just be clear here. We're talking about the women, right?"

Delaney tipped her head. "Basically."

"That's all that's really talked about. Most people like Jack, personally, they just have this disapproval thing going. Like they're jealous or something. But most believe he's a good guy, just a ladies' man."

Delaney frowned. "You say that like it doesn't make any difference to you."

Kim laughed. "Why should it? I don't think it's true, first of all. Well, not any truer than it is for any good-looking guy. Besides, I know what he's really like."

Ah, the mantra of the mistreated woman, Delaney thought. "Which is . . . ?"

"He's a gentle, sensitive guy. Very sincere. I think his reputation just evolved from him looking for the right woman. Everyone dates, you know, but not everyone lives in a town the size of a friggin' supermarket. And not everyone's considered one of the best-looking guys in the county. You watch, the second this town knows he's found the right girl, they'll have nothing to say about his behavior."

Delaney nodded, watching Kim crunch into the pickle, apparently confident that the moment the town would know about this "right girl" was imminent. To Delaney, her defense of Jack sounded suspiciously like a woman justifying her own inconvenient emotions.

"Well, that's good," Delaney said, picking up a potato chip. She didn't much feel like eating it but needed something to do with her hands.

They sat in silence a moment while Delaney debated telling Kim that Lisa Jacobson was at Jack's house just last weekend. She didn't want to be a tattletale, but she liked Kim. If she was involved with Jack, she should know that he wasn't exactly the paragon of sensitivity she seemed to think. It wasn't that Delaney was jealous or wanted to put doubt about Jack in Kim's mind or anything like that. It really wasn't.

I'd *want to know*, Delaney told herself, *if I were Kim*.

"Oh God," Kim muttered through the end of her pickle.

Delaney glanced up to see Kim's eyes on the door.

"What?" She turned in her seat for the umpteenth time and saw Jack coming toward them through the crowd. "Speak of the devil."

Now that she saw him, his arrival made perfect sense. When he'd asked Kim where she was of course it was because he wanted to come to her. Why, she wasn't sure. Unless it was because he was afraid Delaney would say something to Kim about their night on the beach together.

His grin was cocky—even playful—Delaney thought, as he made his way around the tables. He waved a hand to the diners club and pinched the cheek of one of the hassled waitresses, who, to Delaney's disgust, blushed and giggled like a girl half her age.

Delaney wanted to roll her eyes. Instead she turned back in the booth to face Kim.

"What an idiot," Kim murmured.

"Why do you say that?"

Kim *did* roll her eyes. "Long story."

"Well, hello there," Jack said, arriving at their table. "Fancy meeting you two here."

"Yeah, fancy that," Kim said dryly.

"Mind if I join you?" he asked, shifting his gaze to Delaney.

She hated herself for the butterflyesque twinge in her stomach. What a mess this whole thing was.

"Not at all," Delaney said.

"We're almost finished," Kim said, "but you're welcome to the table."

Jack sent a lazy grin Kim's way and sat on the bench next to Delaney.

He was so close she could smell the clean fragrance of his laundry detergent and it took her straight back to that night, that damned fateful night, when they'd danced at the Hornet's Nest. She wished she could move farther away but she was nearly pressed up against the wall as it was. Despite herself, her heartbeat accelerated.

"So what are you girls talking about?"

"Business," Kim said. "We were just discussing various modes of billing and whether or not we should outsource some of the payroll and accounts-receivable responsibilities."

He laughed easily. "I'm in over my head, is that what you're telling me?"

"You're not the only one," Delaney murmured.

He gave her a quizzical look, then shifted it to Kim.

Delaney looked at Kim, too, and found her watching the two of them with undisguised amusement. Which was odd.

"Oh, by the way, what are you doing tomorrow night?" Jack asked.

Delaney thought he was speaking to Kim until she realized they were both looking at her expectantly.

"Me?" she asked, with a classic finger to her own chest.

Jack smiled, sending her hormones spiraling. "Yeah, you."

"I don't know. Why?" She lowered her brows ominously.

"My aunt would like to meet you. And Emily. Said she'd love to have another baby around the house."

"Aunt Linda's going to take care of Emily?" Kim asked.

Delaney glanced at her, noting the excitement in her voice. "I don't know . . ." she said.

"Oh, you should. That would be *wonderful*," Kim added. "Aunt Linda's the best. I wish she would take care of me!" She laughed.

Jack looked at Delaney again, those brown eyes warm on her face. "So what do you say? Tomorrow night? Sevenish?"

Delaney glanced from Jack to Kim and back again. If Aunt Linda was so great, she'd be fool to keep Emily in day care. And Emily was what mattered here.

"All right," Delaney said uneasily. "But now, I

really should get back to work." She dug through her purse for her wallet. This time she wouldn't forget to pay her bill.

"So soon?" Jack asked.

"Oh we've been here a while." Delaney tossed a few bills on the table. "Kim, I appreciate your coming out with me, we should do it again sometime. I'll see you back at the clinic."

"Okay, I won't be long."

Delaney turned to face Jack, as he'd made no move to let her out of the booth, and he looked down at her. Awareness of their proximity swept over her again. The breadth of his chest and the length and strength of his arm next to hers seemed ridiculously masculine, like Mother Nature had wasted a good deal of attractiveness on a man who clearly didn't need so much. They sat suspended for a second, an arc of electricity between them, before Jack laughed.

"Oh, sorry," he said, pushing out of the booth.

Delaney slid out behind him, awkwardly brushing against his chest as she rose. Her nerves spun at the contact. They stood next to each other for a moment after Delaney collected her purse, and she felt small and flustered beside him. She wanted to find a way to say something to him, to tell him she saw right through him, that he should be more careful in playing with women, but nothing came to mind except the way his thigh had run hot alongside hers when they were sitting and the way his hand had looked lying on the table near hers.

"Well," she said after an awkward silence, "see

you guys later." She smiled at Kim and glanced once more at Jack before beelining for the door.

"You fool!" Kim crowed to Jack as Delaney headed out the door. "But oh my God, did you see the way she *looked* at you?"

Jack dragged his gaze from Delaney's stiff, slim back and moved it to Kim's incredulous expression.

"How did she look at me?"

"Like she was a dog and you were wearing sirloin underwear." She smiled with satisfaction. "I've always wanted to use that line."

Jack chuckled and slid back into the booth. "So why am I a fool?"

"Because I was *just getting* to the good stuff," Kim said, throwing up her hands in disgust. "She was involved in the conversation, she was asking questions, she was talking about *you*, you moron."

His brows rose. "She was? What was she saying?"

"It wasn't what she was saying so much as *how* she was saying it. She was relentlessly interested in you. And I swear to God, she acted like she was jealous of how close you and I are."

"She was jealous of someone who calls me a moron?"

"Well, I didn't tell her that. No, you owe me, bigtime. I sang your praises."

"I can just imagine."

"*I* had to. Jeez, my imagination was working overtime." She grinned. "But she ate it up. Asked about all the gossip she's heard about you, about the women you've supposedly been involved with. It was great. She could hardly contain her curiosity. And when I told her what a great guy you were I could tell she was about to say something important, but then in you walked. Dummy."

This was interesting. Delaney Poole, asking about him. Could Kim be exaggerating? Definitely. But she rarely got things completely wrong.

"And what did she say about her husband?" he asked.

Kim leaned forward. "That was the best part." She gave a Cheshire smile. "I got the *distinct* impression that Old Jim is about as close to history as a man can get. And what a creep he seems to be."

"Really?"

"He's cheated on her," Kim said, not without a certain amount of salacious satisfaction. "That's why they're not together. And I got the impression the only reason she's thinking about staying with him is because of Emily, though she seemed pretty concerned about the kind of father Jim could be while being so unfaithful."

Jack's eyes narrowed. So the bastard was cheating on her. The guy didn't deserve her and Emily if he couldn't even appreciate what he had. Anger on her behalf leapt to his chest.

Then a little voice in the back of his head reminded him: *She had cheated too.* With him.

"Well, you never know. Maybe she cheated first."

Kim gaped at him. "What are you talking about?"

He shrugged. "Nothing. You just never know the circumstances behind these things."

She leaned back in the booth and folded her arms across her chest. "You *guys*. You always stick together, don't you? I thought you *liked* this girl."

"I do like her. I just don't know her all that well, and for all we know they've both contributed to their bad marriage."

"Well, according to Delaney, the marriage has been bad the whole five years."

Jack's attention shrank to laser intensity. "*Five* years?" Hadn't Delaney told him two? Or had he just assumed that from something she'd said?

"But it was weird, she said something about him not really being dishonest about it."

"They've probably got some kind of open marriage," he said, the thought curdling his stomach. "That would explain her actions some."

Kim leapt on the comment, and Jack could have kicked himself. "What do you mean?"

"Nothing."

"No, come on, I'm telling you everything. What do you mean?" Her eyes widened. "Wait, don't tell me. Have you guys . . . ? Is *that* why you seem so sure you've got a shot, even though she's married?"

Jack gave her a look. "No. In fact I don't think I have a shot at all."

"I don't believe you. You—something's happened between you two, hasn't it? Oh my God! Wait a minute. Carol told me you met her last spring. She saw you guys at the bar together." She gasped with delight and shock, then put a hand over her mouth.

He shook his head. "Kim, your imagination's running away with you. Say, did I tell you about the job offer I got?"

"*Don't* change the subject," Kim warned with an accusing finger. Then her brow furrowed. "What job offer?"

"From Briarly College. Hugh, a buddy of mine from high school, is their head coach and when one of his assistants suddenly quit he thought of me."

"Briarly College! That's, like, eight hours from here. You can't leave Harp Cove."

Jack raised a brow and shrugged noncommittally. "I don't know. It's an attractive deal."

Kim looked at him assessingly for a moment. "Then you should take it."

He gave a half smile. "I should, huh? Why? You just said I couldn't leave Harp Cove."

"Because it's a good opportunity."

"Maybe. Maybe not."

She hesitated. "It's more money, right?"

He nodded.

"And a better job, certainly. More resources. Some travel, probably. What's not good about it?"

He looked away. "I don't know. I'm still thinking."

"Wait a minute . . ." Kim looked from his face toward the door through which Delaney had just exited. "This is about her, isn't it? My God, Jack, you've got it really bad. I had no idea."

"Kim," he warned.

But he couldn't quite maintain the stern look to go with it, because something in what she said was ringing the bell of truth within him. Was that really why the job offer had seemed such a disruption? When his friend had called he hadn't leapt at the chance. He'd told his friend he'd think about it, feeling unexpectedly reluctant to leave Harp Cove. Could it really have that much to do with Delaney?

The question seemed stupid, suddenly. Obvious.

He picked up Delaney's coke and polished it off.

"Jack. 'Fess up. You *know* you can trust me," Kim persisted.

He snorted and Kim slapped his arm.

"All right. I met her a year ago," he said, "when she was here to check out the town or interview or something. Though I had no idea at the time that she might be back. I sure would've done a few things differently if I had known."

"Like what? What happened between you?"

He looked at her avid face, her hands clasped before her on the table and her plate shoved to one side. He was tempted to talk about it with someone, that much was certain, but it seemed imprudent for that someone to be Kim.

He smiled. "Nothing I'm going to tell you about."

She sat back and after a second, a smile curled her lips. "You know what? That, Jack Shepard, tells me everything I wanted to know."

Chapter 10

Jack met Delaney at the carriage house the following evening to take her to his aunt's. Delaney had just gotten home from running a bunch of errands, and neither she nor Emily were in a good mood after dealing with parking lots and shopping centers, not to mention Route 1, but Jack was. He practically filled the house with light and energy when Delaney opened the door to his knock.

"Ready to go? Where's Emily?" he asked, looking around the front hall. In his hands was a small, fuzzy, pale blue elephant.

Delaney was wiping her hands on a dish towel and feeling trepidation about the whole endeavor. "We're almost ready. We've had an exhausting afternoon. I'm not sure Emily's going to be the most charming baby in the world. Maybe we should wait to introduce her to your aunt."

Jack shook his head. "Naw. Aunt Linda's seen it all. She can calm even the crankiest baby. Trust me."

Delaney raised a skeptical eyebrow.

"Besides, I got her this." He held up the elephant by one leg, and it rattled softly. "This ought to cheer her up."

The look on his face was so optimistic and cheerful Delaney had to smile.

"Oh, well, if *that'll* do it, thank God you've brought it. I've been needing it for months."

"You mock me," he said.

Emily gave a short, frustrated cry, and he looked up the stairs.

"You just watch, *Mom*." He bounded up the stairs.

Delaney heard him enter Emily's room saying something in a croony kind of voice. Emily either cried louder or continued crying and it just sounded louder because the door was open. Either way, the elephant's magic seemed to be lost on her.

Leaning one hand on the downstairs railing, Delaney smiled. The croony voice continued. She could hear the faint rattle of the toy. Emily's wails grew longer.

"You all right up there, Jack?" she called, biting back a laugh.

Emily was hungry, Delaney knew. That's why she'd been in the kitchen, fixing a bottle. Still, it amused her to let Jack try to console her. Amused her in a deep, comfortable way. Someone else was up there undergoing the same frustration Delaney had all day, sparing her from more of it.

Emily wasn't normally fussy, but the days she was Delaney thought she'd lose her mind. Dealing with an inconsolable baby was like being in a tunnel from which she couldn't emerge. She'd reach her wit's end and feel as if she were going to be living that day for the rest of her life. Emily was never going to calm down, the crying was never going to stop, and Delaney would simply expire from aggravation.

Now, with someone else taking the brunt of it, she could view it as the temporary frustration that it was. And she felt herself breathing easier with the perspective.

She went back to the kitchen and took the bottle from the microwave. After testing the temperature on her wrist, she stood looking out the window a moment.

This must be what it's like to have a husband, she thought, allowing herself the rumination like a forbidden piece of chocolate. Someone to share the load with. And the joys, she conceded. She imagined him up there cuddling Emily in the rocker, trying to get her to sleep, watching her face with the same heart-wrenching tenderness that Delaney always felt. Marveling over the delicate eyelashes, the firm, petal-soft cheeks, the tiny rosebud mouth that could open so sweetly into a great toothless smile, or a yawn, either one a miracle.

Sometimes Delaney felt so much love she thought she could explode with it, like she could share it with the whole world and still be overwhelmed with devotion. What would it be like to have even one other person feel that same way about Emily?

Well, that wasn't quite fair, Delaney thought. Her mother loved Emily, too, but not enough to stand up to her father and come visit. She sighed. Maybe some day.

Delaney tested the bottle again, decided it was cool enough, and left the kitchen. Might as well spare Jack the unpleasant part of child care, he'd suffered long enough. But when she reached the foot of the stairs she didn't hear Emily crying. And as she quietly ascended the steps she detected the soft rattle and contented humming of a calm baby.

She rounded the top railing and walked to the threshold of Emily's bedroom. Jack stood by the window with Emily in front of him standing on the sill. Or rather, bearing some weight on her plump little legs while Jack held her body with his big hands. Emily held the rattle and sucked on the elephant's trunk, her brown eyes gazing out the window at, most likely, the flag flapping in front of Jack's house.

Delaney paused silently in the doorway.

"We're gonna meet Aunt Linda," Jack said. "You're going to like Aunt Linda, because . . . well, because everyone likes Aunt Linda."

Emily made a little humming sound as she sucked on the elephant trunk.

Delaney wondered if she would like Aunt Linda. Or rather, if she'd trust her to take care of Emily. Not that she thought any relative of Jack's would hurt her daughter, but Emily could be a strong, willful little thing, and the tiny white-haired lady Delaney was picturing would never have the stamina to take care of her all day every day.

Delaney was somewhat ashamed to admit she hoped that would become obvious to everyone today. As good as it would be for Emily to get individual attention, the idea of Jack's aunt looking at her every day made her queasy with fear. There was so much resemblance, once you looked for it.

Granted, Aunt Linda wouldn't be looking for it, but suppose Jack stopped by one day and it just jumped out at her, the way it had at Delaney that day. Well, that would just be disastrous.

"She lives in the city, where all the cars and people and buildings are," Jack continued. "Maybe she'll take you for walks. Maybe you'll come see your buddy Jack on his boat, the *Silver Surfer*. Maybe one day I'll get you a *Silver Surfer* comic book."

Delaney cleared her throat and moved into the room. Jack turned from the window and held Emily against his chest.

"The city?" Delaney repeated. "Did you just call Harp Cove a *city*?"

Jack smiled ruefully. "Well, you know. To *her* it'll seem like a city."

She scoffed, smiling. "Sure, to a seven m—" Her words skidded to a halt. Good God—her heart thundered in her chest. She'd almost called Emily a seven-month-old, after leading Jack and everyone else to believe she'd be five months now. Her limbs trembled as if she'd just stepped out of the way of an oncoming bus.

"What?" Jack asked.

"Hm?" she looked back at him dumbly.

"I didn't understand what you just said."

"Oh." She laughed. "Just that calling Harp Cove a city is a stretch even to a baby. But here, let me take her. I'm sure she's hungry."

Jack handed her over, and Delaney sat in the rocker with her. Emily made a terrible face when Delaney removed the elephant trunk from her mouth, but the ensuing cry was quickly quieted by the bottle.

Jack watched them with what appeared to be great interest.

"It must be hard for you," he said, looking at Emily thoughtfully, "doing this all alone."

Delaney nodded. "Sometimes. Sometimes it's overwhelming. Like today." She laughed and looked down at Emily's contented face. "But then, sometimes it's this wonderful, private thing . . . this incredible *comfort* that I get all to myself."

Their eyes met, Jack's crinkling at the corners with a gentle smile. "Sounds nice."

"It is." Emily squawked and Delaney shifted her, resettling the bottle in her mouth. "But then there are days like today, when I think I'm going to lose my mind."

"Hm." He nodded and watched Emily feeding a moment more. "On those days, like today, do you ever get, I don't know, angry that your husband's not here to help?"

Delaney grimaced. "Funny you should ask. I felt that way all afternoon."

And she *had*, that was the weird thing. She'd been thinking about Jim and what a complete jerk he would be if he actually wouldn't come up here and help in this situation just because of some *job*. She'd found herself growing annoyed at the very idea and worked herself up into a lather of self-righteous feminist anger at the arrogance of men who thought their jobs were more important than their families, as if the *money* were the hard part and not the nurturing and the caring and the being there when they were needed.

"But," she sighed, "he's got his reasons, and I have no choice but to respect them."

"No choice? That doesn't sound like the Delaney Poole I know."

She looked up and caught him grinning at her.

"I mean, come on," he continued. "I don't know if you've heard, but it's not a man's world anymore."

She laughed. "I'm glad to know *you've* heard. But the circumstances in this case are—unusual."

She looked down at Emily, who had dropped off to sleep.

"Guess she was more tired, than hungry," Delaney said, wishing to change the subject. "Let's take my car. It's got the car seat."

They stood up, and Jack held his hands out for

the baby. Delaney handed her to him without thinking, turning to gather up the diaper bag and new elephant rattle before realizing the mild relief she felt at not having to juggle everything herself this time just to get out the door.

"I'll just go put her in the car seat. Is the car open?" Jack asked.

Delaney turned at looked at him, at his strong, capable arms holding her sleeping daughter, at the comforting, competent look in his eyes—ready to help, ready to solve problems, ready even to unwittingly take some of the burden from Delaney's shoulders.

His brows rose expectantly at the time it was taking her to answer.

"Yeah, uh, yes. The car's open." She turned quickly around and grabbed the blanket that had hung over the back of the rocker. "I'll meet you down there."

He took Emily out into the hall, and Delaney stood in the middle of the room as his footsteps descended the stairs. A second later the front door opened, closed, and Delaney stood by the window watching Jack Shepard carry his daughter to the car.

Aunt Linda was not the small, fragile woman Delaney had expected. After Jack knocked on the thick wooden door in the old apartment building it was opened by a tall, strong-featured woman who looked nothing if not *strapping*.

She wore a denim jumper with a red tee shirt underneath and her long iron gray hair was pulled into a casual bun on the top of her head. Thick leather sandals held sturdy feet.

Delaney looked her over from head to toe before realizing how rude it was, taking in first her height, then her strength, then her sharp blue eyes.

Sharp blue eyes that were simultaneously taking in Delaney and the child sleeping with its head on her shoulder.

"Dr. Poole," she said in a voice that was probably never lowered. This was a woman who would tolerate no secrets. "Good to meet you." She held out a hand.

Delaney took it, feeling soft and inconsequential in the grip of this powerful woman.

"Nice to meet you too," she said. "But please, call me Delaney."

"Oh, no. I was a nurse for too many years to start that. It's Dr. Poole to me." She smiled. "And you can call me Aunt Linda."

Delaney wondered if she was joking. "It's kind of you to consider taking care of my daughter," she said. "I hope Jack didn't put you on the spot about it."

"Nonsense," the woman said in a way that made Delaney feel she meant it—*really* meant it, in the way that some people don't want or appreciate compulsory politeness.

"Aunt Linda volunteered," Jack said, stepping forward and placing a kiss on her cheek. He didn't have to bend far to do it, they were nearly the same height. "I was telling her about Emily. And you."

Delaney looked up at him, wondering what he

might have been saying about either one of them. He liked her baby? She was a pain in the neck? Something simple like he had a tenant with an infant? But of course she couldn't ask.

"Come in, come in." Aunt Linda strode imperiously into the room and threw an arm out toward an old, pillowy couch. "Have a seat. I just made blueberry muffins. Would you like tea or coffee with yours, Dr. Poole?"

She looked back at Delaney with those steely blue eyes, completely confident that of course she would want a blueberry muffin. Delaney wondered if anyone ever contradicted her, but had no desire to do so herself.

"Tea, please," she said.

"And coffee for you, Jack, I know." She disappeared into the kitchen.

Delaney turned in wonder to look at Jack. With such a woman as this in his life how had he ever become such a ladies' man? One would think that with Aunt Linda's influence he'd have nothing but respect for women.

Jack looked down at her and smiled a lazy, knowing smile. "She's great, isn't she?"

Delaney resettled Emily on her hip and moved toward the couch. "Yes. She is."

Aunt Linda reappeared with a pile of muffins in a basket and three mugs on a tray. Delaney felt herself sitting up straighter in her presence.

"So tell me about this little one," Aunt Linda said after depositing the tray on the table in front of them and swinging a dish towel over her shoulder.

She bent over Emily's sleeping form in Delaney's arms. "How old is she?"

"She was born in March," Delaney said.

"*March!*" Aunt Linda leaned closer, picking up one of Emily's sleepy hands. "Goodness, but she must have been a big one. She looks to be at least six or seven months to me."

This woman was far too sharp.

"She's almost twenty pounds," Delaney continued, unnerved, as Aunt Linda straightened and gently placed Emily's hand back on Delaney's lap. "I've got her eating a little cereal, but mostly it's milk—"

"Breast milk?" Aunt Linda demanded, backing up toward a chair and sitting on the edge of it, leaning forward.

Delaney blushed. "Well, yes . . . I . . ." She glanced surreptitiously toward Jack.

"Don't mind him," Aunt Linda said with a boisterous laugh. Emily jerked in her sleep at the sound but miraculously didn't awaken. "He's heard it all before. His sister's got three kids, you know. And I've always got babies here. So, you're pumping."

Delaney was *not* going to have this conversation in front of Jack. She shot a glance over at him, and said, "Maybe we should go over the details later. I mostly want to be sure you're interested in having a baby around the house. With all your experience you know how exhausting they can be."

Aunt Linda gave her a shrewd look. Rather than shrinking under it, as she felt like doing, Delaney leaned forward, grabbed a muffin, and took a bite.

The crumbly roll practically melted in her mouth. She looked down at the delicious thing in surprise.

"No more exhausting than a ward full of sick people," Aunt Linda said. "Or sick children, for that matter. I was a pediatric nurse for the last ten years. So you don't have to worry about me, Doctor. I'm up to the task. The question is whether Emily and I will get along."

She nodded toward the sleeping bundle in Delaney's arms, her gaze softening. Delaney was surprised by the look. With all her no-nonsense talk and strapping sensibility, it seemed babies were a soft spot for Aunt Linda.

"I'm sure you will," Delaney said. "Emily gets along with everyone. And from what Jack says, so do you. These muffins are *incredible*." She popped the last bite into her mouth and picked up the cup of tea.

Aunt Linda laughed her big laugh. "Thank you. But I wouldn't listen to anything Jack says. He tends to put a smiley face on everything he talks about."

Delaney raised her brows and looked over at Jack. "Is that right?"

"I just try to balance out whoever I'm with." He grinned at Aunt Linda.

"Oh, you." She swatted at him with the dish towel. "So, why don't you two go out a little while and leave me here with the baby. I don't want to wake her up, but if you leave for an hour or two, we ought to be able to decide if we like each other well enough."

"Oh, I don't know," Delaney began, looking uncertainly at Jack. She put her mug gingerly back on the table. She hadn't anticipated leaving Emily here. And she *certainly* hadn't anticipated going out anywhere alone with Jack.

"Sure," Jack said easily. "We can go over to the Nest and have a drink. After the day you've had, Delaney, sounds like you could use one."

"Perfect," Aunt Linda said, standing up. "An hour or two and then come on back."

"Oh, but . . ." Delaney looked down at her daughter.

"It's only an hour, Dee," Jack said.

The familiar use of her nickname took Delaney by surprise. She looked at him sharply. How did he know she was called that, first of all? And why did it roll so easily off his tongue?

"Yes, go on, relax," Aunt Linda urged. "You can set Emily down right there on the couch."

"But the pillows—," Delaney protested.

"Don't worry, I'm not going to leave her alone to suffocate. I know all about pillows and stuffed animals. She'll be sleeping on her back and all that good stuff. Now you two go on."

She was so insistent that by the time Delaney could even say another word, she and Jack were out the door, leaving Delaney to wonder if Aunt Linda and Jack were in cahoots somehow. To trick her into a date with her nemesis.

"Well, that was neatly done, wasn't it?" Delaney said, as they walked slowly down the hall to the elevator.

She looked almost dazed by Aunt Linda, the tornado, who had swept them out the door before either one of them could protest. Not that Jack would protest. No, he knew Aunt Linda knew he was attracted to Delaney, and he didn't put it past her to have arranged this nighttime meeting specifically to give them a chance to go out.

Jack hadn't confided his suspicions about Delaney's husband to Aunt Linda, but he had told her he thought there was trouble in paradise. Apparently that was all Aunt Linda needed to hear. *Homewrecker*, he thought, chuckling inwardly.

"What are you smiling about?" Delaney asked.

Jack looked over as he pulled the iron gate closed behind them on the old-fashioned elevator. He pushed the lever to "1."

"Just how 'neatly,' as you say, Aunt Linda managed to get us out of there."

"Yes," she said speculatively, eyeing him. "One might almost think it was planned."

He folded his arms across his chest and leaned against the wall. He couldn't help the grin that spread across his face, though he knew it gained him no points with her. "Why, Dr. Poole, are you accusing me of something?"

She narrowed her eyes and said nothing.

The elevator car lurched to a halt on the first floor. Jack slid open both gates and stepped back to let her exit.

Their footsteps sounded hollowly on the tile

floor of the empty foyer and then they were outside, in the cool August air of Maine's late summer. They stopped at the bottom of the stoop outside the building. Beside them, the clinic's sign showered them in white light.

"So, the Hornet's Nest?" Jack asked.

Delaney looked out into the darkness of the street, light from the sign creating an arc of shine on her hair. "I suppose." She didn't move, however, and after a second, she added, "Are you sure Aunt Linda really wants to take care of Emily? I mean, this wasn't some sort of . . . she wasn't just, you know, pretending to so that . . ."

"So that what?"

She kept her face averted, seeming to study the park across the street with great interest.

"I just got the feeling that she was rushing you and me off, you know, alone. I hope she didn't think . . . that is . . . I hope she's—oh, I don't know." She threw her hands up and let them drop to her sides.

Jack was silent a moment, wondering how to adequately assure her that nobody was doing this as a ruse.

"Listen, Delaney," he began, and something in his tone, apparently, made her turn and look at him. Her eyes glittered pale in the light from the neighboring sign. "Aunt Linda would never use your child to trick you."

"I'm sorry—"

"No, don't be sorry," he said, reaching a hand

out automatically to touch her, but stopping before he did. He put the hand in his pocket. "I understand why you might think that, but no. She's genuinely interested in taking care of Emily. I promise you."

She looked up at him, and the vulnerability in her eyes had him crossing his heart with one finger just to keep from taking her into his arms. "Cross my heart," he added, to complete the stupid gesture.

She let out a long breath. "Okay, then. Thanks. Thanks for not misunderstanding."

"Well, I'm an understanding kind of guy," he said, starting to walk in the direction of the Hornet's Nest.

Delaney started up beside him, and they crossed the street to the town green. The tree branches overhead began to sway, the leaves making a sound like rain, though the sky was clear. Feeling the wind freshening, Jack thought he should invite her down to the boat. The night was perfect for a sail. But then she'd really think he'd planned things, so he kept quiet.

In contrast, the Hornet's Nest was a loud, smoky cauldron of humanity. With the end of tourist season at hand, the place was full of sunburned people drunk on margaritas and Geary's beer. They were, however, lucky enough to score a table in the back, near the doors to the kitchen, just as the people got up to leave.

The table was perfect, Jack thought, because it

was behind the speakers, making it one of the quieter spots in the bar.

They sat and each ordered a beer.

"So," Jack said, as Delaney took a sip from her mug, her eyes grazing the bar and the pool table. "How's Jim?"

That got her attention.

"Fine," she said, eyeing him warily.

"He coming up anytime soon?"

She pushed her hair back from her forehead with one hand. He liked the way it looked afterward, slightly mussed, less controlled. Almost windblown, like that night on the beach.

"Actually," she said, "I'm meeting him this weekend. In Boston."

The image of her on the beach popped like a soap bubble and disappeared. "You are?"

She nodded.

He frowned. "He'll go to Boston, but he won't come here? Isn't that a little odd?"

It was more than odd, he told himself. It was ridiculous. The man didn't—couldn't—exist.

She regarded him thoughtfully a moment. Then said, out of the blue, "That was you on the phone to Kim yesterday, wasn't it? When we were at Sadie's having lunch."

So she felt she had to change the subject. Interesting. He watched her eyes for signs of discomfort or embarrassment. "Yeah, probably. Why?"

"She said it was her mother."

Jack was so busy looking at her face, taking in

the subtle arch of her dark brows and the gentle curve of her mouth, that he didn't immediately absorb what she'd said.

"What?" he asked.

"She said it was her mother," she repeated, looking him dead in the eye. "Now why do you think she would lie about something like that?"

A slow heat crept up Jack's neck and into his face. His mind was blank. Why *did* she lie? To cover up the fact that he was checking in on her, seeing how the conversation went, wanting to know what information she'd gleaned from Delaney.

His pause grew so long Delaney's fine arched brows rose, and the look in her eyes bordered on triumphant. He'd been pushing her about Jim without knowing she had something to push back with. Damn Kim, anyway. She didn't need to lie about that.

"Maybe the call you heard *was* her mother," he said, the thought coming to him like an unexpected guest, though perhaps a little late. "I talked to her while she was there, but she could have gotten more than one call."

"She only got one call."

"Maybe she got one before you got there—"

"We got there together."

"Maybe when she went—"

"She didn't go to the rest room."

Damn, she was quick. Jack swallowed, then picked up his beer and swallowed some of that.

"Besides," Delaney added, "the voice on the

other end was male. I could hear it through the receiver."

Jack cleared his throat and looked at the cocktail napkin on the table in front of him. Then, realizing how guilty that looked, he raised his head and took another swallow of beer.

"I can't imagine why she'd lie," he said finally, turning the bottle of beer around and around in its water ring on the table. "Really."

Delaney gave a small smile. "Me either."

She sipped her beer.

Suddenly a commotion erupted at the front door of the bar. People seemed to be stepping back and gathering around simultaneously, laughing. But when the song playing on the sound system stopped a voice rose over the noise of the crowd.

"Gimme a 'J'!" a female voice yelled. Loud.

Jack and Delaney both stared at the crowd. Over the heads of the tallest Jack could see the large end of a crimson megaphone.

"Gimme an 'A'!" the voice said again.

The music started and someone pulled the plug on it.

"Gimme a 'C'!"

It was then that the crowd parted and there, standing in full cheerleader regalia, stood Lisa Jacobson. Megaphone in one hand and pompons in the other, she strode toward him.

"Gimme a 'K'!" The hand holding the pompons rose into the air with the words.

No one gave her a "K," or any of the other letters, but still she asked, "What have you got?!"

A nightmare. Jack closed his eyes.

"JACK!"

Chapter 11

The next day Delaney finished up the last of her notes on Mrs. Beckwith's bursitis and flipped the folder shut. Emily sat in her car seat making what could at any moment become unhappy sounds.

"Two more minutes, Em," she pleaded, piling up the last of her charts and setting them in the box for Nurse Knecht to file on Monday. If she could just get out of there and on the road, Emily would fall asleep and Delaney would have some time to think about what else she needed to buy.

She was heading to Boston this weekend, ostensibly to meet "Jim" for a minivacation. In reality she was going to shop for her husband. That is, shop for evidence of her husband.

Several things had strengthened her resolve to stay with her husband, as it were, and increase the evidence of him around the house. First, when

Jack had pointed out the lack of masculine items in the house she'd realized that if she was going to continue the charade, she had to at least make it convincing.

Second, Aunt Linda had fallen in love with Emily—and vice versa, it seemed—and was going to take care of her starting next week.

Third, it was obvious *some*thing was going on between Kim and Jack. What, was none of her business, really, but it cemented her opinion about his opportunistic womanizing.

And fourth, the moment Delaney saw Lisa Jacobson in her tight little cheerleader's outfit she'd known she could never in a million years trust a man who would be attracted to a child bimbo like that.

So she decided it would be appropriate for at least a few things to "arrive" that her husband might have sent up, had he actually existed. Last night, after arriving home from the bar, she'd sat down and made a list of things she wanted to get. It was easier than thinking about Jack, she'd reasoned at the time. Because thinking about Jack was what she'd done all the way home.

She pulled the shopping list from her purse now and glanced at it.

Frames were first on the list. At the very least, she'd decided, she should have a picture or two of him around. She had cut out black-and-white photos of a guy from one of her medical journals last night—a nice-looking guy who wasn't too pretty, so his modeling career wasn't likely to propel him into mainstream magazines anytime soon—and she planned to pick up frames to display them on the mantel at home and perhaps on the desk in her office. She'd chosen him carefully so that his build was similar to Jack's. His hair color appeared to be that same sandy blond and even though the photo was black-and-white, his eyes could easily have been brown.

The fact that he was a model for an article on the drug Viagra was only momentarily alarming.

She also wanted to get a decent color television, as much for herself as for "him." She was tired of watching *Destiny's Children* wrestle with her own lie on that tiny black-and-white set. Plus, now that she was practically studying it for insight into her own situation, she needed a TV that would actually show the characters' expressions.

She wanted a boom box, too. Some clothing, would be appropriate, she thought. Books, CDs, shoes, shaving equipment for the bathroom, that sort of thing. It would cost her, but it would be worth it. For one thing, she was saving so much money in rent, she could afford to purchase a few luxuries. For another, those luxuries were even more justified if they served to remind Jack, Kim, Aunt Linda, the diners club, and whoever else was skeptical that there was a husband in the picture.

The day after Jack had fixed the window Delaney had filled out subscription cards to several magazines, including *Architectural Digest* and *The Law Review*, in the name of Mr. & Mrs. J. Poole. Since they shared a mailbox, having those labels stare him in the face once a month ought to keep Jack at bay, she figured.

In addition she had ordered a few things from the Internet that would be arriving with Jim Poole's name on them.

Delaney was just stuffing the list back into her purse when Maggie Coleman appeared in the office doorway. She was dressed in tight, worn jeans and a black Metallica tee shirt that was short enough to show her navel.

"Hey," Maggie said, a big smile on her face. "Haven't seen you in a few days."

"Oh, hi, Maggie." Delaney zipped the list safely away in her purse. "No, I've been having to leave early this week to pick up Emily. I only came back tonight to finish up a few charts before the weekend."

Maggie glanced at the suitcase on the floor next to Emily's car seat. "Going on a trip?"

"Yes, actually, I'm leaving right now." Delaney stood and started gathering her things, hoping Maggie would take the hint and not delay her.

The last couple of times she'd run into Maggie after work she'd had trouble extricating herself from the conversation, most of which revolved around her son Blake and his antics.

"I'm meeting my husband in Boston," Delaney continued. The words felt so strange on her lips that the lie suddenly seemed like a game they were both playing. "And since we only have two days, I don't want to miss a minute."

"Oh good." Maggie leaned one hip on the doorframe and looped her thumbs in her jeans' pockets. One hand held a feather duster, the kind stereotypical French maids used, and bounced it idly against her side. "About time you got to see him. You know it ain't good to let men out of your sight for long. That's what happened to me and Blake's dad. And I swear, most of Blake's troubles are directly 'cause he grew up without a man in the house."

"Is that right?" Delaney picked up the paperwork she was taking with her and stuffed it into the side pocket of her briefcase.

"Oh yeah. You know, they done studies. Blake's a classic example of a one-parent household. That's what the counselor told me last year after Blake took that teacher's purse and stole her car. Said it was a cry for attention." Maggie shook her head, then laughed. "Well, he got some attention for that, lemme tell you. And not the kind he was likely looking for, I don't imagine."

"I'll bet." Delaney gazed at her a moment, at the smile still lingering on Maggie's face, and felt something akin to admiration at how she could continue to see the humor in things Blake did after all the trouble he had put her through.

Delaney had met Blake once as he and Maggie were coming out of the tattoo parlor next door. Maggie'd apparently caught him just as he was about to get *rap* tattooed on his forehead. She'd only gotten him out of there by pointing out that he'd probably go through life with people knocking on his head to see if anyone was home.

Clearly, however, Maggie hadn't been able to intercept him before several other visits to the tattoo parlor. His forearms were covered with them, and his nose, ears, eyebrow, and tongue were all pierced. For all Delaney knew that was not the extent of it, but she certainly wasn't going to ask.

He'd seemed personable enough, though, with Maggie's same broad smile and dark curly hair. But while Blake's problem may have had something to do with not having a father, Delaney also suspected he'd learned early on how to manipulate his young mother.

Or that's what Delaney told herself anyway. It comforted her to think that while she herself was a single parent, becoming one at thirty instead of seventeen, like Maggie, might make a big difference in the outcome of the child. She also found herself thanking God after conversations with Maggie that Emily was a girl.

Tonight, however, Delaney was able to escape Maggie fairly easily by asking her to help carry some things out to the car, making her departure that much more obvious, though she did have to start the engine in the middle of Maggie's diatribe against the cop who arrested Blake for vandalism even though he and Maggie had gone out on a date the week before. This was only after hearing about the math teacher who'd given Blake a D just because she, Blake's mom, wouldn't go out with him after he'd picked her up at a party.

Delaney sighed deeply as she pulled out of the parking lot. She was never going to date, she decided. Not in this small town. Not if it meant dating cops and geometry teachers who pick up cleaning ladies at parties. Maybe it wasn't fair, but Maggie's dating woes—about which Delaney heard quite a bit in each of their conversations—made Delaney feel like avoiding the entire single population of Maine. If she added her own experience with single Maine men to Maggie's, it seemed they all were after the same thing. Getting drunk and having sex. Neither of which was high on Delaney's list at the moment.

Although . . . she thought to herself . . . it had been a long, *long* time since she'd been touched by a man. Heck, a simple hug would feel good some days, when she was stiff and stressed from standing up and dealing with other people's maladies all day long. As nice as Emily's warm clutches and soft touches were, they were still imbued with responsibility. Though she knew she couldn't risk it, she had to admit that spending a few quiet minutes in a good hard embrace would be awfully nice . . .

Which was the only reason Jack Shepard ever looked good to her, she told herself firmly. And was the only reason—with the possible exception of the beer she'd had—that she'd found herself attracted to him again last night.

After they'd left the bar—Jack had somehow escaped Lisa Jacobson with just a few words, none of which Delaney could or cared to hear—she'd almost felt sorry for him. He was so clearly mortified by the experience. But then, he'd gotten himself into that mess, she had to remind herself.

Still, she'd felt herself softening toward him,

even going so far as to joke with him when he'd started to explain why Lisa was the way she was. He was so grateful for her casual attitude she had to catch herself after they'd picked up Emily and driven home from Aunt Linda's before inviting him in for another drink. If there was one thing she *shouldn't* do around Jack Shepard, it was drink. Emily was proof enough of that.

Delaney cruised south on the dark pine-lined Maine Turnpike and turned her attention to the stores she'd have to hit in and around Boston. Thinking about Jack was not productive. She had to concentrate on her immediate future, which consisted of setting up a life that would keep both herself and Emily together and well provided for.

Most of what was on her list she could have found in Harp Cove, but even having only been here a month she knew that people would talk about her purchases. After her conversation with Kim she was more paranoid than ever about what people might be noticing and speculating about her.

Which was why she'd brought with her several boxes in which her mother had shipped items to her from D.C. She would produce the new things she bought from the boxes as if they'd been brought up by her husband. Not that the townspeople were likely to see them, but Jack might, if she left them in a conspicuous location when she knew he was coming to work on the house. After all, *he* was probably the one fueling the gossip about her

husband's absence, so the more convinced he became, the less talk there was likely to be.

Jack walked across the driveway separating his
house from the carriage house, flipping a set of
keys around one finger.

Delaney was gone this weekend, so he was going to use the time to do some of the louder projects
the place required, such as replacing the missing
trim in the baby's room and installing a new medicine cabinet in the upstairs bathroom. He was also
going to paint the bathroom while he had time to
air it out before they returned.

He moved up the front walk, past the pansies
and petunias Delaney had planted in the front
beds, and inserted the key in the lock. Though he'd
been in this house thousands of times, he felt
strangely alien entering it now, with its rightful oc-
cupant gone.

He stepped into the foyer. The door closing behind him sounded surreally loud, like the creaking
of a shutter in a horror movie.

The hallway was cool. A tiny vase of pansies sat
on the half-moon table against the stairwell, along
with several pieces of opened mail.

Jack moved forward to look at the envelopes, not
touching them but noting the return addresses.
They were bills, it looked like—Visa, American Ex-
press, some insurance company.

Nothing from Jim.

He moved into the kitchen and noted the crumbs

on the small table by the wall. Emily's high chair was pushed against the back doorway, the top disengaged and resting in the seat, wiped clean. In the dish-drainer was a mug and a plate, in the sink a few coffee grounds.

The place was homier than he'd ever felt it. He passed a hand over the kitchen counter, briefly touched one of Emily's empty bottles.

He turned and went upstairs, noting the pictures she'd hung on the wall, etchings and watercolors, one pen-and-ink drawing of Emily looking much closer to newborn than she did now. The door to the master bedroom was closed, and he paused outside of it, hand on the knob.

He frowned, fingering the cool metal knob and gazing at the brushstrokes in the freshly enameled door. He imagined turning the knob and going into the room, smelling her scent, seeing where she slept. Did she make up her bed? Were there clothes scattered on the floor?

He smiled to himself. He doubted it. The place was probably neat as a pin, but he wasn't going to open that door and find out. He took a step back, exhaling. He was curious, but he couldn't do it. He wouldn't invade her privacy.

He turned and moved down the hall to Emily's room, where he was to work. He glanced quickly at the doorframe and windows, the areas where he was to install the new trim, then stood for a minute looking at the crib where Emily slept. A blanket lay on the mattress as if pushed off a tiny body and forgotten. A black-and-white mobile hung over one end, and a music box was attached high on the outside of the rail.

He thought about Emily's small but solid weight in his arms, the clinging hands, the bright clear eyes.

He'd never been one for babies. He'd only told Delaney he liked them last weekend because he'd caught her in what seemed to be a rare good humor, and he wanted to spend more time with her. But when he'd picked Emily up, and she'd smiled so quickly, so purely, even with cheeks still blotchy from crying, something inside of him had beamed.

Maybe she was just an exceptionally cute baby, he thought. Maybe he was intrigued because she looked like her mother. Maybe he was getting older and wanted to start a family himself.

At this he scoffed, then attempted to laugh. *Yeah, right. Me, Jack Shepard, pining after a family. The idea is ludicrous.*

But somehow not funny.

He could just imagine what Kevin's reaction would be if he knew the idea of a family had even crossed Jack's mind. Shock, most likely. Then cynicism. He'd never believe that Jack had actually enjoyed holding a baby. Though he *would* believe Jack had done it to ingratiate himself with the mother.

A pain settled itself low in Jack's flank. He pressed a hand to it, wondering if it had anything to do with thinking about his brother's perpetual disbelief in him.

Just for kicks, Jack allowed his mind to wander to the possibility that Delaney's husband never came up, that she and he picked up where they'd left off last summer. What if things worked out so well they ended up getting married? He'd be Emily's stepdad.

Kevin had always relished his role as the only stable male Shepard. What if Jack suddenly joined him?

The thought sent a sputter of apprehension through him.

Hell, it didn't matter, Jack laughed to himself, turning to step purposefully down the hall to retrieve his tools. But instead, he paused, thinking. First of all, it would never happen. He and Delaney were a flash in the pan, a momentary event, a best-forgotten accident. She kept making that clear. Though there was a moment, after going to Aunt Linda's the other night, when he could have sworn she . . .

He shook his head. No, best not to start thinking like that. Next thing he knew he'd be making a fool of himself for her.

Second of all, he persisted, the fact that he liked holding Emily Poole for five minutes while her mother looked on meant nothing. He was as ignorant about babies as a man could be. Just look at what he'd done that day: He'd blown in her face. He didn't even know you weren't supposed to blow in a baby's face.

The bottom line was he just wasn't father material. He knew it. And she knew it. So there was no point in thinking about it. Or her. Either of them.

But then there never had been any point in thinking about Delaney Poole, and that hadn't stopped him for the last fifteen months.

Jack picked up the elephant rattle he'd given Emily that day, when a voice assaulted him from the stairs.

"Hey, Jack! You in here?"

Jack threw down the rattle and spun toward the door, even as his mind processed the voice as Kevin's. Yanking the tape measure from the holster at his waist, he moved to the door needing trim.

"Yeah. Back bedroom," he called back. His hands shook slightly as he pulled the tape along the top of the doorjamb. And he hadn't even been snooping.

Kevin tromped up the stairs and turned at the top to head back down the hall, his eyes grazing Delaney's pictures much as Jack's had minutes before. Eventually his gaze made it to Jack.

"She fixed it up nice," he said, looking past Jack into the baby's room.

"Yeah." Jack sent the measuring tape up one side of the doorway.

"Hey, I brought that cedar chest Dad wanted back in the house."

Jack nodded. "Great."

"I'll need your help getting it out of the truck."

Jack wrote the measurements down on a piece of paper, even though he'd already done that and cut the trim to fit, and shoved the tape measure back in its pocket.

"No problem," Jack said, starting down the hallway.

But Kevin's gaze drifted again into the baby's room, and he soon followed it. Jack turned around and leaned against the doorway.

"Yeah, it looks good in here." Kevin nodded, looking around the room. "You could've gotten more than three-fifty for this place. Does Dad know that's what you rented it for?"

Jack nearly rolled his eyes at Kevin's knee-jerk distrust of him but opted to laugh instead. "Yes, he knows. He told me what to rent it for."

"Yeah, right," Kevin said, almost under his breath.

Jack made an effort to ignore the jab. "C'mon, let's go get that chest. I've got work to do."

Kevin followed slowly behind as Jack moved back down the hall, but at the top of the steps he moved toward the master bedroom. Without compunction he opened the door and looked in.

Jack felt the violation as if it sucked all the air from the hall. His pulse pounded as if all the evils of the world might come pouring from the room, like Pandora's box, but he couldn't help looking past Kevin to the space beyond.

This was where most of Delaney's own belongings had gone. Even though the house was furnished, she'd brought her own bed, drapes, dresser, and cheval mirror, he knew from the move. But now, seeing it all set up in the room that smelled of perfume and fresh sheets, he could see that her furnishings consisted of so much more.

Several long, trailing plants hung near the windows where soft, frilly drapes muted a bright summer sun. A dressing table covered with bottles gleamed like a liquor bar in the corner, and a stack of books and magazines sat on the table next to her bed. The closet door was mostly closed but in the gap he could see fabric and shoes, enough to know that the dresses and shirts, pants and jackets, into which Delaney Poole breathed life, hung waiting for her return.

The room was feminine and soft, so unlike the cool, reserved persona that greeted him when they ran into each other, but so quintessentially the woman he had met, and could not forget, that spring a year ago.

"Kevin, come on, we shouldn't be in here." Jack took several steps backward until he was standing at the top of the stairs.

"Why not?" Kevin turned to him, brows raised. "It's our house. You stipulated in the lease you're allowed to come in whenever you want, right?"

"Yeah, but only to work. And I don't need to work in here. And she knows it."

Kevin laughed at him. "I'm not going to do anything. She'll never even know we were here. Come here a minute." He walked toward the window.

Jack felt a familiar anger bud in his chest and another slice of pain shot through his abdomen. "No, Kevin, come on. Let's go."

"I just want you to look out the damn window a minute. Would you come here?"

Recognizing that the fight was not worth it, Jack sighed and stepped up to the other window. The bedroom looked out over the flagstone patio and across the lawn to the ocean.

"See that point of rocks out there, Jack?" Kevin's voice was like a schoolteacher's.

Jack's eyes slid over to Kevin's pious face. "Of course."

"You know, don't you, that those are the rocks where Great-uncle Josiah's ship foundered off the coast. And that if that hadn't happened, the Shepards wouldn't have landed here, wouldn't have bought up half the coast of Maine, and wouldn't be living here to this very day."

"Kevin—"

"And this room, Jack," he continued, turning around to spread a hand toward the place where Delaney slept. "You know that this is the room where Great-grandfather Elias died."

Jack folded his arms across his chest. "I'd rather you didn't impart that to my tenant, if you don't mind."

"And that house you're living in now, Jack, does it mean anything to you that seven generations of Shepards were born and lived there? Many of them dying there too?"

"I was born in Portland," Jack offered. "And if they keep dying there, maybe it's time to leave."

"Jack, imagine someone coming along and turning this place into some kind of damn—what's it called—breakfast hotel."

"Bed-and-breakfast," Jack corrected. "Good idea."

"Or suppose they tear the whole place down and put up a subdivision?" He thrust his hand out toward the windows again, as if sweeping away the whole homestead.

"A lot of money in that."

"They could turn this place into a *resort*, or—Jesus—or a *mall*, for God's sake." Kevin's color was high and his voice had gotten louder.

Jack glanced out the window. "Who'd build a mall next to a view like that? Most likely it'd be something like a Sheraton. Maybe one of those Marriott residence places."

"*Listen* to me, Jack. What will *our* descendents have if you sell this place?" Kevin nearly shouted. "Will you bring your kids to a shopping center to point out where your grandfather was born? Will you book a room at the Harp Cove Sheraton to tell your grandchildren about Great-uncle Josiah's ship?"

"I don't know if you've noticed, Kevin, but the kid thing isn't looking good for me. I'm already thirty-four—"

"*Dammit*, Jack, can't you stop thinking about *yourself* for even a second?"

"Well, stop bringing me up." Jack straightened, gritting his teeth against harsher words that wanted to emerge. After a moment he added, "I suppose you want me to start thinking about you for a change."

"I want you to think about your goddamn heritage. About the people—*the Shepards*—that will be coming after us."

"You know," Jack said mildly, "*I'm* not the one selling the place. It's Dad's, as I keep pointing out."

"But you're the only one who can save it."

Jack laughed at the dramatic words and the reverent tone Kevin used to utter them.

"Have you tried this tirade on Dad?" Jack asked. "Because it may work on him. But Kevin, you don't seem to understand that it's not just my choice not to buy this place. I couldn't afford it if I wanted to."

"Yes you could."

Jack laughed incredulously. "How do you keep figuring that?"

Kevin hesitated a second, fixing him with a serious eye. "Like I said before, you could sell *The Silver Surfer*. Did you even look at those numbers I gave you?"

Jack stared at him a long moment, then shifted his feet and adopted a flippant expression. He had looked at the numbers. They'd scared him. "And you could sell the *Hornet's Nest*."

"Don't be ridiculous. That's my livelihood. But the boat . . ." Kevin shrugged elaborately, his palms turned upward. "That's just a luxury."

"I'll tell you what's ridiculous," Jack said, striding toward the door. "This whole conversation. Besides," he added, turning once he'd reached the threshold, "I might be taking a job at Briarly College."

Kevin stopped in his tracks. "Briarly College? What job?"

"Remember Hugh Peterson? He's head coach there and offered me an assistant coaching job. I'm thinking about it."

To Jack's surprise, Kevin's face broke into a wide

smile. "But that's fantastic. It's better money, right?"

Jack frowned. Was this his brother, actually being *happy* for him? "Sure."

Kevin laughed incredulously. "Then you could definitely afford this place!"

Of course. It furthered Kevin's own ends. Irked with himself for thinking otherwise, he turned and started for the stairs. "Forget it."

"You know you're being unreasonable." Kevin started to follow and brushed against a stack of magazines on the bedside table. Several slid off the top to the floor.

Jack turned and looked back. "Great," he said, seething back into the room to pick them up. He gathered them one by one, trying in vain to unbend the pages that had wrinkled on the way down, and set them back on the pile. It looked as if she'd been cutting things out of one, several bits of cut paper fluttered from the pages onto the ground.

"Just get out of here, Kevin. You're going to break something, and then she'll know we were in here."

"What are you getting so uptight about?" But Kevin moved toward the door, eyeing him oddly. "You have every right to be in here. *I* have every right to be in here."

"Not when it's rented you don't." Jack put the final magazine back and herded him from the room, closing the door firmly behind him. "And I'll tell you this for the last time: I'm well aware of the history involved here, but I'm not buying the damn place. And you can tell me to sell the boat as many times as you want, but I'm not going to do it."

With that, he shouldered past his brother and strode down the steps.

Kevin's footsteps followed him down the stairs and out the front door. Jack was halfway across the front yard when he turned abruptly back, and called, "And close the goddamn door."

They moved the cedar chest into the main house in silence, Jack boiling over Kevin's presumption. Not that they hadn't had nearly this exact conversation before, but for some reason it had gotten to him this time.

Maybe he was just tired of it. Or maybe Kevin had struck a nerve, talking about children and grandchildren. Coming off his recent experience with Emily and his uncharacteristically open-minded thoughts about parenthood, the remarks had just caught him at a vulnerable moment, that was all.

Kevin was just being Kevin, wanting Jack to mortgage the rest of *his* life so that *Kevin's* children could have this heritage that mattered so much to *Kevin*. He shouldn't take it so seriously, Jack thought.

By the time the heavy chest was in place in the front hall, Jack had talked himself into cooling off. Kevin could harp all he wanted, it wasn't going to talk anyone into giving Jack a mortgage.

As they walked out the front door, Jack stopped on the porch and glanced over to the carriage house. Delaney's car was not there, of course, she was gone for the weekend. But it had become a reflexive habit of Jack's to look for her car when he got up, or when he arrived home. Or came out of the house. Or looked out a window.

He supposed it would be the same for any tenant. After all, they did live very close to one another. It would be natural for him to look to see if the tenant was in the yard, or home and likely to be seeing him . . .

"Thanks for helping with the chest," Kevin said, pulling a set of keys from his pocket and stepping off the porch.

"No problem." Jack turned his gaze in the direction opposite that of the carriage house. Nothing there but trees, however. Another probable reason he always found himself looking at her house.

"Oh and by the way," Kevin added from the walk. "Carol met the new doctor the other day. Said she recognized her."

Jack's breathing slowed to a dangerously low level. "Oh?"

"Yeah, said she'd met her before. She's that girl you met last year, isn't she?" Kevin raised one brow, inquiring. "At the Hornet's Nest? What was her name? Delores?"

"Delaney." It was odd saying her name without her there.

Kevin smiled, remembering. "Yeah. Didn't you guys, uh . . ." He chuckled and gave him a sly look. "You know, have a good time that weekend? Or am I thinking of somebody else?"

Jack frowned, then shook his head slowly. "Must be somebody else."

Kevin studied him a moment. "Really? Carol was pretty sure she'd met her with you at the bar. Said you all looked pretty cozy, then you disappeared."

Jack gazed off in the direction of the trees again. "Yeah, we were at the bar. I remember introducing her to Carol. But we just had a few drinks."

"Uh-huh." He paused. "Nothing else happened?"

Jack looked back at him, looked him dead in the eye, and said without blinking, "No."

Kevin nodded. "And you didn't know it was her, renting the house?"

Jack forced a laugh and glanced skyward. "Nope. Shocked the hell out of me when I saw her. Guess I never got her last name the first time. But then we only spoke a couple of times. I barely know her."

"Huh." Kevin looked thoughtfully at the ground. "Well, you'll get to know her now, huh?"

Jack narrowed his eyes, said nothing.

Kevin turned toward the car and started walking. "All right, see you later." He waved a hand backwards over his head.

"Yeah." Jack said. "See ya."

He watched his brother drive off, then turned and went back into the house. He needed aspirin for the damn pain in his gut Kevin caused. He headed toward the kitchen and reflected that, unfortunately, most of what he'd told his brother about Delaney was true. They'd only met briefly, they'd only spoken a couple of times, they'd just had a couple of drinks, and he never got her last name . . .

He barely knew her. That was the most unfortunate part.

Delaney made it home with just the barest amount of energy to get through the door. Fortunately, Emily was still asleep from the drive, and she could put her directly into her crib, though Delaney was under no illusions that that would last long.

It had been a tough weekend for both of them, which is why she'd come back from Boston early on Sunday. Exhausted and out of sorts, she decided not to waste any more time on a trip designed solely, it seemed, to torture herself.

The whole thing had been a disaster. Not a failure. But definitely a disaster.

The phone rang the moment she sat in the big comfy chair in the living room. Afraid it would wake Emily, she jumped up and ran to the kitchen.

"So, have you been watching?" Michael asked after her whispered *"hello."*

"What? Now?" She sat down on one of the kitchen chairs and wrapped the phone cord around her finger. She really needed to get a cordless phone so she could sit in the living room. She felt as if she never sat in the living room, and it was her favorite room. The one Jack was so proud of.

"No. *Destiny's Children.* You *have been* watching,

haven't you? Sybill's passing her baby off as Ruark's, and they just got married on Friday. Isn't that great? Just like you and Jim!" He cackled merrily on the other end of the line.

Delaney let his laughter dwindle, then said, "Except that Jim doesn't exist and Jack thinks Sybill's a selfish bitch."

"Who's Jack?" Michael asked.

"Who's Jack?" she repeated, incredulous.

"Oh, *your* Jack." He laughed again, sheepishly this time. "Jeez, sorry, Dee. I thought you meant someone on the show."

"No, Jack. Or maybe I should say my Drake."

"Jack watches too? God, is this a great show or what?"

She heard him shift the phone from one ear to the other.

"Are you in bed?" she asked.

"Yeah. Late night, last night. So Jack watches too, huh? That's great."

"No, his mother watches it and tells him about it. And apparently they both think Sybill's a selfish bitch for what she's doing."

Michael was silent, then, "So what?"

"So he therefore thinks *I'm* a selfish bitch for what *I'm* doing." She sighed and slumped down in the seat, pulling her hair back from her face with one hand.

"Except he doesn't know what you're doing."

"I know, but still . . ." She hesitated. And she wasn't going to tell him, so what difference did it make? "I bought a lot of stuff this weekend, want to hear about it?"

"Oh yeah. This was the visit with Ru—, uh, I mean Jim."

"Ha. Ha. Don't you dare start calling him Ruark, or I'm liable to have to make up some lame story about Jim having *two* middle names."

"Sorry. What did you buy?"

She rattled off the list: a large-screen TV with a universal remote; a huge stereo system and a rack of compact discs; some socks, sweatshirts, pajamas, and robe; shaving cream, razors, aftershave and cologne; and frames for her medical-journal photos of Jim Poole.

"Then I stopped at this thrift shop and found a *gorgeous* Burberry's raincoat that I thought would look great on the hall coatrack. And it does. It's fabulous."

"Burberry's? In Boston? You'd think you'd only find L L Bean or something," Michael said.

"Yeah, but Burberry's is better, since Jim's from D.C. And then I went to Cambridge and picked up a tiny little Harvard tee shirt for Emily," she told Michael. "Jim, you know, graduated from Harvard Law."

"So, you're expecting the guy to be riffling through your closets looking for clues, huh?"

"No, of course not. I don't think he'd do that. But if he does, I'm ready for him."

Michael laughed. "Sounds like it was fun."

"It was, in a way." She ran her fingernail over a

sticky spot on the kitchen table. "I loved going through the men's departments at Filene's and Nordstrom, picking out ties and suits, looking at the money clips and cuff links, the leather slippers and travel bags. Who knew men's departments had so much cool stuff?"

"So how much did you spend?" he asked.

She sighed. "Too much. And not enough." She hesitated, debating whether to talk to Michael about her volatile feelings.

"What's wrong?" he asked, reading her mind as he so often did. Why could she never find a guy who could read her like Michael did? Why did it take a gay man to give her that feeling of being truly loved for herself, and cared about?

"The problem is I started imagining all that male paraphernalia strewn about my house. Coins on my dresser, razor stubble in my sink, athletic socks on my floor."

"Sounds like a nightmare," he said. "Sounds like *your* nightmare."

She laughed and felt disappointment sting the backs of her eyes. "I know. But the more I shopped the more I got into the idea of it, of having this wonderful man to shop *for*, of living with all of these things as part of some idyllic kind of life."

She paused and sniffed, mortified to be getting so watery.

"I mean it was ridiculous," she continued. "It wouldn't have happened if the damn men's department hadn't been so full of stuff that men would never buy for themselves. They were definitely catering to the women in those men's lives. I mean, there were these gorgeous, classic suits that you never see outside the fashion magazines. And overcoats and bankers' umbrellas, boxer shorts and tee shirts and sweater vests and collar stays. I kept imagining this man in my house with excellent taste and a closet full of thick woolly sweaters that would look great on a fall day with his dark blond hair."

"Tell me you didn't buy all that stuff, Delaney."

"Of course not. Mostly I just walked around picking it out, as if he might come and find me in the store at any moment. It was sick. I'm sick."

She didn't add that she had gone on from the department store to discover that her "husband" was partial to biographies, which she picked up a couple of, and that he couldn't live without a barbecue grill she'd seen at Sears, so they were shipping it to her.

"Then," she added, and here she had to laugh, "I decided that had he been real and really shopping with me, he definitely would have insisted that I get something for myself too."

"Oh no, here we go. And what was left for you to buy?"

"I got myself a pearl ring. It's beautiful, so simple and charming. He knows just what I like."

"This is getting scary."

She laughed. "Tell me about it. But then, as I was returning to Filene's to check out the home furnishings department, I realized something."

"That you were losing your mind?"

"*Yes*. You laugh but that's exactly how I felt. All around me, in advertising for the store and posters and stuff, were pictures of men with women who were supposed to be their wives, with kids who were supposed to be their children, with other couples who were supposed to be their friends. And standing there, alone in the middle of this incredibly bright mall, I started crying."

"Oh, honey."

"I mean, how pathetic have I become? I'm *pretending* to be married. Pretending to have a life that includes all the stuff I just bought. I'm setting myself up with all the props for a happy marriage, and I'm missing the main ingredient." She trapped a tear from the corner of one eye on a knuckle and wiped it on her pant leg.

"The leading man."

"I mean it, I thought I'd hit rock bottom when I found out I was pregnant from a one-night stand, but this was different. This was deliberate."

Now she was perpetrating a charade so contemptible, living a lie so incredible, it was worse than the circumstances she was trying to make up for.

"Don't tell me you returned all that stuff."

She laid her head in one hand, her elbow on the table. "God, no. Are you kidding? I kept it, if for no other reason than that it would have taken forever to take back."

"That's my girl," Michael said. "And besides, you need a decent-sized TV to watch *Destiny's Children* on."

"No," she said adamantly, shaking her head. "I'm through watching that stupid show. All it does is depress me."

"Are you kidding? Watching a woman get away with exactly what you're doing *depresses* you? You should be studying Sybill's every move. The hell with Jack, the woman's a genius."

Chapter 12

In Delaney's fantasies, she always imagined herself the first to arrive at her small-town country clinic. She would mount the steps on some sparkling summer morning, breathe in the fresh salt-sea air, pull from her pocket the reassuring cluster of keys to her sanctuary, and open the door to her own oasis of healing.

In reality, however, Nurse Knecht arrived at some ungodly hour seen only by fishermen and drunks, and staked out the oasis ready to defend its shores with ever-present scowl and scathing tongue.

So it wasn't her ideal, Delaney thought as she pulled her Toyota in next to Nurse Knecht's big brown Oldsmobile. But she wasn't one to despair of a situation just because it wasn't picture-perfect. After all, she could still smell the sea air, admire the clear blue morning, and ensconce herself in her office until the first needy patient arrived.

This morning, however, the first needy patient was already there.

"Got an abdominal pain in exam one," Nurse Knecht tonelessly informed her as she pushed through the door. "And a postnatal exam at eight-thirty. Kathy Blevins's boy."

So much for ensconcing herself in her office, Delaney thought, wishing she'd stopped for coffee on the way in.

"Is the abdominal pain an appointment?"

"Walk-in." Nurse Knecht scowled. "Been here forty-five minutes."

Delaney stopped on her way back to her office. "Forty-five minutes! Why didn't you call me?"

"You were coming in anyway. He could wait."

Delaney gaped at her. Nurse Knecht returned the look with a stony obstinacy.

"Next time," Delaney said deliberately, "call me. I can come in early if someone's in pain."

Nurse Knecht nodded once, then repeated, "He could wait."

Delaney dropped her bag in her office, wondering if she could possibly hire a different nurse without upsetting the whole town, and made her way straight to exam room one.

She was pulling on her white lab coat as she opened the door, grabbing the chart with one hand and shrugging into the jacket with the other, when she glanced at the name. Her eyes shot to the examining table when both evidences hit her at once.

There, sitting on the end of the table in a paper gown, was Jack Shepard.

He looked as shocked to see her as she was to see him.

"Well," she said, clearing her throat, "hello, Jack."

In fascination she watched as he flushed to the roots of his hair. "Hi," he managed, looking past her as she shut the door behind her.

"I apologize for your having to wait," she said, busying herself with the chart. "I didn't know you were here. I've told Nurse Knecht to call me next time someone comes in early."

He cleared his throat. "No, it's okay."

She opened the chart and sat down on the rolling stool, schooling her face to professional composure. Her heart hammered, and her hands threatened to sweat, but she felt that this was an opportunity. Maybe dealing with him as a patient, and thinking of him as a patient in the future, might help her stay poised around him whenever she saw him.

"What seems to be the problem?" she asked, looking at his chart. It was remarkably short for someone who'd lived here nearly his whole life and undoubtedly had seen Dr. Jacobson for the last ten or fifteen years. Jack was a healthy guy, aside from a sprain here or a tetanus shot there. She felt glad for Emily's sake.

When Jack didn't answer she looked up.

He swallowed hard and glanced at the door. "I, uh, I don't mean to be rude or anything, but . . ."

He rubbed the side of his neck nervously with one palm. "I thought I was going to see Doc Jacobson."

Delaney smiled calmly. He wasn't the first person to say such a thing. It was natural to distrust a new doctor, and she found it quaint that Jack was no different than the children and little old ladies she'd had to comfort before him.

"It's true, he does usually take Monday morning appointments," she said. "But Dr. Jacobson decided to take a long weekend."

Jack's eyes flashed to the door again and then down to his paper gown. His hands gripped his knees as if holding the gown in place for dear life.

"He's fly-fishing, I believe," she added.

She knew what he was feeling, the unfamiliarity of having to trust someone you know in one capacity with fulfilling another capacity entirely.

"Jack," she said gently, "I know our relationship is an odd one, but I *am* a professional. I've treated people before that I knew much better than I know you."

The moment her words sank in to her own mind a blush crept up her cheeks. She knew they were both thinking of that one night when their hands, lips, and bodies had gotten to know each other quite well.

Which *wasn't* what she'd meant. That is, she hadn't meant she'd known people even more intimately, though of course she had, in the context of a relationship but . . . oh hell.

"What I mean to say is," she added, rising and

turning her back on him to retrieve the thermometer off the counter, "you can trust that I am well qualified and impartial, and anything that goes on in this office will remain completely confidential."

Jack sighed heavily. "Delaney—or should I call you Dr. Poole, now that we're in your office?"

She turned and sat back down on the stool. "Whichever you're more comfortable with."

"I don't mean to insult you—I really don't—but I really think it would be better if I waited for Doc." He started to push off the table, but the gown moved too and he grabbed at it, sliding awkwardly to his feet, his hands clutching the paper hem.

Delaney did her best not to notice the generous length of thigh the gown exposed.

"Listen, if you're uncomfortable, I'm certainly not going to make you stay, but are you sure you want to wait? Dr. Jacobson won't be back until Wednesday."

Jack faced her as he edged toward his pile of clothes on the plastic chair near the scale. "It's all right. It's better now. It's just a little—*aghh*." He doubled over, arms folded across his lower body as if someone had just kicked him in the groin.

Delaney shot to her feet and took him by the shoulders. "Jack, come here." Her voice was firm and he moved back toward the examining table. "Now, I understand your concerns, but you're obviously in pain. You've got to let me help you. What does it feel like? Where exactly is the pain?"

He sat back up on the table, his breath coming

back to him as the pain seemed to subside. His face was beet red, and a fine sheen of perspiration lined his forehead.

"It's this shooting, searing pain—*agh, God*—" He gasped.

"Where?" Delaney asked, pushing him gently back onto the table until he lay completely prone. His hands covered an area very near his groin. "Here?" she asked, touching his hands.

He closed his eyes, exhaling. "Yeah. Jesus." He took a deep breath and exhaled again. "It's going away again. Thank God."

She slowly moved his hands, her fingers exploring the area with infinite softness.

"Sometimes it starts higher. Sometimes it's lower than that."

She glanced up at his face, but he was looking at the wall. She could tell from his ear he was still blushing. The sight of it gave her the same tender feeling she'd had when he'd told her about his boyhood knitting. She smiled slightly and looked back at her hands.

Which is when she noticed the unmistakable rise in the paper gown below the area her fingers explored.

I'm in hell, Jack thought. *Pure, unadulterated, mortifying hell.*

The pain had disappeared again just in time for him to become aware of Delaney's hands. He lay for a moment willing his arousal away, then sat up as abruptly as he could manage in the revealing paper gown. If he could just get home, he could probably last another two days.

"Look, this isn't good. I—I'll just wait until Wednesday. Really, how much worse can it get?"

His question was answered immediately by another stab of pain. He tried to conceal it but couldn't, and ended up leaning over his own knees with a guttural moan.

"Jack, lie back and take deep breaths." Her hands were touching him, cupping his shoulders and urging him to lie back. It was ridiculous. He couldn't go anywhere—suppose he had an attack while he was driving? This automatic doubling over wouldn't work very well on the road.

He lay back and took deep breaths. At least his erection was gone, for the moment, anyway, he thought, wishing he could dissolve like an ash onto the floor.

He glanced at her under hooded eyes as she resumed her palpation of the offending area. Her cheeks were pink, he noted. So the experience was mortifying for her, too.

He closed his eyes.

After a moment, she stopped and he heard the metal clatter of wheels on linoleum. He opened his eyes to see her sitting on the rolling stool, chart and pen in hand.

"There are several possibilities," she said, looking strictly at the chart. He watched her throat as she swallowed. "The first, and most obvious thing I should check for is a hernia."

And he thought this day couldn't get any worse.

"No. Absolutely not. It's not a hernia." He shook his head, teeth clenched. "I'm sure of it. I've had one before, and it's not a hernia."

He knew the way doctors checked for hernias, and he wasn't about to let Delaney Poole perform that humiliating examination on him. Not to mention the fact that direct contact with his, uh, privates was certain to produce another completely unsuitable reaction.

"You've had one before?" she asked. "In the same spot?"

"No, over here." He indicated the place on the opposite side of his abdomen. "But this isn't that. Trust me. No." His eyes demanded that she believe him.

"Okay," she said slowly.

Her pale blue eyes looked back at the folder in her hands, and her shiny hair draped against the side of her face when she bent her head. All in all she was far too pretty to be taken seriously as a doctor, he thought. She looked more like some sultry nurse from a Penthouse video.

"Have you had any difficulty urinating?" she asked.

A-ha! So it *could* get worse. He closed his eyes, the image of the sultry nurse fleeing like a startled cat.

He hesitated a long time, measuring the merits of leaving against his likely inability to withstand the pain until Dr. Jacobson returned. Maybe he could make it to the hospital in Bangor before passing out. . . .

"Jack?"

"Yes," he said finally.

She nodded, and her pen scratched something on the chart. He noted the delicate pearl ring she wore on her right hand. Hadn't she said she couldn't wear a ring? That was why she didn't wear a wedding band. They got in the way when she worked. Supposedly.

"Now, I know you're going to want to leave again but I have to ask you some personal questions. Please remember what I said about everything occurring in this office being completely confidential."

Dread formed a cannonball in the pit of his stomach.

She kept her eyes on the chart. "How many sexual partners have you had in the last six months?"

Anger flashed through him like wildfire, and he sat straight up, wincing after the fact.

Delaney stood up, one hand outstretched as if to calm him down with her palm.

"I have to ask these questions, Jack—"

"You think I've got a venereal disease." His voice was loud, much louder than he'd intended.

"I have to explore every possibility—"

"Are you sure you're not just *interested* in my sexual activity?" he asked, sliding off the table and grabbing up his underwear. A tiny pain threatened as he punched one leg into the boxers. "Can't you just get that information from your precious sources of gossip? You seemed to think they were reliable enough before."

"Jack, there's no need to make this personal—"

"That's right," he said, facing her in his boxers and paper gown. The fingers of one hand pressed against the area of pain in his abdomen.

"Whatever it is, it's most likely curable—"

He laughed cynically. "Some antibiotics and everything'll be fine, is that it? And you get justification for every bad thing you've ever thought about me."

"I don't think bad things about you." But she didn't take her eyes from his chart as she said it.

Silent, he clenched his teeth until her attention returned to him.

"You can't even look at me when you say that, can you?" He laughed wryly, his gaze flipping to the ceiling. After a second he brought his eyes back to her face. She was looking at him now.

"All right, I'll tell you," he said, folding his arms across his chest with a paper crinkle, "since you're so anxious to know. I've slept with two women in the last year and a half. Lisa, whom you met, *one time*; and I won't get into what a drunken mistake that was." He exhaled, his eyes not leaving hers. "And you."

She glanced at the floor, then seemed to realize what she did and brought her gaze back to his face.

"Does that fit your profile for someone with VD?" he asked caustically. "Is that all you need to know? Do you even believe me?"

Her chest rose and fell rapidly. "Of course I believe you," she said softly.

But her eyes skittered away once she said it.

He laughed and pulled the paper gown off, reaching for his tee shirt. "I don't think we have the proper doctor-patient relationship for this examination. I don't think we're likely to get any accurate results. If you don't mind, Dr. Poole, I'll just take myself off to the emergency room in Bangor."

He pulled the tee shirt over his head, and she was standing by the time he pushed his head through the neck. He shoved his arms through the sleeves.

"What kind of drunken mistake was I?"

Her words were quiet but clear, and they froze him where he stood. Her eyes looked stricken, even paler in her ashen face.

What *that* what she thought? That *he* thought it was a mistake?

"Delaney—" Confusion swamped him.

"No. Never mind." She turned away.

"But you have to know—"

"*I don't care*," she said, turning, with so much vehemence he stopped talking. "I'm sorry," she added quietly. "Just . . . just let me help you. Let me take one X ray."

A twinge in his groin voiced its opinion to stay. Still, he stood undecided and confused, jeans in one hand, Delaney standing just to one side of him.

"Have you been eating a lot of greens lately?" she asked. "Spinach? Rhubarb? Drinking a lot of coffee?"

He stared at her. What the hell was she thinking? He was caught between anger and confusion. Why did she have such a bad opinion of him? Why did her opinion make any sort of difference to him? What the hell did it matter what he ate?

"Kale," he said, remembering. "I made a big batch of Portuguese kale soup. I've been eating it all week. Why?"

She nodded. "You may have a kidney stone." Her voice was soft but sure. "They're pretty common in men, particularly in the summer when we sweat more and pass a more concentrated urine. If you eat a lot of foods with a high oxalic acid content—like kale, or any leafy vegetable—that would also encourage formation of a stone. Coffee does too. The pain can be intermittent and would be sharp, moving toward the groin. You may even feel occasionally nauseous. Does this sound accurate?"

He gazed at her, at her pale blue eyes trained on him with what could only be described as concern. He nodded shortly.

"Then let me take one X ray, and if it is a stone, I'll get you a painkiller right away. Then, depending on the size, we'll decide what to do about it. Okay? It's probably not too late to avoid surgery."

He didn't say anything, not trusting his voice. He was such a wad of anger, confusion, mortification, and pain he wasn't sure which one to listen to.

"There's no sense driving all the way to Bangor if you don't need to, Jack," she added gently. "You can try it to spite me if you want, but if you leave here in the kind of pain you came in with, you won't get far."

He dropped his jeans back on the chair. "All right." His voice emerged gruffly.

She regarded him soberly. "Thank you."

His eyes shot to hers, but her expression was sincere. "Why are you thanking me?"

"For trusting me." Her eyes were steady. "It means a lot to me that you do, at least as a doctor."

He took a deep breath and let it out slowly. "But you'll never trust me, will you, Delaney?"

She looked away and he saw her cheeks go red again. "What do you mean? What do I need to trust you with?" She turned and moved to the counter, picking up the pen to write something else on his chart.

His brows descended, and he shook his head. "No. Nothing."

She moved to the wall and pushed a button on the intercom. Nurse Knecht's nasal tone invaded the room a moment later.

"Yes, Doctor?"

"We're going to need a urinalysis and an abdominal X ray on Mr. Shepard right away," Delaney said, then turned back to him. "I've got another patient, but I'll get back with you as soon as I'm done, all right?"

"Oh, don't worry about me," he said, feeling like an actor in the wrong play. His lines didn't seem to be getting an appropriate response. "You don't have to hold my hand or anything, I'll be fine."

She moved toward the door, then stopped to look back at him. "I know you will, Jack."

Delaney sat in the back of the diner with a newspaper propped in front of her face and a cup of coffee on the table beside her. She couldn't sleep last night and so had gotten up early, dropped Emily off at Aunt Linda's, and come to Sadie's to try to relax. She was the first patron here, a fact that surprised both Delaney and Lois, the waitress who seated her.

She was wound up because of the events of the previous day, which had been harrowing. It had been busy from start to finish, but beginning the day unexpectedly with Jack had set the tone for the rest of the day.

As it turned out, Jack did indeed have a kidney stone, which fortunately was small enough to pass with a lot of water and painkillers. But something about having to talk him into letting her treat him, having to offend him with the requisite questions, and then feeling the shock that he might consider her to have been a mistake, had started her day off with a lot of doubt. About her abilities, his character, her feelings, but mostly about her course of action—to which she was inextricably committed.

The one bright spot had been the exhilarating discovery that not only had he slept with Lisa Jacobson only once, but he'd *never* slept with Kim—a destructive fantasy she'd spent nights obsessing over since her lunch with Kim. Furthermore, if he were to be believed, he had barely slept with *anyone* since he'd been with her. Just one drunken evening with Lisa.

But even that bright spot was tempered by the fact that it shouldn't matter to her how many people Jack Shepard slept with. The revelation had made her feel too good. Why was she so relieved? What difference did it make that he was perhaps not as promiscuous as the gossips would have her believe? It actually would have made things easier on her if he'd turned out to be a self-professed Lothario.

But no, it was better for Emily that he was not, she told herself. How, she wasn't exactly sure. Maybe because it was good Emily's father wasn't off siring dozens of other babies.

Still, she told herself, he could easily have been lying. She could see where he would be more than reluctant to tell her that he slept around. Besides, what was all that "meet me at the boat" stuff with Kim on the phone the other day if not some sort of romantic tryst? Though it was possible he was just going slowly with Kim. Maybe that's how he did things with women he cared about, instead of just jumping them on the beach. Hadn't Kim said something about him finally finding the *right* woman?

Delaney frowned and took a sip of her coffee. Not for the first time, she wondered what they'd talked about after she left.

Delaney set her mug back on the table and slumped farther down behind her paper as the bells on the front door jangled. She didn't want to be bothered by anyone.

Several male voices entered at once, one raspy voice—Sam's—giving the newcomers away as part of the diners club.

"Set us up, Lois," Sam called. "The wife ran out of coffee this morning, and I'm grumpy as a coon in a brand-new trash can."

"You know I got it brewing, Sam," the waitress called back. "Seat yourselves. I got a plate of doughnuts for you too."

"Ooh, doughnuts," Norman's voice said.

Delaney nearly smiled at the delighted tone.

The bells on the door rang again, and another man entered, speaking as if he'd started the sentence down the street.

"And I got something good for you boys today. Guess who went into the pretty new doctor's office yesterday?"

Delaney froze, afraid to make a sound. Had they not noticed her sitting here?

"Well go on, Joe, it ain't as if we got all day," Sam said, then burst out laughing. The others joined him.

"Our own Jack. Went in yesterday morning before the place even opened. Carla was on her way to the laundry-mat when she saw him skulking around front. Same time Janet Knecht arrived and let him in." Chairs scraped across the floor, and Delaney peered silently around the edge of her paper. Four men sat at the square table in the middle of the room. Lois was crossing the room with a tray full of mugs and a full pot of coffee.

"Here you go, guys. Go to it."

"How 'bout them doughnuts you promised?" Sam asked.

"They're coming, they're coming." Lois waved a hand as she moved back to the kitchen.

"Think he had a reason for going in, or might it just be he wanted to flirt with the new doc?" Norman asked. "Seems strange for Jack to go to the doctor's twice in one summer, 'cause didn't he go just a short while back?"

"Strange indeed," Joe said. "But his going in there crack a dawn like that seems to me he mighta had something to say to her, more'n a medical problem."

"I'm telling you, boys, he's making his move," Sam said. "He knows that husband's never gonna show."

"Oh, hell no," Joe agreed. "And them living right next to each other like that. I'm 'bout ready to wager they been keeping company already."

Sam laughed, a wheezy, raspy laugh. "Keeping company? That what you think, Joe?" He laughed some more.

"Now, you know what I mean, Sam."

"I'll wager they been doing a sight more than keeping company, if I know Jack."

"Now—now—I don't know," Norman said tentatively. "It's not Jack's way to sniff around after a married woman like that, is it?"

"Oh, she ain't married," Joe said, laughing.

A cold sweat broke across Delaney's brow.

"I got to agree with you, Joe. Got to agree," Sam said.

"I heard her husband works for the White

House," Norman said. "For the president of the United States."

"Now where'd you hear that?" Joe asked skeptically.

"I heard it," Norman said. "He's some big wig in the White House, and that's why he didn't come with her."

"Well, I heard her daddy's in the Secret Service," Joe said. "One of those men who guards the president. Maybe that's what you're thinking of, Norman. Her daddy, not her husband."

"No." Norman's voice was unusually assured. "It was her husband. And that's why he's not here with her."

"Old Jack oughta watch out, then, if either of them things are true," Sam said. "Which I doubt."

"Jack isn't watching out for anything. You all saw him and her and that McQuade girl over there in the corner the other day. Seems every time she's in here he shows up," Joe said. "God knows where else he shows up when she's there."

"It's only been twice," Norman said.

"And he's been in to see her twice," Joe said, "at the clinic. Yesterday and that time a few weeks ago."

"That was after Lisa hit him," a fourth voice said. "He didn't have much choice that time."

"Here you go," Lois said. "So who are you guys talking about today, hm? Anybody I know?" She cackled.

"Lois, have you noticed every time that pretty

doctor comes in here, Jack Shepard shows up?" Joe asked.

Delaney heard a plate slide across the table and Lois's voice dropped so low she couldn't hear it. A blush burned her face, threatening to torch her hair, as Delaney realized Lois was most likely telling them of her presence in the corner.

Embarrassment scalded her as she realized they'd know exactly why she hadn't spoken up: because she'd wanted to hear what they had to say about her. There was no way she could leave the diner now without walking right past them, humiliated to the core.

She heard Sam clear his throat. "Well now, how's that wife of yours, Martin? I hear she's making baby clothes for a whole 'nother grandchild."

Maybe she could pretend she'd fallen asleep. After all, she'd barely moved since they arrived. But with the paper up in front of her face she could be stuck here for hours before anyone would think to check on her. And God knew the diners club could afford to stay long after Delaney was due at work.

"Hey," Norman said, "did I ever tell you guys about my wife's dead brother?"

"The one hit by the boat?" Joe asked.

"Yeah. So I told you?"

"You didn't tell me," the fourth voice, presumably Martin's, said.

"Well." Norman cleared his throat importantly. "My wife's dead brother went to see one of them palm readers—"

"A psychic," Sam supplied.

"Yeah," Norman continued, "and she told him he was going to be killed by a boat. So he refused to go out on the water for years. Gave up his job fishing, took a desk job with the Aroostook County police department, wouldn't even walk on a beach."

"But he was killed by a boat anyway?" Martin asked.

"Yep. Driving the Maine Turnpike. He was right there near the Saco exit, matter of fact. Down Portland way. Boat slid right off the back of a trailer and ran him over. Got him right through the windshield of his car."

"Well, I'll be damned," Martin said.

"*He* sure was," Sam muttered. A spoon clucked in a mug, then clattered against the tabletop. "So now we heard that story for the last time, right, Norman? Everyone's heard it now."

"That palm reader was right," Norman said. "That's the point."

There was nothing to do but tough it out, Delaney decided, wishing a boat would come through the window of the diner and take her out of her misery.

But, dammit, it wasn't *her* fault they were talking about her. All she was doing was having an innocent cup of coffee. *They're* the ones who should be mortified, she decided.

She contemplated stopping at the table and telling them all that *she* was the one in the Secret Service and had been sent here to arrest old men spreading false rumors, but she knew she'd never do it. If she did, they'd only have that much more to say about her.

No, she simply had to get up and leave and let them be the embarrassed ones.

She folded her newspaper and the sound seemed to reverberate around the room. She picked up her coffee, drank down the last tepid bit, and grabbed her purse.

With her head high, her back straight, and her face red, she marched past the diners club with a bright and cheerful, "Good morning, gentlemen," and then she was out.

Sunlight broke over her like a bottle in an old Western movie. She shielded her eyes against it and crossed the street to the town green, holding her breath until she was under the trees. She was tempted to sit on one of the green's garden benches and collect herself, but she was still within view of the diner so she kept going.

"Delaney!"

She turned at the sound of her name, only to see Jack pulling up in his truck in front of Sadie's. And there, just behind the plate-glass window, the old men sat and watched, she was sure. It was all she could do not to put her head in her hands.

They'd be crowing about this, she was sure. And now that they knew she'd just sat there, silently, while they said whatever the hell they pleased about her, they'd be even more eager to make wild assumptions about her life. Why hadn't she said more? Pointed out that everything they'd said was false, for example.

Jack stepped out of the car and trotted across the street toward the green.

"Thanks for stopping," he said. He wasn't winded from his short sprint across the road, but his hair was perfectly tousled, and he had a healthy glow in his cheeks.

"You seem to be feeling better," she said, edging left so his body would block any view of her to whoever might be watching from the diner.

"I am," he said with obvious relief. "I think it, ah, passed. Last night. Not without an incredible amount of pain, however. Thank you very much for the Percocet. I think I'm still feeling a little high from it."

"I'm very glad to hear it. That it passed, that is." She shifted her purse from one shoulder to the other. "They generally do, once they get that painful, and if they're very small like yours."

"Thank God for that." He was blushing. "I just dropped it at the clinic for analysis, as you instructed, Doctor."

"Good. I was just heading that way," she said, beginning to turn away.

"Delaney, wait." He reached one hand out, as if to grab her arm, but stopped before touching her. "Do you have a minute?"

She faced him again, her eyes on his neck, unable to meet his gaze. She was disconcerted to be talking to him, to be seen with him, so soon after what she'd just heard, and at the same time she was aware of every inch that stood between them. When she thought he might touch her arm, the nerves from her hand to her shoulder had tingled as if he actually had.

"I owe you an apology."

At this she did look at him, raising her brows and rearranging her purse on her shoulder. "What for?"

"For yesterday. I acted like a defensive ass, and I'm sorry. You were being nothing but professional and I . . . well, I wasn't acting very professional in return."

"It's not the patient's job to be professional." She smiled slightly, her gaze on his downcast eyes. It was easy to look at him when his intent gaze was averted. In fact, she believed she could look at him for a long time if it weren't for the possibility that he might look back at her.

"You know what I mean." He folded his arms across his chest, arms that filled out the short sleeves of his white tee shirt in a way that made her think of fifties drag racers and cigarettes.

She dropped her head. "Yes. I do. Thank you. I appreciate your apology, but it really isn't necessary. Most people get defensive in the face of those sorts of questions."

"Well . . ." He ran a hand through his hair and glanced behind him at a car honking its horn. Catching sight of the driver, he raised a palm in greeting.

"You have a good day, Jack," Delaney said, turning away again. Seeing him standing here in the bright sunshine with his hair ruffling in the breeze, she had a hard time remembering why she needed to keep her distance. And that was not good.

"Delaney wait." He strode toward her again. "I also wanted to tell you . . ."

He hesitated, and Delaney found herself trying to read the expression on his face, as if she understood him, as if they had once been close. For some reason he made her feel as if she knew him quite well, when that was so patently false based on everything she'd heard about him.

Then again, she'd heard a few things about herself today that put a decidedly odd spin on which rumors might be real and which were sheer fantasy.

He looked up at her, his eyes sober and intense, as if he might see something in her face that would either encourage or stop him.

"I wanted to tell you that you weren't a mistake. A drunken mistake, like Lisa."

Delaney looked at the ground again. "This isn't necessary."

"Yes it is." His voice was firm. "I never considered that night anything but a godsend. And I know—I know"—he held his palms up in the face of her impending protest—"I promised never to bring that night up again but I thought this needed to be said. I don't think—I never got the chance to tell you that—what I felt about that night."

A thrill shot from Delaney's stomach to her heart, causing it to thunder wildly.

"Morning, Dr. Poole. Hey, Jack!"

Delaney jumped and glanced over to see Maggie striding swiftly down the walk toward the bus stop.

"Hey, Mags," Jack said.

"Good morning, Maggie," Delaney said.

Maggie waved and rushed on. "I'd stop to talk, but I'm late!"

Delaney looked back at Jack. His expression was frustrated.

"I know this isn't the best time or place to be doing this," he continued. "God knows why I am, maybe it's the Percocet." He laughed. "But I was up all night thinking about it. I really think you should know, you deserve to know, that I wanted to call you a dozen times—more than a dozen times—after that night. But I didn't know your last name or have your number, and I didn't know where you lived."

He stopped talking, and Delaney had no idea what to say in response. Her head was empty, but her body was a mass of jittering nerves.

"Okay," she said slowly.

"But I guess it's just as well, since even if I'd found you, I would have found Jim too." He looked at her so intently her breath caught.

"Jim?—oh yes." She coughed and rubbed her forehead as if her mind had been somewhere else. When in fact, she'd forgotten all about Jim as she'd tried to figure out why Jack was explaining this to her. "Well, of course, Jim. Sure."

"Delaney," he said, his expression unguarded. "This probably comes under the heading of 'things we shouldn't talk about,' but I need to know. Did you think of me at all, after that night?"

She stood rooted to the spot. His expression, so vulnerable, brought such a wave of unexpected feelings to her that she found it difficult to breathe. He wasn't asking if she'd thought of him—God knew she could answer that question unequivocally, she'd *had* to think of him. No, he was asking if she had any feelings for him. He was asking if the night meant something to her.

"Jack, I . . ." her voice faltered.

She could ask the same of him. But then, she'd unilaterally answered the question for him. He *hadn't* thought of her, she'd concluded. The night had meant nothing to him, was something he did all the time, she was but one of many female encounters he had with "summer girls" over the years. She had answered these questions and more, and had considered herself right.

But if she was so right, why did he say he'd wanted to call her? And why was he asking her how she felt about that night?

She glanced behind him and saw diners-club Sam exiting Sadie's. He smiled and tipped an imaginary hat in her direction. Delaney wilted. She knew what kind of picture they made, standing in the middle of the green, talking intently at seven-thirty in the morning. She and Jack both had their arms folded across their chests. They were speaking like adversaries, like people with something to hide, like people the diners club would speculate about ad nauseum.

She, Delaney Poole, was becoming Harp Cove's juiciest scuttlebutt, thanks to the notorious Jack Shepard.

She cleared her throat. "Jack, I'm late for work. I can't talk about this now."

His face closed up, and he withdrew as surely as

if she'd slapped him. "Yeah, sure. No problem. I shouldn't have bothered you."

She regretted it instantly.

"No, it's all right," she said, searching for something to say that might make him feel better. But what could she say? What did she *want* to say?

From the corner of her eye she saw Sam walk to the corner. She flicked her glance to him, saw him purchase a newspaper and turn back to the diner. Delaney knew damn well there were papers in the diner. She'd left one herself, as a matter of fact. The man had emerged solely to make a point to her, she was sure. And the point was, her reputation was history.

"Have a good day, Delaney," Jack said, and turned away.

It was on the tip of her tongue to call him back, but she was caught between the real Jack Shepard and the one whose image lived in Sadie's Diner. Which was more important?

But she knew the answer as soon as she asked herself the question.

She watched Jack smack his palm against the hood of his truck, then open the door. He slid onto the seat, slammed the door, and started the engine, almost simultaneously throwing it into gear.

He'd misunderstood her distraction, thought she didn't care about his feelings, but what could she say? That she did care? She could never tell him that. For so many reasons.

Not the least of which was that it was true.

Chapter 13

Jack stood in the middle of the field wearing gym shorts and a sweatshirt with the sleeves cut off. The late August day was hot and his shoulders flexed as he tossed a football to one of the padded and helmeted students in a line in front of him. The students trotted sideways, back and forth, like a bunch of bulked-up crabs defending some unseen habitat.

Despite the fact that school hadn't started yet, football practices had been going on daily for a week. Since the boys were already gathered at the school, Dr. Jacobson and the principal had decided Delaney might as well start their health class now, before they got distracted with their other courses.

A whistle swung from Jack's neck, and a clipboard lay on the ground beside him. Tan, muscled legs carried him along the line of boys as he watched the players' movements and occasionally tossed a football to one who perhaps looked unready.

Delaney stood watching him, acutely aware of her prim skirt and pumps, her hair pulled conservatively back in a clip at her neck, and her briefcase neatly parked at her side. She was like a parakeet getting ready to walk into a pack of puppies. These boys wouldn't listen to her. They needed to hear what she had to say from someone they could relate to, someone they respected. Someone with shoulders broader than theirs and the ability to run the 440 without breaking a heel, not to mention a sweat.

Jack moved tirelessly among the players. Now tossing the ball; now bending down, four fingers on the ground in a classic set position; now jogging backwards to catch an overthrown return pass.

Delaney's eyes caught on the long stretch of outer thigh. *The vastus externus,* she thought idly, attempting to keep it clinical. Finely developed and toned, the muscles moved like well-oiled machinery under skin tanned and gleaming with perspiration.

He was a picture of health, a man in his prime with a textbook body. She tried to think of this in terms of genetics, of the healthy stock he'd passed on to Emily, but her mind kept regressing to the night when her hands had felt the definition of those deltoids and biceps, when her fingers had known the hardness beneath the skin.

She stood watching a few moments longer, then

made her way along the sidewalk by the side of the school. She looked at her watch. Class was to start in ten minutes, so surely they would finish up soon. She pictured them all tumbling into the auxiliary gym as they were, sweat-stained and revved-up from hours of physical exertion. How in the world would she capture their attention? How could she get her message across without crossing any of the school-board-imposed lines?

She frowned, considering again the blunt measures she'd toyed with the previous evening, when drawing up her notes. "Health" class was a thinly disguised veneer for sex education, in her mind. And sex education for teenagers was vitally important. These boys were men, she saw now even more clearly. In every aspect but the mental they were ready for real—i.e. biological—life. Their bodies were strong, their urges stronger. Their spirits were perhaps their most invulnerable assets, and their willpower their most vulnerable. They needed to know what effects their actions could have. And how to contain them.

Jack blew the whistle in five quick blasts, and the lines of players dissolved into boisterous groups of kids bumping and hitting each other, laughing and smacking each other's heads as the helmets came off. Their boyish faces reconfirmed Delaney's resolve. They needed to know what she had to tell them, and the local school board could just blow a gasket later.

Jack looked up and saw her standing on the top

of the hill. She saw his reaction in his body as he stopped briefly, then moved more slowly, picking up balls and tossing them to a scrawny assistant— obviously a boy too young to be on the team—who corralled them into a canvas bag.

"Showers, *now*," he yelled to a group of boys squirting water at each other from white sports bottles.

"Aw, Coach, it's *hot* out," one of them protested.

"Then make it a cold shower," Jack said, tossing a ball onto the head of a boy still squirting at a rival.

The boy put a hand to his head and whirled, ready to drench his attacker, but his posture turned sheepish when he saw Jack.

"Kyle, I'm serious. You guys have health class after this, remember?"

"All right, Coach."

The boys had wandered close enough now for Delaney to see their faces. Some of them had five o'clock shadows, some nothing but peach fuzz. A couple looked to be about twelve, but she knew they must be older if they were on the varsity team. Some looked as if they could be in college. It was a strange age for kids, with everyone maturing at such different rates. But she remembered well those surging hormones and the frenzied pawing at the ends of dates. Yes, they needed a health class.

Jack gave a few more directions, chastised a few more students for moving slowly, then moved toward Delaney.

Her pulse accelerated as he neared. He looked

larger, for some reason, in his athletic clothes, and perspiration dampened his hair.

Talk about hormonal impulses, Delaney thought. Her physical appreciation of him was directly related to that primal instinct to secure such a man for protection, she was sure. Thank goodness she wasn't one to confuse that biological imperative for anything other than what it was.

"You're very good with them," she said, nodding toward the boys. "I'll bet you're their favorite teacher."

"I don't know about that, but they're good kids. They'll be quick," he said, looking down at her with shuttered eyes.

Delaney was immediately reminded that she had hurt his feelings yesterday. The loss of his openness was like a loss of sunlight—and she was decidedly chilly in its absence.

"Actually I'm glad we have a minute," she said. "Is there someplace we can talk before class?"

He considered this request for a minute, then nodded, and said, "Yeah. My office."

They cut through the auxiliary gym, where class would be held, and skirted a blackboard and table, wrestling mats, and a long set of parallel bars.

Jack's office was small, densely furnished and crammed with football equipment ranging from pads to helmets to balls. One wall was consumed by trophies, newspaper clippings and plaques announcing Jack Shepard as *Coach of the Year* for several years running.

She was curious about the clippings and
plaques, wanting to see what Harp Cove's journalists thought of the infamous philanderer, but they
only had a few minutes, and she wanted to clear
the air with him.

He motioned her to a seat across the desk from
him. It was a rolling desk chair with no arms and a
distinctly wobbly back. Delaney perched on the
edge of it.

"First, I want to tell you how much I admire
what you do," she began, as soon as he sat. "Those
kids obviously think the world of you, and I'm sure
that's no coincidence. I know I once gave you the
impression I didn't think much of your job, but I
do. I really do."

He lounged back in his chair, feet outstretched,
and his hands folded across his stomach. He fit the
surroundings as comfortably as a ball in a catcher's
mitt.

"Okay," he said carefully. "Thanks."

"Second," she continued, "I'm sorry about yesterday."

"What are you sorry about?" he asked. "I'm the
one who shouldn't have brought any of that stuff
up. I don't know what I was thinking. Blame it on
the Percocet."

He watched her with guarded eyes, his expression pointedly unconcerned. Delaney felt suddenly
out of her depth. But yesterday he had been open
and she the one distant, so she forged on.

"I'm sorry that I did not give your question the
proper attention it deserved. I'm sorry I was so dis-

tracted. The problem was, I had just come from the diner where that group of meddling old men were, and I felt . . . exposed, I guess."

His brow furrowed. " 'Exposed'?"

She took a deep breath and let her eyes drop to a brass nameplate attached to a triangular base. *Coach Shepard.*

She was so tired of lying. And especially tired of lying to him. So she continued, "Yes, you see I managed—totally inadvertently—to overhear them talking about me in the diner, and I was bothered by it. I don't know where they got their information, but it was absurd. Almost laughable, really, except that the things being said were not just unflattering but untrue."

"You shouldn't let them get to you like that," he said, his expression becoming slightly less disengaged. "They're just a group of bored old men. Let them have their fun. It's nothing to do with you, really."

She looked up at him, intently. "But it *was*. It was all to do with me. And *you*." The moment she said it, she regretted the admission.

A small grin crept onto his face. "Ah, so that's what had you so upset. They were gossiping about you and me."

"Yes, partly. And then you showed up there, on the green, and I knew they were watching." She shrugged and looked at the scattered papers on his desk. "Well, I was just terribly uncomfortable. I couldn't shake the feeling that their eyes were on me. On us."

"So what were they saying?" he asked, his expression still bordering on amused.

"There was some . . . speculation going on about us, about how close we live to each other and what might be going on. But that wasn't all. They were also talking about my father. And my *husband*. Of all the ridiculous things." She laughed incredulously and threw out a hand. "Talking about a man who—"

With a shock, she stopped herself just in time. She was about to say *a man who doesn't even exist*. Adrenaline shot through her.

He leaned forward, elbows on his desk.

"A man who . . . ?" he prompted.

"A man who they've never even met," she finished, blushing, she was sure, to the marrow of her bones.

Jack shook his head and leaned back with a casual smile.

"I don't know why you're so smug, Jack," she said. "What if Kim were to hear what they were saying?"

He frowned. "She probably has. What of it?"

Delaney looked at him, exasperated. "That doesn't worry you? Are you trying to tell me you don't think it makes a difference to her?"

He shrugged, looked confused. "Why would it make a difference to her?"

"Jack," she said, with a knowing look, "I know something's going on between you two."

His mouth dropped open. "Between me and

Kim?" He laughed. "Whatever gave you that idea? Is that something else you got from the gossips?"

She shook her head. What *had* given her that impression? Well, Kim, mostly. Talking about what great friends they were. And then that phone call at Sadie's she'd lied about . . .

"Delaney," Jack said firmly. "Kim and I are friends, and only friends."

"All right, but still," Delaney said, trying to regroup after this seemingly honest bit of information. From the expression on his face to his unequivocal words, Jack gave every indication he was telling the truth. "You should still know people are talking about you. You should be more careful."

He paused a moment, studying her. "The trouble with you is," he said finally, "you care too much about what other people think."

"And the problem with *you* is you don't care enough," she shot back. She hated being treated like an oversensitive female.

He had been about to take a sip of Coke, from a can that had been on his desk for God knew how long, but he stopped mid-lift.

"You don't seem to understand," Delaney continued. "It's dangerous for me to have people I've never even met dissecting my life, and in a way that has very little basis in fact, because reputations, careers, *lives* can be ruined by gossip. You of all people should know that."

At that he placed the Coke back on the desk.

"What do you mean *me*, 'of all people'?"

She stood up, turning away from his eyes to face the trophy shelves. "Surely you're aware of how much the people in Harp Cove know about you. You're the most talked about person in town, as far as I can tell."

"You haven't been here very long. I've just been in the news a lot lately."

She turned back and shook her head at the grin he wore. "I don't know how you can be so unconcerned."

"There's not a lot else I can do," he said, rising and sitting on the edge of his desk, not far from where she stood. "Just like there's not a lot you can do. Not without making it worse. So what did they say about your father? And your husband? Was it really so bad?"

She looked at his knee, where it bent over the edge of the desk. His foot swung lightly. "They said something about my father working for the Secret Service. And one of them said he heard Jim worked for the White House, was some bigwig there, and that's why he wasn't here."

"That's it?"

She nodded. "Yes, but—"

"Hell, that's not bad. Is either of those things true?" he asked.

"No! But then they went on to say they thought Jim would never show up and that you were—that you would—that you and I are probably . . ." She couldn't even repeat it. "Oh, I don't know, it was all so sordid."

Jack stood up and took her gently by the shoulders so she had no choice but to look up into his face.

"How much of *any* of what they said was true?" he asked quietly. "Hm?"

His eyes were kind, reassuring, but the warmth of his hands through her blouse made it difficult for her to breathe.

"None of it."

He gave her a look, as if his case were made.

"But that was the worst part," she insisted. "If even some of it had been true, I might have felt that there was at least a reason for their talk. But as it was, they were just making it up, saying it to be cruel."

"They weren't being cruel; they were being creative. That's what they do. Nobody believes them. In a way"—he laughed, and gave a half shrug, his hands sliding down her arms to take her hands—"if they can talk about you, they like you. It means you're one of them, not too good for them. You've arrived, Delaney Poole."

"But I'm *not* one of them." She pulled her hands away and crossed her arms over her chest. But she didn't move away from him. She stood staring at his chest, unable to make herself move. Despite herself, she wanted him to touch her again. And she didn't know how she could want that when she couldn't stand the thought of her name being dragged through the mud with his.

"I don't want to be talked about that way," she said finally. "I want respect. And I want my privacy."

"Then you'd better move back to D.C. because as long as you're in this town—or any small town—there's going to be talk." Jack sat back down on the edge of the desk.

They were both silent while Delaney sought to figure out her own chaotic feelings. She wanted him to touch her, and yet she was afraid of what would happen if he did. She wanted to be able to trust him, but something inside her was sure she should not. She wanted the things she'd heard about him to be untrue, but if they were, would she then have to tell him the truth?

She shuddered at the thought.

"The thing you have to remember," he continued after a moment, "is that gossip's only destructive if it's taken seriously. Even if it's true, it's not so bad. Small towns may seem scandalized by some things, but they're probably a lot less shocked than your neighbors in suburban D.C. would be by similar stories. These guys have seen and heard it all, and they relish the telling. That's all."

"That's *not* all, Jack." She looked up at him, willing him to understand. Surely if he understood he'd stop whatever it was he was doing to be "in the news" so much lately. "Just because you don't take them seriously doesn't mean other people don't. I've heard more people talking about you than just the diners club. And they all say basically the same things. When you hear that much talk, you start to believe it."

Jack folded his arms across his chest and tilted his head. "People believe what they want to believe, Delaney." He let that statement stand for a moment before adding, "And you obviously want to believe bad things about me. What I can't figure out is why."

"That's not true," she protested, probably too quickly. "I don't want to believe bad things about you. But every time I turn around I hear something new. So when I hear my name linked with yours forgive me if I become alarmed."

He studied her anew, as if finally understanding the source of her distress. "So, when I talked to you on the green yesterday you were distracted because you were *embarrassed* to be seen with me. Is that it?" His eyes narrowed, his expression angry.

She couldn't speak.

"You're not worried about your dad being accused of working for the Secret Service," he continued. "It's not a bad thing if people think Jim works for the White House. No, you heard a couple sentences containing your name and mine, and *that* scared the shit out of you."

She had difficulty taking a full breath. "Is it so hard to believe I wouldn't want people speculating about us? You should have heard the things they were insinuating."

"Did any of it come close to the truth, Delaney?"

She was about to issue a heated denial—she'd done all she could to avoid Jack since she'd moved to Harp Cove, and no one could say otherwise—when the meaning of his words penetrated. He meant did they know about that night over a year ago. Did they say anything about Delaney Poole and Jack Shepard taking off from a bar to have sex on the beach.

Her mouth went dry and her palms wet. Her eyes shot to his. "None of it had anything to do with truth," she said lowly.

His eyes were hard. "Then be glad. Be glad they're making stuff up because if the truth ever did come out, no one would believe that either."

He stood up, and she backed up a step.

"But don't worry, Delaney," he said quietly. His eyes were laughing at her, and not in a nice way. "Your *secret* is safe with me." He chucked her lightly under the chin.

She grabbed his hand and lowered it from her face, glaring at him. "How *dare* you bring that up again."

"How dare you so conveniently forget it," he said in a tone that showed he had lost patience with her. "You can make all the disparaging comments about me you want, Delaney, you can believe every last derogatory word you hear, but we both know you're not as lily white as you like to pretend."

"And we both know—along with the entire town of Harp Cove—that your reputation is not unfounded."

For a second they stood there, inches apart, Delaney's hand holding Jack's at her side. The electricity between them was incredible, and Delaney found it impossible to tear her eyes from his.

The skin-to-skin contact with his hand sent a physical yearning through her body that was nearly uncontrollable. Adrenaline, anger, and desire all warred within her to produce a feeling just like the one she'd had that night at the Hornet's Nest—times ten. Because this time it had been well over a year since anyone had touched her. And this time she knew just how good it would feel if Jack did the touching.

His look was unwavering, but she could not tell if he was angry. He was close, so close, she couldn't think, and his skin was hot in her hand. She wished he'd say something.

Instead, he took a slow step closer until his body was nearly touching hers and her back was against the shelves. He raised his other hand and traced the curve of her cheek with one finger.

"My reputation has nothing to do with me," he said softly. "Or you."

Every nerve in Delaney's body came alive. Her eyes scanned his face, his brows, his stubbled cheek, his finely shaped mouth, and lingered on his lips. God help her, she wanted him to kiss her. She wanted to feel his hands on her so badly she could have leaned right into him. At the same time she desperately wanted to move away.

She just couldn't.

He moved forward and touched her mouth with his, softly, so gently he might have been kissing her good night. His hand cupped the back of her head and their hands, once gripping each other in anger, held to each other palm to palm.

His tongue traced her lips, and she allowed herself to open to the touch. His head tilted, and the kiss deepened. Delaney's anger vanished like a puff of smoke.

Her hand rose and grabbed the front of his shirt, the other still gripping his tightly. His tongue entered her mouth, and his hand moved down her back, pulling her body hard against his. She wanted to press herself into him and felt him pressing into her. Her arm encircled his neck as they kissed hungrily, violently, passionately.

At the same moment someone knocked on the door.

Reality avalanched upon her. Delaney turned her head, one hand pushing weakly against his chest. Her cheeks and chin burned from his beard. Her breath came in near gasps.

Jack sighed and stood stock-still for a second, his cheek against her hair. Then he stepped back and their hands relinquished each other.

Delaney's fingers stretched taut, and she pressed the palm to the side of her skirt. Every nerve trembled. What was she *doing*?

"What?" he barked to whoever was on the other side of the door.

"We're all in the gym, Coach," a boyish voice called.

Jack's eyes met hers, dark and unreadable. Hers were hot with guilt, she was sure. And desire.

"We'll be right there," he said, watching her.

The ensuing silence was physical, pressing on her chest like a fist. They looked at each other a long moment.

"That can't happen again," Delaney said finally, her voice an octave lower than usual.

She thought she saw his eyelids flinch at the words.

"I'm sorry," he said flatly.

But it wasn't clear whether he meant he was sorry for what just happened or sorry that it could never happen again.

Or sorry that it had been interrupted.

He moved back around the desk and sat down, one elbow on the desk, his hand covering his mouth. He looked ... disconcerted, Delaney thought.

"This is just the sort of thing I'm going to discuss today," Delaney said. Her voice quavered slightly. "With the boys. These purely sexual urges and how to resist them."

"Purely sexual urges," he repeated, then laughed without humor.

She cleared her throat. "That's right."

"You're well qualified."

She couldn't even laugh at the irony. She bent to retrieve her briefcase.

"You know you never answered my question, Delaney."

She straightened and looked over at him, her spine ramrod straight. "What question was that?"

"From yesterday. About whether you ever thought of me, after that night."

He looked so open, sitting at his desk. So real and warm and vulnerable—though that was absurd, Jack was nothing if not confident—that she couldn't help but think about what the gossips had said about her, about how none of it was true, not even the slightest basic fact. Could it be that the gossips just made things up as they pleased all the time? Could Jack really be as innocent as he claimed?

She took a long silent minute zipping up her gaping briefcase.

"I just thought," he added, "when you apologized earlier, I just thought maybe you were going to answer it now."

She paused, unable to come to a conclusion. If the gossip was false, and Jack was as he seemed at this moment . . . if she could not cling to his philandering as the reason to keep Emily from him, what would she do? Would she have to make the decision to share her with him?

The thought stopped her. She was afraid of sharing Emily. She was using Jack's reputation to keep him from his daughter.

She wasn't keeping the truth from Jack to protect Emily at all.

She was doing it to protect herself.

Shame scalded her, and she didn't know what to do about it. The revelation was painful in its intensity.

"Maybe," she said slowly, thinking that at this moment she owed him some truth, at least until she could figure out what ultimately had to be done, "maybe you can take what happened here today as your answer, Jack."

He looked pensive. She slung her bag over her shoulder and moved toward the door.

"Delaney?"

She stopped.

"You should pay less attention to the gossips. All right?"

She dropped her head, staring at the scratched chrome doorknob. "And you should pay more."

She heard him laugh.

"It's been going on so long now I'm used to it," he said. "And it hasn't hurt me yet."

She turned then, a thousand replies in her head, not one of which she could utter.

Oh but it has, she thought. *It already has hurt you, Jack. It's kept you from your child.* The truth of the thought cut straight through her chest.

But it wouldn't forever, she thought grimly. It couldn't. Not if she were to do the right thing.

Their eyes locked for a moment more, before she pulled open the door, and said, "I'll see you in there."

Jack pulled into the end parking space at the one tiny strip mall Harp Cove boasted, though calling it a "mall" of any sort stretched the bounds of credibility.

The Tuckahoe Shopping Center contained all of three stores: a laundromat, a bank, and a card/stationery store that Jack frequently speculated would soon go out of business. He'd been speculating that, however, for several years now, and nothing had changed, including the dismal number of cars in the parking lot whenever he passed by.

He'd often wondered what sort of stuff the store could carry to keep it alive, other than cards you could get at the grocery or drugstore, and had his answer partially answered when his wallet disintegrated in his hands in front of Kim at lunch.

"Jesus, Jack, did you get that for your high-school graduation or something?" Kim asked, as he held the two separated halves in his hands.

"I don't remember," he said, trying to catch the bank receipts, business cards, and folded bits of paper that dripped from the ruined pockets to the floor.

"Obviously," Kim snickered, chewing on a fry, "it's been a while since you bought one."

"I'm not sure I even bought this one. Where can you buy a wallet in this town?"

"The Paper Mill, on Route 1."

"The Paper Mill? That card store near the laundromat? Who goes in there?"

Kim arched a brow. "I do, and you will too. They've got wallets there."

So here he was. He entered the store and nearly gagged on the perfumey smell of the place, which a large rack of candles near the front seemed to be responsible for.

"Hi," a voice from behind the register said. "I'm Ashley. Can I help you?"

Jack glanced over to see a redheaded girl painting her fingernails. She barely looked at him.

Recognizing her as one of Lisa Jacobson's friends, he ducked into an aisle and called, "No thanks. Just looking."

He followed the long narrow aisle crammed with cards to an endcap, where he found two identical wallets.

Apparently they were low on stock right now.

He picked up a wallet and leafed through it, becoming aware after a second that the salesgirl had moved and was rearranging a shelf not six feet away from him.

He turned his back to her and flipped through the other wallet, confirming that it was the same as the first. Why were they so big? Who carried this many pictures? he wondered, letting an accordion of plastic drop nearly to his knees.

He glanced back over to see if the salesgirl was still nearby and saw her attempting to look busy by a shelf of stationary, as if she thought he might be a shoplifter and needed to keep an eye on him. Surely she was younger than Lisa. She looked as if she were about fifteen years old, he thought, wondering for the thousandth time what he'd been thinking that night he'd taken Lisa home from the Hornet's Nest.

How much trouble had come from that, he thought, remembering again the mortifying night she'd shown up at the Hornet's Nest in her cheerleading outfit. Not to mention the morning she'd brought someone else's tee shirt to him as if he might possibly have left it—or anything at all—at her house. And as if he could conceivably be caught dead in a Backstreet Boys tee shirt. She'd just wanted an excuse to come by and hadn't even cared that he'd known immediately the shirt wasn't his.

He sighed, looking at the wallet and remembering how Delaney had looked standing up in front of his team that day she'd come to teach the health class. She was all elegance and composure as she'd silenced the team and launched into the lecture with the words, "It *can* happen the first time, there's no such thing as blue balls, and the good girls really don't."

He smiled thinking about it and was brought up short by a soft hand on his arm.

"Can I help you find something?" The salesgirl looked at him closely, as if trying to place who he was.

Jack slapped shut the wallet he was looking at and said quickly, before she could recognize him, "I'll take this one and be on my way."

She looked momentarily taken aback. "Okay." She bounced her hair over her shoulder as she turned and led him back to the cash register.

She rang up the sale, took the wad of cash he pulled from his pocket and put the wallet into a bag. Then she snapped the receipt tape off the register and shoved it into the bag.

"Thanks a lot," she said, still looking at him curiously. "Have a great night."

"Thanks," he murmured and left the store.

He was sitting in the car in the blue-green light

of the laundromat, wondering what he'd purchased in his haste to get out of the store, when he spotted the picture encased in the plastic film of the wallet's photo slot.

He fumbled for the overhead light in the truck and yanked the model's photo from the liner.

"Well, I'll be damned," he murmured.

In his hands was a picture of a man—a model included to hint to the unusually dense that here was where you put your pictures—who was the spitting image of old Jim-Joe Poole. Jack knew it was him because he had spent quite some time a few days earlier studying the framed photo Delaney had recently put up on the mantelpiece in her living room. Jack's thought at the time was that the man was too pretty and the picture too studiously casual to be real. A kind of glamour shot for men.

On the other hand, he'd considered, maybe they had that sort of thing down there in Washington, D.C. God knew what yuppies liked to spend their money on these days, and he was certain Jim-Joe Poole, if he existed, was a yuppie.

But now, here he was looking into those same eyes, at that same sandy hair and clean-cut, all-American face, smiling the exact same triangular smile as he had on Delaney's mantel—all overlaid with the words *Exceptional Value!*

Chapter 14

Jack drove slowly, way too slowly, down Route 1 from the shopping center toward town. He was onto something big, he knew it. Delaney said her husband was a lawyer, could he also be a *model*?

Jack laughed out loud at the thought. Not so much because it was funny, but because it was ludicrous. Delaney wasn't the type to marry a model. She wasn't the type to be in a place where she might even *meet* a model. But she was definitely the type to see herself with a lawyer, and Jack felt certain that if she were going to create a life to look the way she thought it should, she'd create a lawyer for a husband. Someone with multiple Ivy League degrees, a stable income, and ambition written all over him.

She wouldn't, for example, draw up a small-town high-school gym teacher dogged by rumors of a dubious character.

He'd had his doubts all along that Delaney's sudden husband really existed, but this almost cinched it. Almost, he thought, because the one incongruous thing in all of this was the fact that Delaney just didn't seem like the lying sort. Not that she'd done such a great job of it so far. "Jim-Joe" being the best evidence of that.

Still, it would be such a large lie. And such an illogical one. Why go through all that just to hide the fact that you're a single mother? Just say you're a single mother and be done with it. Let people think what they would.

But, he reminded himself, this was Delaney Poole. The Delaney Poole who became agitated over the ramblings of a few old men in a diner. Who warned him to be careful about what the gossips said, as if he had any control whatsoever over what they chose to make up.

He crept down Route 1, which was blessedly empty, and decided to take the turn toward town. He didn't feel like going home yet. He wanted to know exactly what he'd say to Delaney the next time he saw her. He also wanted to find some more wallets to see if he could find more pictures of Jim-Joe. So he'd stop at the five-and-dime to pick up some laundry detergent, look for a wallet, and maybe hit Sadie's for a cup of decaf afterward.

He parked by the green, remembering Delaney's distraction that day he'd foolishly tried to tell her how he felt. Well, maybe it wasn't foolish, even though he was sure it was the painkillers that had made him feel he could ask her how she felt about him. After all, she had kissed him in his office. No matter what spin she put on it, or what she may be telling herself now about it, she had *responded*.

He may not have a Juris Doctor from Harvard, but he knew when a woman wanted seducing. And Delaney Poole had wanted that kiss. Of that much he was certain.

The five-and-dime was incongruously bright after the drive in the dim cab of his truck, and he found himself nearly squinting under the glare of the fluorescents.

"Hey, Jack," Mitzy Webster said with a short wave from behind the lone cash register. She leaned back against the counter cleaning her fingernails with an orange stick, her gray hair lumped in curler-shaped rolls and her ample torso covered in a faded red apron.

"Mitzy, you're a bright sight on this dark night," he said with an automatic smile.

"Why, thank you, Coach." Mitzy laughed as he kept walking.

"Hey, you guys carry wallets here?" he asked, stopping.

She shook her head. "Go to The Paper Mill. Only place I know's got 'em."

He nodded and continued walking. "Thanks."

He strolled down the detergent aisle and picked up a bottle of Tide. Then, on a whim, he walked to the back of the store where he knew the dusty "Hang In There" cat posters and eighty-nine-cent watercolor sets resided.

Frames were what he was looking for as he rounded one aisle of craft supplies and plastic brushes to another full of shrink-wrapped canvases and balsa-wood embroidery hoops.

He was about to give up when he rounded the last aisle. There he was rewarded by a shelf of frames spanning the entire wall with Jim-Joe Poole's face smiling out at him. *Three for $5!* a blue banner atop the shelf proclaimed.

He stood there, stunned. Brass and chrome, glass and simulated wood grain, from 3×5 to 8×10, all held Jim-Joe beaming at the public from an autumn-leafy scene, a similarly expressioned golden retriever by his side.

This time, instead of *Exceptional Value!* printed across the picture, the words *Documents! Photographs! Diplomas!* were Jim-Joe's message.

Jack let out a slow breath and moved toward the shelf.

He took one of the frames and studied the face. "This shot would have looked nice on your mantel," he imagined telling Delaney as he handed her the frame. "Or maybe the bedroom, since it's so informal. Would this man even *know* the way to your bedroom?"

What would she say? What *could* she say? And should he tip his hand that he knew she was lying, or should he look for more proof?

He supposed it was *possible* her husband was a model . . .

He frowned as he flipped through some 5×7s on a lower shelf and found another version, slightly different, but still featuring Delaney's husband, sans dog. In addition to his law degree, Jim-Joe apparently had an exclusive contract with Bradley Frames.

He should be careful, Jack decided. He should be sure. He should take a couple of these home and compare them to the pictures of Jim-Joe in Delaney's house before he said anything to her.

Down the aisle was a cart with some torn plastic wrap and cardboard in the bottom of it. Obviously a cart a clerk was using to stock the shelves. He took it, threw the trash on the floor and put the Tide and several frames in the basket.

His heart beat rapidly in his chest, as if he'd broken into someone's house and was hoping to take something before they came home. But *he* wasn't the one doing anything wrong. He was just trying to solve a mystery, and in the process possibly release Delaney from whatever fear had possessed her to concoct such a story.

He made his way down the line of frames, looking for more pictures, found a couple 3×5s and tossed them into the basket before making the turn to head for the register.

There, as he rounded the corner, was Delaney Poole. Shopping.

Delaney stopped dead in her tracks when she saw him. Emily lay in her car seat in the basket of the shopping cart, looking, Delaney had just been thinking, a lot like Jack.

Since that day in his office she had studiously avoided him, alternately hoping the whole thing would blow over and chastising herself for not admitting to herself that she owed him the truth. But still, she was kicking herself over how she'd allowed events to transpire that day.

Why oh why had she said that, she'd asked herself more than once, about the kiss being his answer as to whether or not she'd thought of him since that night on the beach? That made it sound as if she'd thought about him *romantically. Physically. Longingly*.

Which she hadn't. Not really. Well, okay, not outside of some very private, unrealistic, and purely fanciful, loneliness-induced fantasies.

Most of the time she'd thought of him only in terms of Emily, which these days caused her to break out in a cold sweat, feeling as she did that perhaps a change of attitude toward Jack Shepard was at hand.

But now, here he was. And he was looking at her strangely.

"Uh, hi," she said. Emily squealed happily, responding to the sound of her voice.

For a second Delaney imagined blurting out that Emily was his daughter right there in the middle of Murphy's five-and-dime. What a memorable moment that would be. But aside from the inappropriate setting, she wasn't ready. She needed more time. To plan. To decide. To be sure.

"Hi," he said. He seemed to be studying her, his eyes intent, his brows drawn, his expression . . . confused. Or something.

"Doing some shopping?" She motioned toward his cart with one hand. Her eyes dropped to the contents of the shopping basket. Laundry detergent and frames. Why did he have so many frames?

"Yeah." He too looked down at his items, then back up at her with that same odd expression.

She nodded. "That's good. I'm, ah, shopping for—"

She stopped, flushing red. She'd been shopping for a bulletin board and some duct tape but had been sidetracked by a pair of men's shoes that could almost pass for real leather wing tips if one didn't look too closely. They sat, even now, in the basket next to Emily's car seat, box-free and tagged with a bright orange *Clearance* sticker. Emily's pacifier had dropped into the well of one.

Jack looked in her basket too. "Shoes?" he supplied.

"Well, I was looking for a bulletin board and some duct tape because one of the legs on Emily's crib is loose." She frowned down at the ugly wing tips. "The shoes were an unexpected bonus."

"They don't look like your style."

She laughed. "No . . . no, they're for Jim, of course."

She swallowed, looking at the homely things. They were supposed to be mere shadowy presences in the front-hall closet, a subtle reminder in case Jack ever happened to open that door.

Jack's gaze rested on them a moment. "For some reason I had Jim pegged as more of a Cole Haan man, what with the Burberry's raincoat on your coatrack and all."

"Well, sure. He likes quality. It's not like he usually gets his shoes at the five-and-dime. Never, actually. I just saw these and thought, well, if he ever came up and forgot his shoes or something. He wouldn't have to worry about what happened to these or anything."

"*If* he ever came up . . . ?" Jack repeated.

"No, *if* he ever forgot his shoes," she said, exasperated. Emily blew a raspberry, her hands rising and falling with the sound.

At least if she someday, somehow told Jack the truth she'd be rid of the wretched Jim, who aside from not existing frequently made no sense.

"So, you doing some framing?" she asked. "Looks like you're doing half the town there."

"No, no," he looked thoughtfully at the frames, "they just caught my eye." After a second, he added, "In fact, why don't you come take a look at them with me. You might want to get a couple yourself."

"Actually I just bought frames," she said, wondering how on earth to get out of this inane conversation and out the door. The more she looked at him—at the way his lips curved with his words, the way his hands looked on the cart, the way his chest seemed so comfortingly broad in his tee shirt—the more she remembered the kiss. And on at least one very basic level the more she remembered the kiss, the more she wanted another.

"I think these'll interest you anyway." He tilted his head toward the aisle behind him. "They're right here."

"No, really. I've got to go. I've got to put Emily to bed."

Jack looked into the basket at Emily. "She looks pretty happy to be here, another minute won't hurt. Come on."

On cue, Emily beamed up at him and let fly another delighted trill.

He smiled, grazed her cheek with a finger, then turned his basket around and headed back from where he'd come. Frustrated, Delaney followed. She couldn't just walk away, after all but, goodness, he could be stubborn. Was he trying to get her into a secluded aisle so he could try to kiss her again? Is that what he wanted?

The idea shot a spasm of outrage and desire through her limbs.

"Jack, I don't know what you're thinking, but I want you to know," she began strenuously, rounding the corner in a fit of righteous indignation, ready to tell him she had no intention of letting him have his way with her whenever he damn well felt like it, when her gaze hit a wall full of smiling Jim Pooles.

She nearly staggered from the shock. Instead, she inhaled so quickly she choked on it. A coughing fit ensued, so dire her eyes watered.

"You all right?" Jack asked, touching her back.

She nodded, coughing.

"Want some water?" He patted her between the

shoulder blades, just hard enough for Delaney's pulse to accelerate at the contact.

"No, I'm—all right," she choked out, moving away from his hand as she gained control.

They both looked up at the wall.

A carpet of Jims—averagely handsome and without much of a future in modeling, *she'd thought*—spread from one end of the aisle to the other. She leaned heavily on the handle of the shopping cart, her eyes streaming and her heart frantic in her chest.

"So, you were saying. You wanted me to know?" Jack prompted from beside her.

Delaney's mind was blank as she stared at the Jim mosaic before her. She had no explanation. The only one—the truth—seemed so obvious she could not imagine how to contradict it. How could he not know now that she'd lied? About everything. And from there it would be one simple guess as to the reason why.

She wondered if people who spontaneously combusted did so for reasons just such as this one.

"By the way," Jack added mildly, "you said your husband was a lawyer, right? He ever do any modeling?"

Delaney took a deep breath—necessary since she'd stopped breathing the moment she'd stopped coughing—and turned toward him.

"I know this is going to sound strange," she said in a remarkably dead voice, "but that's not my husband."

Emily made a low gurgling sound, the kind Delaney might make if she were sitting in a tub propelling a toy speedboat through the water.

Jack's eyes rested on Delaney's face, his expression supremely calm. "I never thought it was."

What did *that* mean?

"It's my husband's brother. His twin, actually. He's a model." She looked back up at the wall, thinking that this was what Sybill would do. It was amazing, the more audacious the lies, the easier they seemed to come. Maybe the soaps were onto something. "They're a very good-looking family."

Jack folded his arms across his chest. "Your husband's brother."

She nodded.

Emily's motorboat accelerated.

"His *twin* brother," Jack clarified.

She nodded again. Emily's legs kicked frantically.

"And he's a model."

She nodded once more.

Emily's hands rose above her head and she squealed. *Touchdown!*

"Delaney," Jack said, his tone both doubtful and cajoling.

"It's a remarkable likeness, isn't it? Between the two of them?" Her hands squeezed the handle of the shopping cart. She would worry Jack might notice her knuckles turning white, but he was too busy studying her face. "It's caused quite a bit of confusion over the years. Not the least of which when Jim and I were dating."

"What's his name?" Jack asked.

She looked at him. "Hm?"

"The brother. What's his name?"

Documents! Photographs! Diplomas! the frames promised as her gaze drifted back to the wall. She thought of her high-school diploma, which made her think of graduation, which made her think of the prom after which she'd gone to a party, gotten drunk for the first time on Southern Comfort and threw up on her date, Carl Wilkerson.

"Carl," she said. "His brother's name is Carl."

"Carl," he repeated.

She nodded.

"Carl Poole?" One eyebrow lifted.

Her expression froze but she continued nodding like a half-wit. Carl Poole . . . car pool . . . good Lord.

After a second she let her eyes drift toward his. She had to tell him the truth, she thought. And soon. Because the lies were killing her.

"That's right," she said wearily. "And now I really do have to go. Enjoy your frames, Jack."

"I want to kill off Jim," Delaney told Michael.

"Kill him off? What for? I was just beginning to like him."

"He's in the way."

"Of *what*?"

Delaney sighed and lay back on her bed. A crack in the plaster ceiling above her looked like a sketch of Jack Nicolson's profile. She was surrounded by Jacks.

"I'm thinking . . ." she hesitated, then resumed, "I'm thinking I might have to come clean, Michael."

Silence gripped the line.

Delaney shifted the receiver. "Hello?"

"I'm still here. I just don't think I heard you right. 'Come clean'? You mean you're going to tell him the truth?"

Delaney took a deep breath. "I think . . . yes, I think that's exactly what I mean." She squished up her face, unable to maintain the decisive tone. "Maybe. What do you think?"

"I, ah . . ." Water ran in the background. "I think that's great," Michael said. A muffled sound came through the receiver. "Sorry," he said after a second, "I had to splash cold water on my face. For a second I thought I might faint from the shock."

"Very funny," Delaney said.

"Are you *sure* you want to tell him?"

"Why? Don't you think I should?"

"It's not that. It's just . . . well, what are you hoping for? Has he suddenly turned into father material? Are you thinking he'll want to jump into Emily's life and be a dad?"

"I don't know. I just don't know how I can justify *not* telling him anymore. I told you about the gossips, what they said about me. What if everything they said about him is just as false?"

"Well, you didn't just hear stuff from those old coots in the diner, right? What about that cleaning woman? Margie?"

•

Delaney ran a hand through her hair, spreading it out on the pillow behind her. "Maggie. Yeah, but everything she said was always said so affectionately. That was one thing I never got, how she could say he was such a bad boy and still seem to like him so much."

"I imagine it's easier if you're not the mother of the rake's child."

"The rake." Delaney chuckled. "Makes him sound positively dashing."

"Well, honey, from the way you've described him I'm thinking that's what he is. Are you sure you want to tell him because of Emily? Or could there be some other, oh, more personal, reason?"

Delaney frowned. "What are you saying?"

He inhaled. "I don't know. It just sounds like, well, after he kissed you and all ... and you've been alone a while ..."

She sat up. "Wait a minute. Are you saying you think I want to tell him because he kissed me? Is that what you're saying?"

"I'm just saying it seems like things have changed. Since the kiss."

"That's ridiculous."

"Hey, don't blame me. I just call 'em like I see 'em."

"Well stop it."

He chuckled.

"Besides, I haven't definitely decided to tell him. There are still a whole lot of unanswered questions about him. Important questions." She would have called one up as an example but she couldn't think of one just then. "Killing off Jim will make things a heck of a lot easier. There'll be that much less of a chance of me making a mistake, for example, and my options will still be open."

"Right."

"Really."

"*Okay!*"

She crossed one arm over her chest and rested her phone elbow on it. "So, all right, smartypants, how do you think I should do it? Kill off Jim, that is."

"Smarty pants?"

"Well?"

Michael sighed. "So you're dead set on this? So to speak . . ."

"Why are you sounding so negative? Seems to me you were the one who wanted me to tell the truth from the beginning."

"Well, yeah. But . . . all right, to be perfectly honest, I was kind of getting into it. The twin thing was classic. A brilliant ad lib. I wanted to see where you went with it."

"Where I *went* with it? Jeez, Michael, it's not like I'm scripting this. I'm not *Destiny's Children*, for God's sake. Though frankly I think I could be."

Michael laughed. "I'll say. I mean, you've got the List, right? And the imagination. And tell me you haven't made notes on at least a couple of conversations you planned to have with Jack."

"The only note I've made is to avoid *having* conversations with Jack."

"Well, you could do worse than *Destiny's Children*, you know. Like, for example, Sybill just married Ruark, you know that, right? And suddenly she's showing like she's eight months pregnant."

"Oh, to have a soap-opera pregnancy," she sighed. "Over in two months."

"No kidding. So Drake corners her and asks what the deal is. Whose kid is it. And she tells him it's Ruark's, of course, but he doesn't believe it. He says he'll be watching, and if that baby doesn't have blue eyes, he's going to *know*. Because they both have blue eyes, right? Ruark and Sybill. And you can't have a brown-eyed kid if you've both got blue eyes."

"I went to four years of medical school, Michael, I know that."

"But *Drake's* got *brown* eyes. So, you know, if the baby ends up with brown eyes, there's his proof."

Delaney started to feel a little queasy.

"What color eyes does Jack have?" Michael asked.

She turned her head and looked at Magazine Jim and his identical twin brother, Carl, on her bedside table. Magazine Jim was black-and-white, and the picture was a little too distant to reveal eye color, something she'd taken into account when she'd cut him out.

"Brown. Jack's eyes are brown, like Emily's," she answered. Her gaze shifted to Jim's twin. "Oh my God."

Full-color identical-twin Carl was another story. His eyes—smiling with buoyant insincerity—were blue. Light, robin's-egg blue. Just like hers.

And not at all like Emily's.

Chapter 15

"I was talking to Carl the other day." Delaney leaned against the doorframe to Emily's bedroom while Jack lay on the floor under the crib with two metal brackets and a drill. Emily was asleep in a bassinet in the kitchen. "You know, Jim's twin brother."

Sybill had nothing on Delaney.

Jack crooked his neck to look at her from under the crib, his eyes amused. "Uh-huh."

"And I was asking him about those frame pictures. You know, if he had to pose for them specifically or if the frame company just bought portfolio pictures, kind of like clip art. And he said it was the funniest thing, they made him wear contacts."

"Contacts?" He stuck two screws in his mouth and fitted a bracket against one crib leg.

Jack had shown up unexpectedly that evening

after she'd gotten home from work to fix Emily's crib. Delaney barely remembered mentioning the loose leg to Jack—had apparently done so during the awful five-and-dime episode—but she was glad he'd come. It gave her a chance to head off any suspicions he might have had about Emily's eye color after seeing Jim's "twin." That was why she'd been relieved to see him, she told herself. Because she could stall a bit longer, think a little more about killing off Jim.

Looking at his capable hands now on the baby's crib gave Delaney an unexpectedly warm feeling. There really was something to having a man around. They could fix things. Well, *she* could fix things, she amended in a spurt of compulsive feminism, but it was so much easier to have someone else do it. A man, for instance.

"Yes, they made him wear contacts," she continued. "*Blue* contacts. For some reason they liked the way he looked, but not with brown eyes. Because you know he's got brown eyes just like Jim's. And just like Emily's, come to think of it." She laughed lightly.

"Uh-huh." Jack switched the drill from his right hand to his left, working for some angle he couldn't quite make with the bulky tool.

"Isn't that funny, that they're so particular? Who would think the color of his eyes would make such a difference? I mean, would people not buy a frame with a picture of a brown-eyed guy in it?"

He took the screws from his mouth and shifted

his body sideways. "Hard to believe." He put the screws on the floor next to his head.

Delaney watched his hips as he moved. She liked looking at where his tee shirt tucked into his jeans, at the flat stomach below the muscled vee of his chest. The tendons in his arm stood out as he tried to position the drill to screw on the bracket.

"Do you want me to hold that?" Delaney asked, bending over to look at him under the crib.

"Yeah, would you mind?" He put the screws back between his lips.

She knelt next to him on the floor and took hold of the bracket and leg of the crib.

He reached up and moved her fingers to a higher spot. The touch made her blush for some absurd reason.

Taking a screw from his mouth, he held up the drill again, and this time she watched the muscles in his neck as he lifted the tool.

"Damn," he muttered around the second screw. "I think I'm going to have to use a screwdriver. Can you hold that for just a second? I've got to run over to the house."

"Sure." She nodded, watching him scoot out from beneath the bed. "But I've got a screwdriver. In the drawer in the kitchen."

"Phillips head?"

"Both." She smiled. The Capable Woman.

"Great, I'll be right back."

Jack trotted down the stairs, Delaney's smile fresh in his mind. There was something about her face when she smiled, even when she just flashed that quick, fleeting smile. It always reached her eyes, crinkling them in such a way that made him feel as if he'd done something delightful. Maybe it had something to do with being Irish.

He turned into the kitchen and pulled open the top drawer at the edge of the counter. Sure enough, it was the Everything Drawer. He used to work on houses during summers when he was in college, and every kitchen inevitably had a drawer where Everything went. Paper clips, rubber bands, scissors, corks, twist ties, newspaper clippings, coupons. You name it, it ended up in that drawer.

Including—he saw, pulling out a sheet of notepaper filled with a column of writing—a list of what appeared to be personal attributes. He studied the piece of paper, starting with the first word on the list: *Jim*, underlined several times.

His eyes flew down the page. *Jim* was followed by: Lawyer, Married five years, Emily—four months, b. March 10 . . .

A thunk sounded from above.

Handsome, he read on. Tall, 6'2" . . .

Rapid footsteps sounded on the stairs.

"Jack!" Delaney called.

Jack threw the paper back in the drawer, closed it, and opened the one next to it. Serving spoons, spatulas, cheese grater, he noted with relief. He began pawing through the implements, making as much noise as possible.

Delaney rounded the corner with one hand on

the jamb, nearly skidding to a halt beside him. Her eyes were unnaturally wide and her lips were parted breathlessly.

"Did you find it?" she asked, voice tinged with panic.

Inexplicably, he felt nearly as agitated as she looked. What he'd found was—well it was *proof*. Wasn't it? Intractable, unexplainable, raw, shocking truth that she had fabricated her husband. Why else would you need to keep track of such things as what he looked like, or how long you'd been married?

How he could be shocked after suspecting for so long he wasn't sure, but he was.

"No, I think I'm in the wrong drawer," he said, pushing the utensil drawer shut with a hand that shook with astonishment.

"It's in this one," she said, indicating the one he'd just been looking in. "Did you look in this one?" Her eyes were pinned on him as if his answer meant the difference between life and death.

"No," he said quietly, shaking his head.

He wanted to soothe the frenzied look from her face, take her in his arms and ask her to tell him the whole story. What was it that made her go to such lengths to appear married? What sort of insecurity would prompt a person to invent a husband? Certainly it was an insecurity that Delaney Poole—beautiful, intelligent, successful Delaney Poole—shouldn't have.

She wilted with his answer. "Really?" she asked,

relief that might as well have been a neon sign in her eyes.

He shook his head.

She edged around so that she could turn her back to him and open the drawer, but he made it easy on her and moved toward the front door.

"You know what?" he said, feeling the sudden need for some air. "I think I'll just go get mine. It's, you know, big, industrial strength. A little household one probably wouldn't do the trick."

"Oh, okay," she said. Eagerly, he thought.

"Yeah, I'll just be a minute."

She followed him into the front hall and he opened the door.

Rain pelted down in sheets. When had it started raining? And why hadn't he noticed?

He glanced at the coat rack where Jim's Burberry raincoat had hung for the last several weeks.

"Mind if I borrow that?" He gestured toward the coat.

"No. Sure," she said, pulling the thing off the rack and handing it to him. She couldn't be rid of him fast enough.

Married five years . . . he thought, *Emily—b. March 10* . . .

Why would she have to remind herself of her daughter's birthdate? The thought crossed his mind as he slid his arm into the sleeve of the coat—and his hand popped so far out the other end many inches of bare skin spanned the space between wrist and sleeve.

Jack looked at Delaney, *Tall, 6'2"* . . . running through his mind.

Delaney looked at his arm, a kind of shocked dismay on her face.

"Isn't this Jim's coat?" Jack asked.

She nodded mutely.

"And isn't he tall?"

She nodded again.

Come off it, Delaney, he wanted to say. He wanted to take her by the shoulders and shake her, just enough to make her look at him, really look at him, and see that he was someone to trust.

"Six-foot-two, right?"

Her eyes closed for a fraction of a second longer than a blink. Jack had never seen anyone actually pale as if they'd seen a ghost, the way people always characterized it in movies, until now. Delaney blanched.

"It doesn't matter," he said, opening the door again. He couldn't look at her. Couldn't stand the despair and confusion on her face. He didn't want to be the one who pushed her, the one who threatened her carefully controlled secret.

He wanted to be the one she confided in. Willingly.

"I'll be right back." He edged toward the threshold of the door, motioning toward his house. "I'll just get that screwdriver. Hope the coat doesn't shrink any more in the rain." He forced a laugh, then turned away, rolling his eyes at the dismal attempt at humor.

Her eyes were on him as he jogged across the
drive to the back door, he could feel them. She must
be wondering what he was thinking, if he suspected, if he'd seen the list in that drawer and was
putting the pieces together. Maybe, he thought, by
the time he got back she'll have figured out the jig
was up anyway so she might as well admit it; but
he doubted it. She was not one to give up on things,
that much he thought he knew about her.

He pushed open the back door and squished
into the utility room. His hair felt plastered to his
skull, and rivulets of water dripped from it down
his forehead and neck. He jerked his head as if he'd
just surfaced in the water, flipping the hair from his
face, and moved to the closet. He bent to retrieve a
tool kit and pulled from the molded-plastic insert a
sturdy Phillips head.

Emily—b. March 10 . . . he thought again. That
was the piece that didn't make sense. If she made
up the husband she could make up the wedding
date, and there'd be no reason to worry about
Emily's birthdate. So why fudge it? The only reason
you'd do that is to keep someone from guessing—

Jack froze, his entire body going numb. The
screwdriver dropped onto the tile floor.

No, he shook his head. No, that was ridiculous.
He rubbed a hand over his face as he bent to pick
up the tool. But he had to tell himself to breathe.

He'd worn a *condom.*

An ancient condom that had been in his wallet
for God knew how long . . . and they'd made love
more than once, his arousal returning without him

even leaving her body, he'd wanted her that much . . .

He felt dizzy and reminded himself to breathe, inhaling sharply as he pressed one palm against the cool metal of the washing machine.

He remembered, all of a sudden, Aunt Linda going on and on about how advanced Emily was. A remarkable baby, she'd said. So mature for her age. In all her years as a pediatric nurse she'd never seen *any* five-month-olds sit up on their own. . . .

And what had Delaney been talking about this evening? Jim Poole's eye color—or rather his evil twin's eye color. She was explaining why his eyes were blue.

No, he corrected himself, like a detective working through a killer's motivation, she was explaining why *Emily's* eyes were *brown*. Like Jim's, she'd said. *Like his.*

A surge of nausea took him by surprise. He dropped the screwdriver on the washer and moved to the utility room's small bathroom. Pushing the door open so hard it slammed against the wall, he bent over the sink and pushed the water lever to cold. He bathed his hands in the icy water, then splashed some on his face, as if he needed to be wetter after the downpour outside.

He straightened, water running from his chin onto his tee shirt. He stared at himself in the mirror. Was it the face of a *father* who stared back at him?

Delaney stood with her hands against the closed door and her forehead resting on the cool wood.

He knew. He *had* to know. He must have seen her list—why would he look one drawer over after turning that corner? No, you'd start right there on the end, wouldn't you?

Not if you started next to the stove, another part of her mind reasoned.

She lifted her head. Yes, he could have started in the drawer next to the stove, then moved to the utensil drawer and not even gotten to the drawer with the list.

But then . . . *the coat.* And—oh, God—he'd said he knew Jim was tall. Six-foot-two. She'd never told him that. She might have told him Jim was tall but she couldn't even imagine a conversation where she would have gotten so specific. Six-foot-two was on the list. The damned, stupid, foolish, idiotic *husband list.*

She dropped her head against the wooden door again, wishing she had the guts to pound herself bloody against it.

He knew. He had to.

Her heart was wedged into her throat, and her head was pounding. What could she do, how could she fix this? Surely there was something she could do to head him off, distract him from the obvious.

She lifted her head again, heart sailing with elation. She knew, she'd tell him Jim died. She'd go back to her plan to kill off Jim, and then Jack would have to wait to ask her any questions. Wait until she could come up with some suitable explanation for all that he might have seen and all that he was most probably thinking.

She ran to the phone. She would call Michael now, run the idea past him, and then when Jack came back with the screwdriver she'd be on the phone in tears. Then she'd hang up and tell him the awful news she'd just received.

Surely he wouldn't doubt a widow. Certainly he wouldn't question her on the subject when she was distraught over the death of her husband. At the very least the ruse would buy her some more time. And then . . . then, after she'd thought of a way . . . then she'd tell him the truth. Maybe.

She picked up the phone and dialed Michael's number. One ring . . . two rings . . . three rings . . . She hit one fist on the wall and swore.

"Pick up the phone, pick up the phone," she muttered to herself as the phone rang one more time.

The answering machine picked up. She splayed her palm across her forehead.

"Michael, it's me," she said in a voice that betrayed every ounce of panic, "call me as *soon* as you get this, the very moment you hear—"

The phone clicked. "What is the *matter* with you?" Michael's voice came on the line.

"Oh thank God," she breathed.

"Jesus, Dee, did someone die?" He was serious. Concern colored his voice.

"No, but someone has to. I've got to kill him—Jim, that is. And I've got to do it *right now*. Jack's going to be back here any minute, and I've got to be in tears over the death of my husband."

"What on earth are you talking about?"

She wasn't making sense, not to someone who hadn't been inside her head for the last ten minutes, but she couldn't stop or slow down her thoughts long enough to explain.

"Just, if I start getting upset and crying and carrying on, go with me. Jack knows, I think. He tried on the coat, on my coatrack, and the sleeves were way too short. And he *knew*—he knew that Jim is tall, six-two, he said that. I never told him that, but it was on the list. So I'm sure he saw the list in my drawer. Oh my God, oh my God." She raked a hand through her hair. "I'm going to have to tell him. He probably already knows, so I'm going to have to tell him. If I don't, he's going to think I *never* planned to tell him. Which I didn't. Oh God, I'm a bad person, Michael. I'm not a good person."

"Delaney, listen to me. You can't kill off Jim."

"What?" She could practically hear the brakes in her mind screeching as she absorbed his words.

"You can't kill off Jim and tell Jack the truth—"

"Why *not*?" she squealed. Her eyes were probably rolling back in her head, a la Linda Blair in *The Exorcist*.

"Because—"

The phone beeped, signifying an incoming call.

"Wait, hang on a second, I've got another call." She hit the hook and switched lines.

"Hello?" Her voice was shrill and she wondered

belatedly why she hadn't just ignored the incoming call.

"Delaney?" Jack's voice.

Her heart hammered in her chest, and her cheeks burned as if he were looking at her and seeing the lies she'd told all over her face.

"Yes?"

"Oh, it didn't sound like you."

And it didn't sound like *him*, she thought. His voice was somber, constrained, as if he were miles and miles away, across a distant, turbulent ocean, in another country with another language and archaic technology, where the phones might be tapped and he'd committed some crime.

Either that or he was holding the receiver away from his mouth.

"It's me," she said. "I'm just on the other line, a friend called, and said he had some news, bad news," she added, remembering her mission in calling Michael. But Jack didn't pick up on it.

"Listen, I can't come back over right now. I've got—something came up."

Her mind—spinning with ways to complete her story—stopped abruptly.

"You can't?"

"No, uh, sorry. I'll come back, finish it later. It's just, something came up. Like I said."

"Oh. Okay." She thought, *What does this mean?* "But your drill's here."

What did that *mean*? It meant she was becoming unhinged. He could live without his drill for one night.

"Yeah, I know. I'll just come back later. I'll finish it later."

He sounded weird. Or was she just imagining things?

"Okay." She bit her fingernail. Something she *never* did.

He cleared his throat. "Yeah. Okay. I gotta go."

"Okay." She thought she should say something more, let him know the awful news she was about to get, about Jim's untimely death, but maybe that could now wait until he came back to finish the crib.

"Bye," he said, and hung up without waiting for her reply.

He definitely sounded weird.

Slowly, she hung up the phone. She was just turning away to go who knew where, someplace she could think and figure it all out, when the phone rang again.

"Hello?" she answered. Maybe it was Jack, telling her why he sounded so weird. Bad news of his own, maybe. Something, please God, other than that he'd discovered the truth about her. The truth that she was a liar.

"Did you forget about me?" Michael's voice, sounding peeved.

"Oh God, Michael, I'm sorry. It was Jack, and I just—"

"You didn't *tell* him, did you?"

He sounded alarmed, Delaney realized through the haze of her own preoccupation.

"You didn't tell him Jim was dead yet?" he asked again. "Please tell me you didn't."

"No, why? What's going on?"

"Because Ruark's dead," he said. "*Destiny's Children* just killed him today, so Sybill had to tell Drake the truth."

Chapter 16

Ruark just died and Sybill had told Drake the truth.

Jack ran his hands through his hair, his elbows on the table, a short glass of whiskey in front of him.

His mother had called the moment he'd hung up with Delaney and in the ten minutes it had taken him to get off the phone with her she'd told him all about it. All about how his life was just like that damn soap opera.

Not that his mother knew he was, in fact, living it. No, she just thought he'd be amused by it.

The worst part of it was that he wasn't even the good guy. No. He was the idiot, asshole Drake. The one who'd deserved to be lied to about his child. The one Ruark outshone in every way— responsibility, income, stability, supportiveness.

Then Ruark died and Sybill had to tell the asshole Drake the child was his because she was convinced the child needed a father, even if he was a class-one jerk.

Not so Delaney, he thought, numb with shock. Delaney thought so little of Jack she'd decided a *made-up* husband would be better for Emily than the real thing. A *made-up* husband would be better than him.

He shook his head, feeling as if his eyes were suddenly open to the kind of person he was. Or rather the kind of person he was perceived to be.

But what had he done? What had he ever done to her to make her think so little of him? The worst thing he could think of was the thing that she, too, was guilty of—a one-night stand on the beach.

Ever since she'd gotten here, however, she'd held him at arm's length. Every time she saw him she was as nervous as a cat and anxious to be rid of him. Why *was* that?

Because she had a secret. She wanted the child to herself.

Why? Because every piece of negative gossip she heard about him she believed. Because to her he was just Drake. He was the irresponsible, womanizing sperm donor who didn't even *want* to be told about his child.

Was *that* the kind of man Delaney thought he was?

If she listened to the gossips, she would. And Delaney listened to the gossips.

But what kind of person would hide a child from its father? And how could he be in love with a woman who would do such a thing? Who would live next door, see him in town, look him in the eye nearly every day and *lie*. All to keep him from his child.

His child . . . he thought again. Emily was *his child*. The truth of it hadn't sunk in. When it did, he would be terrified. Horrified. Hit-the-ground-running scared. Wouldn't he? If he would, then why did he keep picturing the way Emily beamed at him whenever she saw him? And why did he keep remembering that deep feeling of satisfaction, that sensation of having done something wonderfully *right* the day he'd first made her smile?

He should be furious with Delaney, he thought. But he wasn't, strangely enough. Upset, sure, but not angry.

She was afraid, that was why she'd done it. He could see it so clearly in her. She was *always* afraid, as far as he could see. It was one of the things he'd wanted to help her with from the day she got here. It was one of the things he thought he *could* help her with.

She *needed* him, he realized. Because without him she would always be running. From him. From herself. From anything that didn't fit into her carefully constructed plan.

He sat up straight and pushed the glass of whiskey away. He hadn't really wanted it anyway, never liked the taste, but he'd been so shaken he'd thought it would calm him.

Now he knew he had to think. Clearly. Soberly. Because the most important event of his life had just occurred. And he had to decide what to do about it.

The writing was on the wall. Delaney sat at her kitchen table, staring at the wall where the phone hung, thinking she might as well take a Magic Marker and write it right there on the wall. *It's the truth, stupid.* She knew what she had to do. She had to tell Jack the truth.

But how? Just walk over to his house, sit down, and start talking?

She shivered and looked over at the bassinet where Emily still slept. No. She had to plan it. She had to make it as gentle, as palatable as she could. She would set the scene. Have him over for dinner. Quiet music. Emily dressed up and cute—

No. Emily at Aunt Linda's. Delaney wasn't going to parade her daughter out before The Man in a pretty frock like some floozy to be taken if she's pretty enough and rejected if she's not.

So . . . quiet music. A good meal. Some wine, just for relaxation. She would start with some conversation. They seemed to do that pretty well. Strike up a mood of camaraderie. Maybe confide some of her feelings about him—

No. No feelings. She didn't want to turn her feelings into a bartering tool, or have them look like she was using them to convince him to accept Emily. Not that she knew what her feelings were, exactly. She just knew she had some. Unsettling, is what they were, and that wouldn't be helpful anyway.

Besides, she wasn't going to convince him to accept Emily. She was just going to tell him about her, and he could do what he damn well pleased. Walk away if he wanted to, the womanizing cad. Philandering coward. Sure, it's all well and good to sow your wild oats, but when it came to harvest time . . .

She stopped herself. It was all too easy to take off on the familiar tirade, but when it came down to it—*the truth, stupid*—he wasn't like that and she knew it. Some part of her brain—her intuition, maybe—was standing back, watching her believe all that stuff she'd heard about him to justify what she'd done, when all along it knew that he was trustworthy. *She* knew that she could trust his integrity.

She closed her eyes for a second and swallowed hard. What a fool she'd been, to have ended up in a spot like this. She'd been taken by surprise, that's what the problem was. When he'd walked into her office that first day she hadn't known what to think, what to do. And before she could change her mind the words were out of her mouth and could not be unsaid. *Presto*, she had a husband. What could she do but follow through? But then one thing led to another and before she knew it . . . here she was.

Delaney opened her eyes, pressed both palms to the tabletop and stood up. Taking a deep breath, she turned and walked toward the front door. The rain had stopped so without any further thought, without allowing even a momentary doubt, she marched across the driveway separating their houses, up the front walk, and grabbed the heavy brass knocker in her hand.

But she couldn't let go of it. She stood there, knocker raised, staring at the polished wood of the door, and couldn't move.

What was she doing? She couldn't do this. She couldn't invite him to dinner. For God's sake, *he knew*. The moment he opened the door he would look at her and she would pass out from shame and mortification.

Suddenly the door opened and the knocker was yanked from her grasp. Delaney was jerked forward into Jack's chest, and the knocker landed with a solid *clank* against the metal stop.

She gasped as she tripped up the threshold. He grunted as her hand hit his chest. He grabbed her arms and she righted herself, stepping back so fast she forgot about the step and almost fell over backwards. He grabbed her arms again.

She laughed briefly, hysterically.

"What are you doing?" he asked, dropping her hands as soon as she was steady.

She sobered instantly. "I didn't expect you to open the door."

"Well I saw you pass by the window, and when I didn't hear the bell I decided to look and see where you went."

Too late, she noticed the doorbell.

"I was . . . I was thinking."

"Okay . . ." He looked at her. His expression was unreadable, which was a bad sign. Most of the time Jack's mood was right there on his face. Smiling, frustrated, embarrassed, blushing, laughing, teasing . . . Would she never see that again? Once she told him, revealed herself to be dishonest, would she be looked at forever with this veiled, distrustful expression?

"I just came to invite you to dinner," she said, spitting the words out quickly. There was no way she could recover any sort of grace at this point. "Tomorrow night. I hope you can come. It's important. You know, to me. To you too, I think. That is I think you'll think—"

"Okay," he said, nodding.

Neither of them smiled.

"All right." She nodded too. "Good. See you tomorrow." She turned and started to go, then stopped and turned back around. "Seven-thirty. Okay?"

He watched her, looking large and strange in the doorway. Who *was* this man? she wondered. Who was this stranger to whom she had to entrust the most precious thing in her life?

"Yeah, okay," he said.

"Okay," she said, and turned to leave again. She felt as if she were walking on someone else's legs all the way across the lawn. She wanted to look back to see if he was watching, but she didn't dare. The way things were going she'd trip on a hedge and fall flat on her face. Which might not be bad. Maybe he'd feel sorry for her. If nothing else, she knew Jack was compassionate.

And trustworthy, she knew that too. He might be angry with her, but he would strive to do what was best for Emily, she was sure of it. For the first time since she'd moved to Harp Cove and realized Jack was there, she felt complete confidence in his honor. He wouldn't try to take Emily away. He wasn't going to turn out to be a psycho. He wasn't the type to try to screw somebody because he was mad.

She moved into the kitchen and gazed down at her sleeping daughter for a minute. Then she walked up the stairs and stood in the doorway to Emily's room, looking at Jack's tools on the floor beneath the crib.

The fact was, he might be angry—he probably *would* be angry—but he would do the right thing.

And that, she thought with a shamed yet comforting conviction, was the realization that sealed the deal.

Jack Shepard *was* father material, she admitted, staring at the leg of the crib he'd been fixing. And she was a fool not to have seen it earlier.

The next morning Jack watched from an upstairs window as Delaney put Emily in the car seat, threw her briefcase in the passenger side, got in the driver's seat, and pulled down the driveway. He saw her turn signal light about ten yards from the turn and smiled grimly. That was his Delaney, cautious to the end.

Once she'd turned and he'd waited about fifteen minutes, he made his way down the stairs and out the back door. He let himself in her back door and moved silently through the kitchen.

He didn't linger this time, looking at the crumbs in her sink and the dishes on her table. He didn't look at the mail or even glance at her bedroom door as he ascended the stairs. No, he went straight to the hallway wall and the pen-and-ink drawing of Emily he'd noticed that day he was in the house working. The one drawn of Emily as a newborn.

His pulse hammered as he neared it. He could see before he could even read it that the print was signed in a spidery hand in the lower left hand corner, just as he'd remembered. He stopped before the print and looked closely at the writing.

And saw what he'd hoped he'd find. The artist had not only signed but dated the print. *2/00.*

February. A full month before Emily was supposedly born.

He let out a long-held breath and ran his fingers through his hair, momentarily holding his head.

Then, just to be sure, he headed for the nursery. He remembered seeing one of those frames with the date and time and other particulars of a baby's birth engraved on the sides. He'd thought it was hanging near the closet, but when he got to the spot there was nothing there but a nail hole.

He narrowed his eyes and looked around the room. Closet, baby's dresser, chest, crib, changing table, rocker. He glanced at each thing, then settled on the chest. He crossed the room and opened it.

Blankets and baby linens. The perfect spot, he thought. He dug carefully through the piles and was rewarded halfway down with the feel of something solid. Snaking his hand between the linens, his fingers felt cool metal and he pulled the pewter frame from its cossetted hiding place.

Emily Jacquelyn Poole, he read. His breath caught in his throat at the middle name. *January 10, 2000, 7:27 A.M.,* 7 lbs. 3 oz., 20 inches.

January 10, 2000. Just under nine months after Delaney Poole's visit to Harp Cove.

As he stood there with the evidence in his hands, trying to decide what to think, how to feel, what to do, he became aware of tears welling in his eyes. He watched as one fell from his eye to hit the frame's glass and roll down one of Emily's perfect cheeks.

Delaney rushed past the receptionist's desk toward her office to fill out the last chart of the day. She was late. Mr. Prouty's lab results had come back and had needed a lot more explanation than she'd thought they would. Then Cheryl Flanagan had come by without an appointment because her baby, Roxanne, had conjunctivitis. Millie Sewell had refused to take no for an answer when she'd requested Valium. Then Lester Blackwell had come in with a sprained ankle.

So she was late. Really late. And she had not been able to shake the knot in her stomach all day. How she was going to get a meal down before telling Jack the truth she had no idea.

"Oh, Dr. Poole!" Cindy, the high-school student who worked as a receptionist in the afternoons during the school year, hailed her from behind the counter. "I took a message for you."

"Not now, Cindy," she said, pulling a pen from her pocket to make a note on Mr. Prouty's chart.

"But it's important! He said it was really, really important." Cindy pushed through piles of paper on the desk, most of which looked like homework, with a few doodles and notes thrown in on top. "Wait. It was just here. A-ha!" She whipped a pink While-You-Were-Out pad from beneath the debris, then frowned at the blank sheet on top. "I know it was here."

Delaney reined in a heavy sigh. "Do you remember who it was from?"

"Wait. I'm sure it's here . . ." She continued to push papers around, peering under them as if people she didn't want to disturb were living underneath, then shuffling them around some more.

"Cindy, I've got a lot to do, and I've got to get out of here. I'll be in my office if you find it." Delaney turned and strode across the lobby.

"Dr. Poole!" Cindy called.

Delaney inhaled and turned back around.

"I just remembered, I put it on your desk." The girl beamed at her.

Delaney forced a smile. "Great. Thank you, Cindy."

She went to her office and shut the door. She just needed a moment's peace to finish this chart, then she could escape before anyone else came in. She could only pray there would be no emergencies before she got out the door, because Dr. Jacobson was on call tonight.

Delaney had stopped at Aunt Linda's at lunch,

as she always did, and asked if Linda could keep Emily a few extra hours tonight. It was important, she'd said, or she wouldn't have asked. She didn't want Aunt Linda thinking Delaney was the kind of mother to go off gallivanting while her daughter was left with whoever would take her.

Fortunately, it wasn't a problem. It seemed things were coming together quite neatly for the evening. She only hoped The Revelation, as she'd come to think about it, went as smoothly.

Her stomach clenched once again at the thought of it.

She rounded her desk and sat down in the swivel chair, rocking back slightly with the chart. After a second of writing she became aware of the pink message slip in the middle of the desk and she leaned forward to pick it up.

Jim called, it said in curly, girlish script. *Said he figured it all out.*

Delaney stared at the piece of paper. *Jim* called? Jim who? She tossed the message down on her desk and went back to studying the chart. But after a second, curiosity got the better of her and she picked up the note and walked back to the front desk.

"Cindy, is this the message you were talking about?" she asked.

Cindy's face showed relief. "Yes. Good. Thank God I didn't lose it, you know? He sounded like it was really important."

"You didn't put Jim's last name, though. I'm not sure who this is."

Cindy's brows drew together, and she looked at Delaney oddly. "It was your husband. Jim."

Delaney flushed to the roots of her hair. "My *husband*. Oh."

"Yeah. He said to tell you your husband called and he'd figured it all out. Or something like that." She cocked her head, watching Delaney. "And he said to call him."

Delaney stared at the pink sheet. "Did he leave a number?"

"You don't know your husband's phone number?" Cindy asked.

"Well, yes, of course I do," Delaney said, wadding up the note and shoving it into the pocket of her lab coat. "It's just that . . . he's traveling, and I thought maybe he'd left a hotel number. Or something."

Cindy's face cleared. "Oh. No, he didn't say he was traveling, I don't think." She frowned again. "But he was kind of pushy. And he said something like, tell her not to do anything stupid. Which I thought was kind of rude. Don't you? You don't let him talk to you like that, do you?"

"No," Delaney said, pushing the hair back from her forehead and turning away. "No, I don't let him talk to me at all."

It had to be Michael, she thought. There was no other explanation. She went back to her office and dialed his number.

One ring . . . two rings . . . The answering machine picked up.

Delaney hung up. She'd call back tomorrow and tell him what she'd done. Something told her she'd really be needing to talk to Michael after this evening was done.

Chapter 17

The evening was cool, so Jack threw a sweatshirt on over his tee shirt, then stopped and looked at himself in the mirror. After a second he stripped off the sweatshirt and the tee shirt and put on a polo shirt. A second after that he pulled off the polo shirt and put on a long-sleeved rugby shirt and decided, the hell with it. She wasn't going to make any decisions about him based on his shirt. Which was unfortunate because he had some nice shirts.

He stopped in the kitchen and pulled a bottle of wine from the rack by the back door. A nice red Bordeaux. That ought to help them both relax a little bit. For sheer relaxation effect he'd have preferred to take a bottle of tequila and a straw, but that would hardly give him the responsible demeanor he was hoping to project tonight.

For that, he planned to tell her about the job offer

at Briarly College. He hadn't given Hugh an answer yet but he had to soon. It was more money, better benefits, and could possibly put him on track to coach at bigger, wealthier, colleges in the future.

Not that he'd ever been interested in the kind of big money, high-stress football that characterized a lot of schools' athletic programs, but taking the job would make him appear to be a much more successful man. Granted, it was a good distance away, and he'd have to travel to see Emily on weekends, but if he took the job, he'd have more money for child support. He'd also have decent insurance benefits for his daughter, and working at a college, especially a good one like Briarly, could help Emily when it came time for her to think about her education.

The bottom line, though, was if he were a woman, assessing a man's suitability as a father, he'd be looking for someone successful. Someone with a bright, lucrative future in front of him. Someone who could support a family. Even if he was a few hours away.

Especially if he were a woman with a list of attributes for a fake father on which the words *Big Bucks* appeared.

Because what other reason would she have for inviting him over tonight? She'd figured out that he'd seen that ridiculous list, and she knew she had to tell him the truth. Was there any other possibility?

The only other one he could think of was that she'd decided she had feelings for him, but he couldn't let himself believe that. For one thing, the disappointment would be too great if he expected a revelation like that, and it didn't happen. For another, it wasn't going to happen.

The question was, how would she tell him? About Emily, that was. How would she couch it? Would she even *accept* child support? Would she hope for or dread his involvement in Emily's life? And if she did want him to be an involved parent, would he be able to do that without also striving to be involved in *her* life?

He stared down at the bottle in his hand. Maybe the question was what did *he* want. Because what Delaney wanted had obviously been to keep him out of Emily's life. Until now, when she was cornered.

He shook his head, ignoring the sting of anger that she'd written him off so quickly, and turned for the door. What he wanted he couldn't have. Her. Without inhibition. Without obligation. Without lies. Like she'd been the first night he met her. But that was impossible now.

He strode across the lawn, relishing the fresh snap of the breeze. Lifting his eyes to the evening sky, he noticed that the stars were not visible overhead. Another storm was coming, he noted, smelling it on the breeze. Thunderstorm, probably, because tomorrow the temperature was supposed to drop off.

It was a dark and stormy night . . . he thought, hoping the weather did not portend anything dire in store for him this evening.

He knocked at the front door, feeling as odd as if he were rapping on his own front door. Usually he let himself in the back door to work. Or found Delaney in the yard or in her kitchen through the screen door.

She took a while to answer, and when she did, she looked harried.

"Hi, sorry, come on in," she said, wiping her hands on a dish towel. She barely met his eyes, just opened the door and looked outside behind him. "Oh, it smells like rain." She sounded surprised.

She wore an apron over what were obviously her work clothes. He hoped he didn't look as if he'd changed clothes three times before coming over.

"Yeah, I just noticed that myself," he said, stepping over the threshold and looking around like a stranger. "Thunderstorm, probably."

The place was filled with the scent of roasting chicken, and there was music playing in the living room, where a fire was burning. The whole place had a warm ambience that gave him a near-physical pang. What would it be like to come home to something like this every night? he wondered.

"Is that wine?" she asked.

He started, raising his hand as if he hadn't noticed the bottle placed there. "Oh yeah. Here. I hope you like red. It's a Bordeaux."

She studied the label. "Bordeaux's my favorite."

She still didn't look at him, just turned and took the bottle back to the kitchen.

"Make yourself at home," she called from the kitchen. "That should be easy, huh?"

He laughed, sounding quite unlike himself. "Yeah," he said. Boy, he was clever tonight.

"Can I bring you a glass of this wine?"

"You bet." He wandered into the living room and, for want of anything else to do, took up the poker to readjust the logs in the fireplace.

A second later she appeared with two glasses. She still wore the apron and barely met his eyes as she handed him the wine.

"I'm running a little behind," she said. "Work was crazy today. I had three walk-ins in the last hour."

"Oh." His mind was empty of conversation. He looked at her, and all he could think was whether or not she had something to tell him. And if so, when? And how? "Well, don't worry about it. Being behind, that is. I'm in no hurry."

She dipped her head and sipped the wine. He sipped his, too, taking as large a gulp as he could manage without appearing uncouth. He didn't think he'd ever been this uncomfortable around a woman.

"Why don't you sit down," she suggested. "I've just got a couple more things to do in the kitchen."

"Take your time."

He sat in the armchair by the hearth and looked into the fire.

In the kitchen, Delaney sucked down the last of her wine and poured herself another full glass. If she didn't calm down soon, she was going to find herself throwing up in the bathroom. Her stomach was a knot, her head felt as if someone had wound a roll of duct tape around it, and if she didn't get out of her stockings soon, she was going to end up spontaneously ripping them off at some undoubtedly awkward moment. And there'd be plenty of those.

She ripped up handfuls of lettuce leaves and threw them into the salad bowl. Then she scraped the cutting board full of carrots, celery, radishes, and tomatoes onto the mix and doused it all with salad dressing.

She should be moving more slowly, she thought, gulping down some more wine. Once she finished the salad it would just be a matter of waiting for the chicken to finish roasting, which would, unfortunately, be another forty minutes because she'd gotten home so late.

Why hadn't she just made cheeseburgers?

Salad done, she pushed the bowl into the refrigerator and pulled a box of crackers from the cabinet. The brie she'd had sitting on the kitchen table since she got home had drifted into a perfect room-temperature slouch. She tossed some crackers around the rim of the cheese plate and stood back to survey the table.

For the first time since she'd left Washington, she'd pulled out her table linens. Tablecloth, place mats, linen napkins complete with napkin rings. Two candles stood unlit, waiting for action, amidst water, wine, and cordial glasses. Evidently she'd been thirsty when she set the table.

She put the cordial glasses away.

An hour ago the table had looked pretty. Now it

looked self-conscious. Homemaker-y. Like she was advertising herself as some kind of domestic wonder. She was terrified that once she told him, he'd get the idea she wanted him to accept *her* as well as Emily into his life.

And wouldn't that just scare him to pieces, she thought. Instant family. He'd probably run screaming from the house.

She was just contemplating undoing the linens when he sauntered in from the living room with an empty wineglass. His eyes were on the elaborately decorated table.

"Oh! I'm sorry. Let me get you some more." Delaney moved quickly to the counter where the bottle—now mysteriously half-empty—stood. "This is very good wine."

"I'm glad you like it." He leaned one hip against the counter nearby and looked remote and calm as he watched her.

She took another sip of wine, filled his glass, then topped her glass off while she had the bottle in her hand. She didn't know where it all was going but certainly not to her head. No doubt it was being burned off by the adrenaline of having Jack in the house and being unsure whether or not he was aware of the bombshell she was about to drop on him.

It didn't help that he looked so damn good either. He wore a black rugby shirt and jeans. He looked good enough to curl up against, and she was just scared and tired and confused enough to want to do that. She could almost feel how warm and solid his chest would feel as she laid her head on it and nestled into the comfort of his arms. If only she could count on him to do that instead of be angry at her when she told him the truth. But she had to face it, if the tables could somehow be turned, she knew she'd be angry.

She glanced up at him suddenly, as if he might have read her thoughts, and found him looking at her.

"What?" he asked, obviously alarmed by the look on her face.

"Nothing! Would you like some brie?" She moved to the table and picked up the plate. Several crackers dropped off the side and skittered across the floor.

"Here, let me . . ." Jack bent and picked up the crackers, then turned in a circle, looking for the trash can.

"Under the sink," she gestured with the plate, sending several more crackers careening off the edge toward his feet.

He laughed. "If you want me to sweep the floor, just say so."

She laughed with him, grateful for the moment of levity. "Sorry. I'm just not—coordinated today. Shall we sit in the living room?"

"Okay." He motioned her to precede him, and she walked toward the living room. Was he watching her walk? she wondered. Probably not. No doubt he was too consumed by the enormity of her lie to think about anything but what an awful person she was.

They reached the living room, and she placed the plate on the table next to his chair, then perched on the edge of the opposite one.

He leaned back in his seat and dug a cracker into the cheese. She'd forgotten to put a knife on the plate, she realized, though it was probably just as well since she might have accidentally stabbed him with it, the way she'd been flinging crackers around in the kitchen.

"So . . ." he said, looking at her as he bit down on the cracker.

She laughed lightly, for no reason, she realized belatedly. "So," she repeated.

Maybe she should tell him now, she thought wildly. Get it over with and save herself the trouble of having to force a meal down her dread-constricted throat. She glanced at him and felt terror—actual terror—grab her chest and rob her of air. He wasn't even looking at her; he was studying the cracker.

"Jack," she began.

He looked at her immediately, his eyes intent. Firelight flickered in their depths, and she felt like a prison convict caught escaping in the glare of a spotlight.

Her eyes shifted to his near-empty wineglass. He was drinking nearly as fast as she was.

"Let me get you some more wine," she said, jumping up and grabbing his glass. She polished hers off on the way to the kitchen too.

There was only one glass left in the bottle he'd brought, but she had bought one too. Not as good as the one he'd selected, but still red and a much bigger bottle. She peeled the metal hood off and rummaged through the drawer for the corkscrew.

She was about to pull the thing out with her teeth when she remembered she'd left it on the counter. She jabbed the screw into the cork and twisted, then pulled. Half a dried cork came out, showering the counter with cork particles.

"Damn," she muttered.

"Here, let me."

Delaney jumped and nearly dropped the huge bottle on the floor. He was standing just behind her, close enough to jangle her nerves even further.

"Oh, you scared me." She laughed and stepped back.

"Sorry." He smiled and her eyes strayed to his lips. Such fine, firm lips, she noted.

He turned half-away and twisted the corkscrew into what was left of the cork. She imagined what it might be like if she were comfortable with him, if they were a couple. He might be in here opening wine and she might join him, wrapping her arms around him from behind and laying her head on that solid, powerful back.

It would be nice to be that at ease, she thought, shifting her gaze to stare into her empty wineglass. The rim of the bottle appeared in her line of sight as Jack filled her glass.

"Cheers," he said, depositing the bottle on the counter and lifting his glass toward her.

"Cheers," she said, and pressed a too-bright smile on her face.

"To us," he said, and just as her stomach began to lift, he added, "Neighbors."

She moved her glass toward his but instead of the two glasses clinking together, their fingers hit and a jolt of surprised awareness went skittering up her arm.

She pulled back and took a deep gulp of the wine. He did the same.

The taste of the cheap wine clashed dramatically with that of what Jack had brought, and she was glad she'd given him the last of the good stuff.

"So," she said, then realized that was exactly what he'd said in the other room. She racked her brain to come up with something to follow it up with. "It should only be another fifteen minutes or so before we eat." She glanced at the timer that said clearly, in large digital numbers, 22:00 minutes.

He looked at it too. "Good. Great." He nodded.

They each sipped their wine.

"Where's Emily?" he asked then. "Sleeping?"

"No, ah, she's . . ." She hadn't anticipated this. If she told him Emily wasn't here, would he think she'd had something else, something more . . . libidinous, in mind?

"On a date?" he supplied.

She looked up at him, at the smile that crinkled the corners of his eyes and made his whole expression warm, accepting.

"Don't even joke about that," she said.

He laughed, and she couldn't help but smile as he did.

"Seriously . . . ," he persisted. "Is she upstairs? Can I go see her?"

She turned to the refrigerator and pulled out the salad. "Oh, she's with your aunt Linda tonight," she said, pouring dressing all over it. Too late, she realized she'd already done that. The lettuce in the bottom of the bowl was swimming in the stuff. "I just didn't know how I'd get dinner finished and all that with her here. I've got to pick her up by ten."

She pushed the salad back into the refrigerator.

"Oh." He raised his brows, obviously surprised. "Well, I could've watched her while you cooked."

She looked at him. If he knew what she had to tell him, that was kind of a leading statement to make, she thought. She could take that to mean he *wanted* to take care of Emily, wanted to get to know her, be part of her life.

Then again, maybe he didn't know. Maybe he really hadn't opened that drawer . . . She looked toward the offending drawer where the list, now in cinders, had been stashed.

They were standing next to each other, each leaning against the counter, looking across the kitchen. To the right was the elaborate table. Straight across was The Drawer.

"Let's go into the living room," she suggested.

"Sure."

They walked back into the living room, Delaney wondering if he felt as silly as she did going back and forth. She stopped at the mantel and looked into the fire. It burned with a hearty flame.

Jack stood next to her, and though they weren't touching, Delaney could almost feel his arm against hers, as if she could take a deep breath and move enough to touch him. For that reason alone she did not want to budge from the spot.

"So—" Delaney said again, turning toward him.

Just as Jack said, "Delaney—" and turned toward her.

Suddenly they were facing each other, not one foot apart, and the look on his face told her he'd been just as aware of her proximity as she'd been of his.

"Yes?" Delaney murmured, unable to take her eyes from his face. Her heart hammered as she looked at him. She was afraid her expression might match that of a deranged stalker, but she couldn't look away.

Slowly, he put his wineglass on the mantel. Then he took hers and set it down next to his.

"Delaney," he said again, taking her gently by the shoulders.

And that was all it took. That touch, his warm palms against her shoulders, and she leaned into him. She had a brief, vague moment of noting the surprised look on his face, before he reciprocated, bending down and capturing her upturned lips with his.

Desire shot through her, as hot and as sudden as if she'd embraced a fireball. She raised her hands to his collar and pulled down on his shirt, pulling him to her, his mouth open and searching on hers.

The feeling was explosive. She'd thought about

it, remembered it so well from that night on the beach and that day in his office. But nothing could compare to this feeling, this loose, uninhibited feeling of sheer desire, brought on and facilitated by the knowledge that she was going to tell him everything. No secrets would stand between them after tonight.

She told herself that if they could just make this connection now, if she could remember how she felt—and remind him how he felt—that night on the beach, then the revelation of Emily would not be such a shock, and he would not be angry with her.

But as she felt his body press its length against hers she knew that remembering how she'd felt that night on the beach was not going to be a problem. In fact, she'd remembered it far too often, and many times when she'd been desperate to forget it.

No, this wasn't for Jack, this kiss. This was for *her*.

She molded her body to his and felt his hand slide down to the small of her back, pulling her hips against his. He was aroused, she noted. Most definitely, extremely aroused.

Outside a crack of thunder sounded. Delaney jumped and their lips separated. But rather than look him in the eye, she stood on tiptoe and put her arms around his neck, kissing the skin below his ear and letting her gaze drift out the side window.

Lightning followed shortly, and the leaves of the trees bent with a sudden wind.

She tightened her arms and felt his tighten in return. His cheek pressed against her hair.

Was she doing the right thing? What was it, exactly, she *was* doing? Was this going to make it easier to tell him? Or harder? If he knew she'd been lying, did this mean he understood?

She didn't know. She couldn't think. All she knew was that the feel of his body was better than anything she'd felt for months. Her skin cried out to be touched, much the way it had that night before they'd ended up on the beach.

Thunder sounded again, simultaneous with lightning, and rain hit the ground like someone emptying a huge bucket from upstairs.

"It's close," he said, low against her ear.

She debated what to do. Should she stop things now? But it felt so good . . . so incredibly, soul-stealingly good. She wasn't even sure she was capable of unpeeling her arms from around his neck.

The sky rumbled again, and this time the crack of lightning was accompanied by a snap and an ominous sizzle. The lights flickered once and went out.

Neither of them moved.

"Jack," she whispered. But she didn't have anything to say, she just wanted to say his name.

He pulled back just enough to take her face in his hands and kiss her. Deeply. Thoroughly.

Delaney was so lost in the kiss she nearly staggered when he stopped, looking at her gently while one thumb caressed the skin of her cheek. Light from the living-room fire illuminated half of his face, one eye glittering in the warm light and the other shrouded in darkness, as if they represented good and evil. The known and the unknown. The face we present to the world and the one we hold back, she thought. That was when she realized she was drunk.

"Delaney," he said softly. "Are you sure?"

It was a moment straight from her memory, straight from that night on the beach. Was he thinking the same thing? Did he remember every nuance of that night the way she did?

"We've had a lot to drink," he added, "and I just want—I need to be sure—"

She laid a finger on his lips to silence him. She didn't want to stop now. She wanted to feel him on, inside, and around her. Wanted to know that he wanted her, wanted to feel his desire before she told him and quite possibly risked losing him for the sake of the truth.

And that was it, she realized. She wanted him one last time, while he wanted her, before she told him the truth that might alienate him forever.

"I'm sure," she said, laying a gentle kiss on his lips.

But he wasn't having any gentleness. He swept her into his arms, kissed her roughly, then pulled her down to lie on the rug in front of the fire.

He grabbed a pillow and afghan from one of the chairs, placed the pillow under her head and spread the blanket out on the floor. After situating them both on the afghan, he stretched out next to her, and his fingers found the buttons of her blouse. She raised her hands to help him, but he moved them away. Then slowly, one by one, he unbuttoned her shirt.

Once the buttons were undone, he pushed the fabric of her blouse away, trailing one finger over the rise of first one breast and then the other. Delaney's nipples hardened, and she felt a shiver run across her skin as he did it. He leaned over and placed a kiss on the crest of the breast nearest him, snaking his hand smoothly around her back to unhook her bra.

She nearly smiled at how efficient the movement was, but the expertise also had her quaking with apprehension.

Gently, he removed her shirt and her bra, then moved to the side zipper of her skirt. Delaney heard the low *zip*, and he pulled the garment off, rolling her hose down over her legs after that.

Delaney had never felt so aroused in her life, lying still while Jack Shepard took her clothes off, item by item, until she was lying naked on the floor by the fire.

He said nothing, but his eyes were drinking her in. She could tell by the movement of his hands. From her shoulders, across her breasts, to the tops of her thighs and back up, light touches of his fingers threatened to make her explode with desire.

"I want to see you," she whispered into the dark. "I want to feel your skin on mine."

Jack stopped, then slowly sat up. In the flickering light of the fire she watched him pull his shirt over his head. Then he stood and pulled off his shoes and jeans and socks.

His body was lean, just as she remembered it, and firelight made intriguing shadows in the hollows and planes of his body. When he lay back on the floor she turned toward him, but he stopped her.

"Shhh," he said softly. "Wait."

He rolled her on her back and continued to run his fingers down the length of her body, across her breasts and down to her thighs and back. Delaney began to tremble, so badly did she want to touch him. Just when she thought she couldn't stand it anymore, his lips found her breast and his fingers delved into the hot apex of her thighs.

Delaney gasped with the sudden sensation and reached out to take his head in her hands as his lips pulled on her breast. She arched up to meet him, and his fingers moved deeper inside of her.

She wanted him, she thought wildly. Oh God, she wanted him *now* and with a greater hunger than she'd ever dreamed possible.

"Jack," she breathed, then gasped as his fingers found the spot. She arched again, and her hand swept down his body to find him, hard as a rock and pearled with dampness.

She touched him, and he let out a deep, animal sound of pleasure. He moved his lips to hers and took her again in a deep, claiming kiss.

"Oh God, Jack," she breathed against his mouth, guiding him toward her. "Please . . ."

He rose above her and her hands gripped his shoulders. His manhood grazed the place his fingers had just been.

"Delaney, what do you want?" he whispered, touching her again lightly.

She inhaled sharply.

"Do you want *me*, Delaney?"

"Oh yes," she replied, arching up beneath him.

He held back, and she nearly whimpered with frustration and desire.

"Say it," he said. "I need to hear you say it."

"I want you, Jack," she said, and he plunged inside of her, his shaft sliding effortlessly into her heat, her fire, her boundless desire. "Oh God, I want you," she said again, as his hips drove against her and she clung to his neck, her legs rising to encircle him.

Their bodies met and moved with frantic abandon, Delaney pulling him deeper and tighter as his arms and chest flexed above her, and his hips dived against her with increasing urgency.

She felt him reaching the peak of arousal, his head thrown back and a guttural sound of pleasure coming from his throat, when the stars broke around her, showering her with the most incredible orgasm she'd ever had in her life.

She moaned aloud and clung to him, but at the last minute, on the last thrust, he pulled out of her and spent himself on the blanket beneath them.

Then he rolled to the side, taking her with him, and held her tightly against his chest, both of them breathing hard.

After several minutes of silence, Delaney shifted her head and whispered, "Jack."

She had to tell him, she thought, her mind spinning like a top. But should she tell him now? What if he thought she'd only made love to him because of what she had to tell him? What if he thought she'd planned this whole thing?

"Mm," he said, raising a hand to the back of her head to finger her hair.

"Oh Jack," she sighed. She couldn't do it. She didn't know how. She was scared to death he was going to hate her afterward.

He shifted so he could look down at her face in the dark. "What is it, Delaney?" he whispered back.

"Nothing." She clutched his arm with one hand and pressed her face to his chest.

"It's all right," he murmured, stroking her hair.

Delaney's heart, which had only just started to return to a normal rhythm, accelerated again. Did he mean he knew? Should she ask him? Was that the coward's way out? Asking *him* to tell *her*?

Of course it was.

She was through being a coward. "Jack, there's something . . ."

His arms tightened around her.

She tightened hers around him. "I need . . ."

Just *say it*, her mind screamed. But she felt as if a wall had been constructed and she couldn't get the words through it.

"What do you need?" he asked. His tone was gentle, careful.

They were both silent a minute, listening to the sound of the rain on the windows.

Then she sighed. "Nothing."

She couldn't do it, simply couldn't make the words come out of her mouth. Maybe she could write him a letter. Call him on the phone so she didn't have to look at him. But those were all cowardly ways out. Ways that would make things more a mess than they were even now.

"I want you to know," he said into the silence, "that I've been offered a better job. With a decent salary and benefits and future. And I'm going to take it. It's at Briarly College—"

"Briarly!" Her voice sounded shockingly loud in the darkness. She sat up and at the same moment the lights came back on, light from the lamp on a nearby table slicing across their makeshift bed. "In Massachusetts?"

He was *leaving* her? she thought wildly. He'd slept with her only to tell her he was moving eight hours away?

He knew she had to stay here for the next three years. He knew all about the NHSC deal she'd made. And yet he was still going to take a job hundreds of miles away?

He *couldn't* know about Emily. He must not have seen the list. If he did he wouldn't make plans to move. Unless . . .

Shock made her skin go cold.

Unless that was *why* he wanted to move. He was running away. He was hightailing it out before responsibility could catch up to him.

"Delaney," he said, sitting up and facing her. He reached for her hands but she yanked them away.

"Jack," she protested, thoughts sputtering from her mind but not reaching her lips. She was about to ask him why he wanted to leave now, of all times, what had he found out and what was he afraid of, when suddenly a figure appeared in the doorway and the light switch was thrown, illuminating the overhead light and blinding them both.

"A-*HA*!" a voice declared.

Delaney jumped nearly out of her skin. Shielding her eyes from the light she could just make out the form of . . . *Michael*?

She gaped at him. "Oh my God. What in the world are you *doing*? *Here*?"

Jack looked from Michael to Delaney and back again, his face slack with astonishment.

"Mi—" she began, but Michael cut her off.

" 'My' is right! My, my!" he said loudly, again in that oddly theatrical voice. "It's me, Jim! Jim-Joe!" He planted his hands on his hips like some kind of superhero. "And I want a *divorce*!"

Chapter 18

Jack's stomach hit the floor. *Jim??* Jim *existed?* Jim was *here?*

For a second he thought he was going to pass out, but that was probably the wine.

He'd been wrong, then. About everything. Jim existed, Delaney was married. Emily wasn't his after all.

Disappointment rocked him. But whether it was for not having Emily or losing Delaney or the destruction of the dream he'd constructed for the three of them, he couldn't tell, couldn't separate it. But it didn't matter because he'd lost it all.

He dragged his startled eyes to Delaney's face. She stared at Jim with an expression that could only be described as desperate.

"Oh no you *don't* want a divorce," she said to

Jim. She stood, snatching up the blanket and wrapping it around herself.

Jack had only a second to move before she yanked it out from under him like a magician's tablecloth. He moved out of the way, then grabbed a pillow from the other armchair and covered himself with it.

"Delaney—" he began.

"I'm not divorcing anyone," she continued, her voice thick with emotion. Tears stood in her eyes as she threw an arm out accusingly at Jack. "He's leaving, do you hear me? He's moving away. *Far* away. He just told me."

Jim looked understandably perplexed. "But . . ." He gestured toward the spot where the two of them had been, naked, on the floor. "But . . ."

"I don't care what this looks like," Delaney said, tears dropping from her lashes to wet her face. "But I am *not* divorcing my husband."

"Wait a minute," Jack said, then glowered at the man in the doorway. "You're saying *you're* Jim Poole? You're Delaney's husband?"

The man, of slight build with curly blond hair and blue eyes, nodded. "That's right," he said, with considerably less conviction than when he'd arrived. "I'm Jim Poole, and I'm shocked at what I see here. Shocked." He looked at Delaney, confusion more than anger on his face.

Jack rose and moved to the pile of clothing next to the fireplace. Dropping the pillow, he bent, pulled his pants from the pile and yanked his wallet out of the pocket. Inside, he still had the picture of Jim-Joe. *Exceptional Value!* He pulled it out and compared it to the man in front of him.

"This is you?" Jack demanded, tossing the picture at him.

The man bumbled it against his chest, then looked at it. He frowned, and cast a sour look at Delaney.

"Oh, Dee," he said, shaking his head. "What a putz."

Jack reached down, plucked up his boxers, and slipped them on. "What does that mean? Is that not you?"

Jim scowled. "Does it *look* like me? Please tell me it doesn't."

"So it's not a great picture," Delaney said, pulling the folds of the blanket closer around her. "He's at least stable. And trustworthy. And not afraid of responsibility." She glared at Jack. "I am *not* going to fall for a man who won't be around, a man who's undependable . . . who would desert us . . ." She pressed her hands to her wet cheeks and pushed the tears away. "I just won't do it."

"Too late," Jim Poole murmured, setting Jack's wallet on the hall table.

"What are you talking about?" Jack faced her, looking down to where she knelt before the fire. "I told you about that job to show you I *am* responsible. And dependable."

"But you're taking that job to get away from me," she said. "Don't try to deny it."

"Delaney, why on earth would you think that?" He didn't understand her at all. "Do you think I want to move away? Do you think I want to leave my home, this town, everyone I know? And after all I've done to be near you, to get through to you, do you think I want to leave *you*?"

He glanced over at Jim, then shook his head. He had to get out of here. He didn't know which end was up anymore.

"But this is crazy," he said, bending over to pick up his pants. "Talking about us as if there is an 'us.' I don't know what's going on here, but it's clear you've got your own troubles to deal with."

He punched a leg into his jeans.

Delaney took one step toward him and stopped. "Wait. You don't want to leave me?"

He laughed, yanked the jeans up over his other leg and looked from Jim to Delaney as he buttoned them. "What difference does it make? Delaney, you're *married*." He cast a baffled look toward her husband. "You might want to jump in here, Jim."

"Just tell me," she insisted.

"Tell you what? That I want you? That I'm crazy about you? That I'm crushed because your husband's here?" He laughed cynically, picking up his shirt. "No. I'm not going to tell you any of those things. To tell you the truth I don't know what I want. No . . . that's not true. I don't know what *you* want." He glanced over at Jim, who was watching them with undisguised interest and not a trace of anger. "Or you," he added.

"What I want?" Delaney asked, her face reddening. She looked guiltily at Jim, then back at Jack. "You really want to know what I want?"

He stopped, shirt in hand. "Yeah, I really want to know."

She took a deep breath, then let it out and looked away. Silence hung heavy in the room.

Finally, Jack sighed. "Never mind. Listen, I—we—shouldn't have done this. I'm sorry for my part in it. It's just, I thought . . ." He stopped, looked at the floor, at Delaney's tangled clothing, then back up at her. "I just, I didn't think you were actually married." Jack passed an apologetic look to Jim. "I'm sorry."

Jim shrugged. "Hey, it's okay with me."

Jack looked at him doubtfully. He sounded like he meant it. "It's *okay* with you?"

Jim made a face at Delaney. "Dee, come on. Say something here."

"Michael," she said suddenly.

Jack turned swiftly toward the door, but no one else had arrived.

"Thank you," Delaney continued. "You're the best friend I could ever have. Thank you so much for what you've tried to do here. But right now the only way you can help me is to go get Emily. Do you mind? I'll call Aunt Linda and tell her you're coming. Take my car, it's got the car seat. The keys are on the hall table."

"Michael?" Jack repeated.

"And where might I find Aunt Linda?" Jim, who was apparently Michael, asked.

"She lives in the brick building right next to the clinic. Apartment two. You'll find it, the town's not that big. Oh God, and will you turn off the oven first? I forgot all about the chicken. I'm so sorry, Michael, I'll explain everything when you get back."

Jack looked from Delaney to her friend and back. "And when will you explain everything to me?"

Delaney sighed and sat back on her heels. "Right now. I just need to know Emily's taken care of first."

"I'll get her," Jim-Michael said. "And I'll turn off the chicken. But can I say just one thing first?"

Delaney looked at him skeptically. "No."

"Just one thing," the man said, smiling and holding up one finger.

Delaney made a reluctantly acquiescent move with her head.

"Jack," the man said, turning to him.

Jack looked at him in surprise. Jim-Michael knew who he was?

"Be gentle with her. She really was trying to do the right thing. And . . . " here he looked warily at Delaney, "trust me on this, big guy. She's been in love with you since the begin—"

"Michael!" she snapped, rising.

"Since the beginning! That's all!" the man said, backing up. "I'm going now. I'll take the long way home."

And he was out the door.

Delaney promptly picked up the telephone and alerted Aunt Linda that Michael was on his way to pick up Emily, all too aware of Jack's piercing gaze on her every move.

Jack confronted Delaney, adrenaline nearly making him twitch. He could feel it in every limb. "What's going on?"

Delaney turned and sat in the armchair, gathering the blanket around her as if it might shield her from whatever came next. Her eyes were on the fire.

"Maybe you should sit down, Jack."

He shook his head. "I don't think so."

The two of them remained silent as Michael tiptoed elaborately past the open doorway.

"I'm gone now. Really!" he sang and slammed the front door behind him.

Delaney looked up at Jack. Her hair was mussed, and her eyes appeared bluer in her flushed face. "I have a few things I need to say that . . . well—"

"Don't beat around the bush, Delaney. Out with it."

His voice was harder than he'd intended, but he couldn't help it. His future was teetering on the brink of some drastic change, and he wanted to know which way to jump to catch it.

Her eyes widened, and she looked at him anxiously. "I've lied to you. I've been lying since I saw you again. I'm not married. That . . ." She inclined her head toward the door through which her friend had just left. "That was my friend, Michael. He knew all about what I was doing and came here because I . . . I was . . ." She searched for a word.

"Because you knew I'd seen that list in your drawer."

Her eyes snapped up to his, her mouth open. "So you *did* see it."

"Yes, and what in God's name was that all about? You *made up* a husband, Delaney? Just made one up? What were you thinking?"

She averted her eyes, looked disconcerted. The cool, composed Delaney Poole he'd seen for the last few weeks was gone.

"I don't know. I guess the whole problem is I wasn't thinking. You see, I didn't expect to see you here. I didn't think you lived here. I thought you lived in that town, in Massachusetts. Wellesley or—"

"Wellfleet."

"Right." She nodded. "So I was shocked when I saw you here, that first day at the clinic, and it just popped out. That I was married. And then there it was. What could I do but carry on with it?"

Jack scoffed, threw his shirt on the chair, and paced toward the hall, arms thrust outward. He turned at the door and looked back at her. "Oh, I don't know. Say 'just kidding'? Tell the truth? What did you think was going to happen?"

"Well, but you see there were other circumstances."

"And what were those other circumstances, Delaney?" He stopped, crossed his arms over his chest and looked at her, barely breathing.

She took a deep breath and opened her mouth.

"Tell the *truth*, Delaney," he added roughly.

A glimpse of her old spark appeared and she shot him an angry look. "I was *going* to."

"Good."

"Emily," she said, looking at him with hard eyes.

But after a second she lost her nerve and the look faltered.

His heart hammered in his chest. "Emily?" he prompted.

She looked at the floor. "Emily . . . is your daughter."

He thought he'd prepared himself. He thought the truth would be a simple confirmation of his suspicions. But no.

The truth was a shock.

He cleared his throat. Then cleared his throat again. He crossed his arms over his chest, then uncrossed them and put them on his hips. Then he turned his back to her and leaned against the doorjamb. He stared blankly into the closet.

"I was as shocked as you are," she said behind him. "I mean, you know, when I discovered I was pregnant. Because of the condom, of course. But you . . . you were the only, uh, possibility." She was silent a moment, then added, more quietly, "We can do a DNA test if you'd like."

He laughed, a grim, empty sound, and shook his head.

He heard her exhale.

"Jack." He could hear her move across the room and then her hand touched his shoulder. He jumped. She removed it. "I'm sorry. I'm sorry I didn't tell you right away, but I was . . ."

"Afraid," he supplied, amazed his voice emerged as steadily as it did.

"Yes." She sounded surprised. "I did try to call, from home. Washington, that is. When I found out I

was pregnant, but I wasn't sure of your last name."
She laughed, incredulously. "I thought it was Shepard, but I wasn't sure. And I wasn't sure how to spell it. I called a few, but none sounded like you and I was so . . . ashamed. Of it having been a one-night-stand, you know, that I had trouble asking questions when I did reach people. I think now one of the people I reached must have been your aunt Linda. Does her middle name start with 'J'?"

He didn't answer at first, not trusting his voice. Then said, "Joan."

"It probably was her," she sounded relieved that he'd answered. "But then when I got here, and I didn't know you. At all. And I heard . . . so much stuff . . ."

At this he turned and looked at her, his back against the doorframe. "The gossip."

Delaney's heart melted. The look in his eyes wasn't angry. He wasn't enraged or self-righteous or accusing. He was hurt.

She swallowed over a sudden lump in her throat.

"You met me, you looked at me in a new light, and you decided I wasn't," he splayed his hands, shrugged, "good enough."

"No," she said, shaking her head vehemently. "No. I saw you for a *second* and made a snap decision. I was afraid you might not be who you'd seemed that weekend I was here. It had nothing to do with who you really were, Jack. Who you are now to me. I didn't know. I . . . jumped to conclusions."

His brows drew together. "Tell me something. If I hadn't found that list—hell, if Jim, Michael, whatever his name is, hadn't shown up—would you have told me? Were you *ever* planning to tell me, Delaney?"

His voice had nearly broken on the last question and it was all Delaney could do not to touch him. She wanted to comfort him, wipe that sad look from his face, but she knew she was the last person he'd want to do that now.

"Yes, yes, I would have."

He looked at her, a slow sad look, and shook his head. Smiling grimly he said, "We're telling the truth, now, Delaney. There's no point in lying anymore."

She looked at her hands, writhing together in the folds of the blanket in front of her. "I believe that is the truth," she said. "Honestly. But it's a little hard to say. I mean, that was the whole reason I invited you to dinner tonight. To tell you. But then I got so wrapped up in my fears again, and the lies I'd already told. It was confusing, keeping everything straight." She put a hand to her forehead. "God, there were times I thought I was losing my mind." She tried a light laugh.

Jack turned and stared back into the closet. Delaney's smile died.

She stared at his back. His shoulders rose and fell with his breath. She wanted to reach out and touch the vague indentation of his spine, the smooth skin of his shoulder blades, the backs of his arms. She wanted to brush his hair with her hand

and relax the tension in his neck. She'd been so wrong about him, so completely, unjustly wrong. But he would never believe she saw that now.

Minutes passed, when his shoulders started to shake. Delaney looked at him in guilt and horror, her heart threatening to split right open. Good lord, had she made him *cry*?

Then he let out a snicker, tried to stifle it, and finally let go a guffaw.

Delaney's mouth dropped open. He was *laughing*?

"What?" she said.

He covered his face with one hand and took a deep breath. The exhale turned quickly back into laughter.

Her lips curved, but she was unsure whether she was amused or annoyed. "What? What is it?"

He gestured toward the closet and she saw, peeking out the partially open door, the heel of one of the five-and-dime wing tips. She felt laughter tickle the back of her throat.

"How much else did you buy?" he asked, turning to look at her. His eyes were watery with mirth. "The coat, the shoes . . ."

"I've got a gas grill coming from Sears," she admitted.

He burst out laughing.

She couldn't help it, she joined him.

"And Jim?" He gestured toward his wallet on the hall table where Michael had left it. "How did you pick him?"

"Out of a magazine. A medical journal. Who

knew he'd turn up in your wallet? Not to mention all those stupid frames?"

Remembering the Jim display at the five-and-dime sent them both into more laughter.

Jack leaned his head back against the doorframe, laughing and wiping his eyes. "Jesus," he said, finally gaining control. "You're not a very good liar, Delaney, but you sure are persistent. Your persistence alone is the only thing that had me doubting my suspicions."

"So you were suspicious? When did you start to think I was lying?" she asked.

He glanced down at her. "Almost immediately. Once I got over my disappointment, that is."

"Your disappointment?"

"That you were married. I was so happy to see you, that day in the clinic. After Lisa, you know."

She smiled wryly. "Yeah. I was scared to death, seeing you."

His smile turned sad and she wished she hadn't said it.

He took a deep breath and crossed his arms over his chest, his expression sobering. "So what happens now, Delaney?"

She wasn't sure what he meant. With her? Or with Emily? "What do you *want* to happen?"

He swallowed. "I want to be part of Emily's life. I don't know much about being a dad, never thought I'd be much good at it. But I want to try. I really want to try."

She tried to smile but felt emotion weigh it down. "Then I want you to. It was never my intention to keep her away from good influences." This time she did smile, ruefully. "It just takes me a while to see where the good influences are."

He nodded, looking unconvinced.

"And as for being a parent, well . . ." She laughed lightly. "I've only got a seven-month head start on you. You'll catch up, and we'll figure it out together."

Too late, she realized what she'd said. "Or rather," she amended quickly, "we'll figure it out at the same time, you know, the parenting thing. We'll—we'll talk about it and stuff."

He looked at her critically.

She exhaled. She was muddying things up again. *Oh the hell with it*, she thought.

"I just don't want you to think," she said plainly, "that we're a package deal. That if you want to be a father to Emily you have to be . . . well, with me. That's not what I meant."

He was quiet a long moment during which time Delaney tried to anticipate every reaction from his wanting nothing to do with her to wanting everything to do with Emily.

Finally, he said, facing her but looking down at the floor. "What if I want the package?" His eyes rose to hers. "What if I want you both?"

Delaney's hands rose to cover her mouth, and her eyes filled with tears. She'd never wept so much in her life. And for so many different reasons.

"Do you mean that?" she asked, her voice a near whisper.

"Delaney . . ." He took one of her hands in his.

"I've wanted you from the very first time I saw you."

She put on a doubtful expression. "You don't even remember the first—"

"I was on my boat, and you were walking on the dock," he said, giving her a small but serious smile. "I remember every minute. And Delaney, I believe I've been in love with you every minute since that morning too."

Tears of joy spilled over her cheeks. "Oh Jack . . . Even after all this? After all I've done?"

He looked down at her hand. "Even after finding out you're a liar and a cheat . . ."

She looked at him, mortified, until he raised those warm golden eyes to her face and she saw the laughter in them.

She smiled. "Jack, you don't know how much this means to me. I've been so—"

"Afraid," he supplied again, this time with a smile. "I know. But those days are over."

"I know," she said. "I'm not afraid anymore, Jack. I'm in love."

Epilogue

Sam walked into the diner with an extra spring in his step that morning. Frost was on the windows but it was warm inside, and smelled of coffee and fresh doughnuts.

"Boys," he said, taking off his cap and tossing it onto the table in front of Norman. Joe and Marvin looked up while Norman took the hat from over the sugar dispenser. "Have I got some news for you."

"Not like I got for you," Marvin said. "Turns out Betty down at the laundrymat's mother is going to Florida. She met some man on that Internet thing and is going to meet him." He gloated as Norman and Joe reacted to the news. "Can you beat that?"

Sam nodded his head. "Yes, sir, I can. What I got's better even than that. And I got it from the horse's mouth. Most of it, anyway."

"Which horse is that, Sam?" Joe asked, scratching his grizzled gray head.

"Jack Shepard." He sat smugly in his seat as Lois deposited a fresh mug of coffee in front of him.

"Jack? What's he done now, the rascal?" Lois asked, tucking her tray against one hip and leaning a hand on the back of Marvin's chair.

The morning was cold, so the diner was full of people warming up before hitting the road, or the water, as the case may be.

Sam took a deep breath, enjoying the moment of anticipation.

"Well, I'll tell you." He paused, making them wait. It was all in the delivery, he thought. You had to dole fresh news like this out just right, for maximum impact. "Jack Shepard is getting married."

"What?" It seemed to be a collective gasp. So many people said it Sam couldn't tell whom to answer. Instead he smiled at the group before him, as well as at the faces from other tables that had turned toward him upon hearing what he'd said.

"That's right. You heard me right. Jack Shepard's getting married, and it's a free cup of coffee for anyone who guesses who he's marrying."

Eyebrows rose all around the room.

"That Lisa Jacobson?" Norman ventured.

Sam shook his head.

"That New York girl, Kim whatshername," Joe said. "From the clinic."

Sam shook his head again and looked at Marvin. "Marvin? Any guesses?"

"Hell, I don't know, Sam." Marvin pushed his glasses back up to the bridge of his nose.

"Nurse Knecht!" someone called from a neighboring table, and the whole place laughed.

Sam looked over and saw the impish face of Maggie Coleman. "Good guess, Maggie," he said, chuckling, "but I'm afraid you're wrong too."

"Well who *is* it then?" Norman asked.

"Jack's marrying the doctor," Sam said triumphantly.

The rest of the room burst into excited murmurs, but Norman's brow creased, and he leaned across the table toward Sam. "Jack's marrying Doc Jacobson?"

Sam sighed. "No, Norman, the pretty young *female* doctor. Dr. Poole."

"Ohhhh." Norman sat back, enlightened. Then frowned again. "But she's already married!"

"Well now, maybe she is and maybe she isn't," Sam said cryptically. He pulled a napkin from the black-and-chrome dispenser and wiped a drip of coffee off the table in front of him.

"She getting a divorce?" Marvin asked.

Sam shook his head and wadded up the napkin. Throwing it into the ashtray, he said, "Nope."

"Then how can she be getting married?" Joe asked.

He picked up his coffee. "Turns out she's never *been* married," Sam said, relishing the even louder murmurs of the crowd.

"Why that's wonderful!" Norman said. "Then

she can marry Jack without worrying about it."

"That is the truth, but that ain't the best of it." Sam sat back and blew on his hot coffee.

"I didn't even know they was dating," Joe said, scratching his head again. "I know he flirted a lot with her, but hell, he's near about flirted with me."

General laughter accompanied this statement, as people from neighboring tables turned openly to listen to Sam.

They could wait, Sam figured. He sipped his coffee, then said, "Lois, I think I need a doughnut or two to go with this cuppa joe."

"Sam," Lois said with a resolute shake of her head, "I ain't leaving until you tell me what's better than Jack Shepard getting married to the doctor who's never been married even though she *said* she was married."

Marvin pulled off his glasses, grabbed a napkin, and began cleaning them. "Why would she say she was married when she wasn't?" he asked.

"The kid," Joe said, nodding sagely.

"That's right." Sam looked at Joe, who beamed at having been correct.

"So Jack's gonna adopt the kid prob'ly, right?" Marvin asked. He placed his glasses back on his face, moon-eyed once again as he looked at Sam. "That'd sure make his aunt Linda happy, wouldn't it, Sam?"

"That it would have Marvin, but the truth made her even happier. You see Jack," Sam said, pausing a moment to sip his coffee and luxuriate in the anticipation of their reaction to his next bit of news, "is the *father* of that baby."

"What—you mean—now how can that be?" Joe said. "She only just got here with that baby a couple months ago."

Sam smiled enigmatically and the crowd hushed, awaiting his next words.

"She got here last spring," Sam said, "a year ago, for a weekend. I remember seeing her hanging about. Seems to me she bought some things at the hardware store. Stuff for Jack's boat, I believe. I remember thinking at the time, *who is that pretty girl and why is she buying stuff for a boat?* Then I saw her and Jack on his boat."

"You did?" Norman looked at him as if he'd performed some sort of miracle.

"Yep, I did. I saw them on that boat," Sam said, satisfied with the expressions of admiration on the faces of those around him. He always, *always* came up with the best gossip. Even if he had to embellish it a little bit. "They looked just as romantic as can be, and I thought to myself, those two look good together. Like they belong together, you know? That's what I thought to myself. And I'll bet you that's where that little baby was conceived . . ."

"You mean Jack Shepard is the *natural* father of that baby?" Lois asked.

Sam looked up at her, a twinkle in his eye. "That's exactly what I mean. Course they're selling the boat now."

"No way." Lois was openly skeptical.

Sam raised one eyebrow and gave her his best You-doubt-me? look. "You go on down to the dock today, missy, and you'll see a 'For Sale' sign on the *Silver Surfer*. And do you want to know why?"

"*I* do," Norman said.

Sam returned his attention to the appreciative. "Well, then, I'll tell you. Because they're buying the Shepard place. Jack's buying it from his old man, and they're going to live in it. He and his pretty doctor wife and baby."

"Well, that's just wonderful," Norman said again, grinning at Sam and then Joe and then Marvin. "Ain't that wonderful?"

"Sure, it is," Sam said. "Finally made that old sourpuss Kevin Shepard happy, too. See he'd been after Jack to buy the place. So Jack and his gal are going to live there and—"

He was about to tack on some wonderful, if fictional, details about what they planned to do to the house and the new car Jack was getting soon and then he was going to speculate about the fact that *maybe*—it was *possible*, after all—the pretty doc might even be pregnant again, when the happy couple themselves appeared.

He saw them first through the plate-glass window, walking across the green toward the diner. They were holding hands, and Jack held the baby, bundled up in a big pink baby parka against the cold.

"And what, Sam?" Norman asked.

Sam nodded toward the door. "And here they come."

The bells on the door jangled, and in walked Jack and the young doctor.

The place fell into a dead silence.

Jack's steps slowed as he entered, and the doctor stopped in her tracks as all eyes came to rest on them. Then after a second, a lone pair of hands started clapping. They were quickly joined by all the others in the room, and Sam immediately stood up. Even he couldn't stop the grin on his face.

Soon Jack and the pretty doc, looking nothing less than startled, were staring into the face of a standing ovation. Then the baby started clapping her little mittened hands together, and the crowd laughed.

Jack smiled first and put his arm around the doctor's shoulders. She looked up at him, then back at the crowd and gave a tentative little smile.

That's when the congratulations started and before long the couple was swarmed by well-wishers.

Sam smiled with satisfaction. His work here was done. For today anyway.

"Lois," he said, turning toward the waitress beside him. "How 'bout them doughnuts now?"